The Ontelles Odyssey

John Lawrence Burks

xulon PRESS

The Ontelles Odyssey
by John Lawrence Burks

Printed in the United States of America

Library of Congress Control Number: 2002108847
ISBN 1-591601-58-4

www.xulonpress.com

PART I

THE ORDER OF PETRAPOLIS

Chapter One

I am Zeb, King of the planet Ontelles, which is located in the Tal star system of the Triad galaxy. Being the youngest son of poor parents, I grew up as a herder of elbs during the time when the sword and beast were the methods of war. I was fortunate to be a herder of elbs, as they are the most valuable animal on Ontelles. The elb is a small furry creature that eats grass and small plants. Their fur is used by the very rich and the warriors. Ontelles is a very cold planet, even during the summer months and the warmth of the elb fur is a valuable and coveted item. A man or even a woman's station in life is determined by the quality and length of his or her elb robe. A robe of fifty pelts of matching color is a most precious possession. Only a few Ontellians are able to own such a robe. But as a herder of elbs, I was able to gather fifty pelts of a pure white color. This task took more than fifteen years. At last my mother tailored a robe for me that was one of the finest robes ever to be seen.

On my twentieth birthday, when all male children on Ontelles must leave their parents and become warriors, I took my elb robe and sword, a double-edged blade which I forged myself in the village foundry, and went to say farewell to my parents. They were waiting for me outside our stone and wood hut. Mother kissed my forehead and Father kissed my right-hand, which is the hand that holds the sword. I left the small village and headed towards the mountains.

A man is never to return to his parent's home after his twentieth birthday. If a man-child returns, he is to be seized, cut into four pieces and thrown to the animals and birds of the wilderness. One piece is placed on each side of the village. The people of Ontelles are very superstitious and read the signs of the stars. The flight of birds or the lifting of smoke from a fire could be a good or evil omen to those skilled in divination. The people of the wilderness villages give lip service to many gods, yet living truth is foreign to all except a very few who live in a mystical city called Rift.

That early morning in front of our home, the wind was blowing steadily from the north and it was very cold. My birthday is in the middle of the winter, and this was an especially difficult situation. There is an old saying on Ontelles, *"Born in the summer or the spring, tis a joy to be a boy, but born in the winter when it's cold aplenty, a son's in dread of reaching twenty."* Most of the Ontelles men twenty years or older were born in warm months because those born in the winter rarely survive to the spring of their twentieth year.

According to the laws of Ontelles, once I reached the mountains, which is a two- day journey on foot from our village, I would have to stay until I found an Ontelles warrior and would then have to challenge him to combat. If victorious, I would cut off his head and take it to the capital city of Ontelles. This was the great walled city of Petrapolis located on the plains of Blood far to the west. By foot, from the village, it would have taken a half-year to reach, but by beast it would take only three months. If a man was fortunate enough to kill a warrior who owned a beast, he became the new owner of that animal and could make it to Petrapolis without much difficulty. To those who know nothing of my world, a beast is a creature with long shaggy fur of various colors. They also have long, slender legs, and a large head with razor sharp teeth. A beast can carry a man at great speeds on level ground and, in combat, attack other beasts and warriors with its teeth. Once I reached the walled city of Petrapolis, I would present the dead man's head to the soldiers that guard the city gate, for there is only one entrance into the city. The head is examined and the dead man's village, name, and birthday are recorded in the official death log (this is easily done since each child born on Ontelles is required to have this information burned on the back of his neck eight days after birth). I would then be pronounced a warrior and be given a new name by the warrior council. The next ten years would be spent in Petrapolis or in warfare in distant lands. At the age of thirty, every warrior must take a mate. Then he must return to the village of the first warrior he killed to live out that warrior's life.

This system of going to the dead man's village was established long ago so that villages would stay populated, and it was also a way for parents to find out if their sons were dead or still alive. Therefore, when a man came to live in the new village with his mate, his name was the name of the dead warrior even though he had another name burned on the back of his neck. For instance, on the back of my neck is my village, my birthday and my birth given name which is Tobe. I go by the name Zeb because that was the name of the first warrior whom I challenged and killed. Now according to this custom, if some young man challenges me and I am killed, his name will be changed to Tobe and at the age of thirty he will return to my parent's village with his mate and my birth name. My parents, if still alive, will welcome this man as their son, even though he is actually my killer. These are only a few of the customs and ways of my world. They are considered holy, and no man is allowed to deviate from the ways of Ontelles or he will be killed, divided into four pieces, and scattered on the four winds.

I kept my eyes toward the horizon that early morning on

my twentieth birthday, fighting back the tears that grew there. The double suns of our binary star system were lifting above the curvature of the planet like molten iron in the village foundry. I pulled my elb robe tightly about my neck and with pride looked at the awe-inspiring color reaching down to the top of the white elb fur boots laced to my calves with long leather cords. The eyes of my parents seared into my back, but I dared not turn around. Other inhabitants from the village looked on from their huts and called out blessings and success in the coming adventures. I nodded in response but looked at no one, keeping my eyes forward. When I reached the edge of the village, many of the onlookers had gone back inside because of the cold wind. As I began to erase the memory of the village from my mind I heard a voice call my name, "Tobe! Tobe!"

I pushed the warm elb hat from my left ear, heard the call again, looked towards the voice, and saw the young girl, Desiree, standing next to a giant lowben tree. Wrapped around her slender body she wore a pink elb robe, boots and hat.

"Tobe! Speak with me before you leave," she called out, hands cupped around her mouth. She beckoned me to come over to the lowben tree she stood beside.

"No, I can't, but you may walk with me for a way if you wish!" I yelled back hoping the wind didn't carry the words away. She nodded and left the shelter of the lowben tree and ran to my side. She was full of innocence and beauty. Her long blond hair was flowing from under her fur hat as she ran, and when she smiled, it brought joy and gladness to my heart. After she reached me, we just walked in silence until the village was out of our sight. She reached her hand into the pocket of my elb robe and found my hand. It was then that we both stopped, turning to look into each other's eyes. She cocked her head to the side like she always did, smiled her sweet smile and said, "I love you Tobe and I always will."

This was a declaration more than just a statement. "I love you too," I repeated, even though I had promised not to say those words, knowing that it would only make things more difficult.

"Be victorious in the mountains and reach Petrapolis. In four years I will leave and we can meet at Petrapolis; I will wait for you until we can marry."

I nodded and smiled sadly, for on Ontelles, when a girl turned twenty she likewise left her village and traveled to the capital city with her father. There he would leave his daughter, and she would join the other girls in the city as community property to all the warriors. She would remain in Petrapolis until she was chosen as a mate or until the age of thirty. If she was not chosen by her thirty-first birthday she would be killed, cut into four pieces and scattered on the four winds. Therefore, no one above age thirty or under twenty lived in Petrapolis. It was a city of warriors and single maidens to be enjoyed to the fullest of anyone's imagination.

I was grieved by Desiree's words, because even if I made it to Petrapolis and Desiree also reached the city, I wouldn't be able to make her my mate until I was thirty years old. During that time Desiree would have to wait at least five years in the capital city and be abused by virtually every warrior. I squeezed her hand in mine and kissed her mouth as our lips almost froze together in the cold wind. I finally released her, brushing noses, and turned away towards the mountains. The last look in her eyes was pitiably haunting, begging me to take her and violate the law of Ontelles. As I made my feet move, Desiree stayed, and I heard her say she loved me once more as the distance between us grew. She did not see the tears in my own eyes as they dropped and froze on my cheeks.

The wind howled and blew that entire morning as I moved through the wilderness toward the mountains. I can't remember a time of feeling more saddened and alone. My mother and father had been through this ten times already with all my brothers and sisters. Although I was the last to leave, I had the impression they were glad I was going. They were two people who lived for Ontelles and her culture. Their whole lives revolved around keeping the city of Petrapolis supplied with all it needed in order that what went on there might continue. All the villages of Ontelles were required to supply sixty percent of their crops, herds, and other assets to support the capital city. If a village refused or even cheated in what was owed, an army of warriors from Petrapolis would come and level the village. My father once told me the story of when he was a young warrior and there had been an uprising in a Topan coast village. He was placed in charge of suppressing the revolt; as he told me the gruesome details of how the inhabitants were punished, I developed a dark spot in my heart for my father and for the ways of Ontelles. How could my father be capable of such cruelty, and why did the people who hated this world have to die in such a way? My father and I were out in the wilderness around a fire when he told me this story, and I still remember the glow in his eyes and the grin on his face while he related all the fine details. After he had finished his story, I asked him why he had been so harsh on the people who had revolted. He jumped up and took a thick stick from the fire, and with it still burning in his hand, he broke it over my back yelling, "Never question the ways of Ontelles or I will kill you!" I shook with fear and promised never to question again.

Now I was leaving him forever, and I was questioning again, but this time I knew he couldn't beat me. "I hate you father; I hate you Ontelles; I hate you and I hate your ways! I don't want to kill anyone, and I don't want to go to Petrapolis!" I shouted to myself. "But what other choice is there! I have to live here; and become like my father and everyone else." I fell to my knees crying again for the second time and began to beat my chest. This condition held for a while until a strange dizziness overshadowed my eyes and I fell forward in blackness.

The suns of Ontelles had set and a powdery snow was falling. The wind was barely blowing but still strong enough to shake the trees. The elb robe had kept me warm as I slept, but now that the suns were down I needed to get up and keep moving or freeze. I stood and began to walk. Inside my pocket I discovered a small bag of seeds my mother must have placed there before I left home. Slowly my strength was revived by the nourishment.

The night was cold and seemed never to end. My legs kept moving and at times I had to use my sword to hack a way through the thick but brittle bush of the wilderness. Finally the night ended and the orange suns of Ontelles began to rise behind me. I found a ledge of rock to lie behind and dug a hole in the snow. Inside the hole I rolled up inside my elb robe and fell fast asleep.

The afternoon of the second day, I awoke and resumed my journey towards the mountains. The giant peaks were looming before my eyes and I knew great dangers and mysteries were hidden in the passes and valleys of those mountains. According to instructions given by my father, I basically knew where I was going. I had the map of Ontelles imprinted in my mind. It was first placed there when I was only a little fellow and my father and I were relaxing around a fire one evening with my brothers in the wilderness. We were all talking about the days when we would become warriors. My father was a big man with a full gray beard and a jolly laugh but his mud-colored eyes seemed to reveal the real man within. They were cold, steely eyes, and when he became angry they could almost burn holes into anything.

"Father, tell me where is Petrapolis?" I asked wondering about the tales he had been telling us of the city when he was a young warrior.

"To find Petrapolis, we must begin with Petrapolis." My father then held out his huge hand with the palm up. I saw every line and wrinkle in the light of the fire. He pointed to the center of his palm and stated that here was Petrapolis. And Petrapolis stood in the center of a huge flat plain called the *Plain of Blood*. In the Ancient Days it was called the *Wilderness of Death*, because of the many battles fought there. Bordering the Plain of Blood were two mountain ranges that joined together far in the north and also in the south. As my father drew the lines of the mountain ranges in his palm, I pictured Petrapolis as a small diamond in a huge oval ring.

"In the mountains, my son, live the warriors who exist only for the hunt and challenge of combat with the nuggets." (Nuggets being the name for those that are twenty years of age and need a warrior's head for access into Petrapolis.) "There is also a rebellious city somewhere in these mountains. This city is called Rift but no one knows where it is. Many warriors have tried to find it in order to inform Petrapolis so it can be destroyed, because the people of Rift are very evil."

"Why are they evil?" I asked hoping this question wouldn't lead to a beating. His eyes darkened but he answered my innocent question.

"Because they won't supply warriors or pay the taxes that they owe."

"Where is our village?" I quickly asked hoping to change the subject, for there was a nervous twitch developing around his left eye and his dark eyes were beginning to burn with hate.

"That city will be destroyed one day and maybe you, my son, will lead the legions from Petrapolis."

"But where is our village in relation to Petrapolis?" The fire in his eyes began to subside, but he gave me a long look before he began to retrace the mountains on his palm.

"We are east of the mountains, halfway between the mountains and the Lepis Ocean. When you are old enough to travel to Petrapolis all you do is head west through the mountains then onto the *Plain of Blood* and you will reach the great city."

"What is over there?" I asked, pointing to the west side of the imaginary map on his palm.

"West of the second mountain range is the wilderness of Topan and it is a land of villages that stretches to the Topan Sea, just as the Lepis Wilderness is populated. There are no villages located on the *Plain of Blood*, only the city of Petrapolis."

"What is the Topan Wilderness like?" It was at this moment when my father began talking about the rebellion he had put down and my question that caused me to be beaten with the burning stick.

On the evening of the second day I reached the first pass leading into the mountains. The pass was a hollow saddle in a low-lying ridge. Beyond the saddle, jagged peaks seemed to float on white clouds that hugged the pointed summits. The double suns were just dropping out of sight and the receding light touched the sky with hues of orange and red. Just as I sat down on a flat rock I heard a voice from behind me. I turned in fright and there stood the ugliest man I had ever seen. He was two heads taller than me, even though I was larger than any of my brothers. He had one eye that remained shut. Apparently there wasn't anything in the socket. He had a bushy red beard and was missing his front teeth. He also wore a red elb robe that stunk and was stained with what looked like dried blood. In his right hand was a sword that was twice as long as mine.

"Are you a nugget, boy?" asked the giant of a man. I knew if I answered truthfully I would have to challenge him and surely he would kill me.

"No, I'm a herder of elbs and several of them wandered off in this direction," was my fraudulent reply, which even surprised me as to how easily it came out.

"I've seen no elbs wander through this pass and I've been here for the last ten days waiting for nuggets." Then he pointed with his sword over to two bodies that lay crumpled and frozen in the powdery snow. "Are you sure you aren't a nugget? You look old enough."

"Next year I will be one, but this year I need to find my elbs," I replied, hoping he wouldn't demand to check the birth date on the back of my neck.

"I think you are lying to me, boy. I haven't seen any elbs in ten days."

"Elbs are afraid of strangers and besides, not to be offensive, your body odor is enough to keep even a wild beast from attacking you." At that he began to laugh uncontrollably, grabbing his stomach as if he were in pain.

"All right, I believe you. Maybe they circled around in the night since I do keep a large fire. You may pass, but first I want that elb robe you are wearing. I've never seen one quite like it, even in Petrapolis."

I hesitated in what the giant demanded. To give something up after working fifteen years for it wasn't easy.

"Listen, I don't want to stain the pretty white fur with your blood, so you better hand it over but quick."

"I'll freeze without an elb robe!" I stammered thinking maybe I was going to cry.

"I'll be nice and give you mine," he replied before he began to laugh again. My eyes watched the vapor clouds as his foul breath hit the cold, thin air. Then, reluctantly, I took my elb robe off and handed it to the red-bearded giant. He threw his filthy robe at my feet and excitedly put my robe on over his armored breastplate and iron-studded shoulder pads. After I covered myself with his repulsive robe, he pointed to my sheath. "Now hand over your sword.

I don't want you sneaking up on me and trying to get your elb robe back."

After a short hesitation to protest, I finally realized my hopeless situation. I pulled my sword from its sheath. He grabbed it and in one circular motion lifted it above his head and swung it against a large rock, shattering the blade. I had spent an entire summer hunting for the choice iron rocks to make that sword, and now it was gone just like my elb robe, all in a moment of time. Life was so bizarre at times and seemed to be thoroughly unjust.

"Now move it boy, or I will be tempted to skin your hide," said the giant as he tossed the remains of my sword over his shoulder. I watched it disappear in the virgin snow, then turned and walked away in despair.

I resumed my journey down into a mountain valley as darkness began to fall on the quiet and lonely terrain. The sky was clear and I realized it was going to be a cold night. I decided to keep moving for fear that the giant would follow and kill me if I were to try to sleep. Halfway into the night, hunger and exhaustion weakened me almost to the point of collapse. Trying to fight it, I stumbled on in a delirious state until I tripped on a root that stuck out of the snow. My head struck a sharp object as I fell and a warm flow of blood streamed from the wound in my forehead. I began to envision lying in the snow and never getting up; drifting into a long sleep. The pain of the cold, hunger, and wound was overpowering. There was only a desire to stay where I was and drift away in sleep, until I heard a strange voice.

"Tobe, get up or you will die." When I heard these words I opened my eyes and noticed the snow around my head was stained rusty from my blood. "Get up or you will die."

This time I looked up and there stood a human form; yet what I saw wasn't human. Although it was still night, the trees and the ground around me were lit by a brilliance that emanated from this being.

"Who are you?" I asked.

"First you must get up, then I will answer your questions."

I managed to stand and noticed this person or being was wearing only a thin white robe. "Aren't you cold?" I asked.

"Would you give me your robe if I were to ask for it?"

"Yes, but what would I use to keep warm?"

"You can have whatever you want, but first we need to take care of that wound on your forehead." I stood there in an incredulous state as he then reached forward with his right hand and touched my wound. Feeling a tingle, I reached up and found only smooth skin where the cut had been a moment ago.

"Who are you?" I asked in amazement.

"My name is Vertunda and I'm a servant to the one who is the creator of all things."

"Creator! Are you telling me you serve the creator of all things? And what god would this be, for there are many gods?" I asked, stumbling over my words. Vertunda stood there with a smile much like that of an adult smiling at the frolics of a little child.

"There is only the One God. The one who made both you and me. Your questions will be answered, but since you don't have understanding of true knowledge at this time, I may not be able to answer them all."

"I believe you are a servant of this one god and you are right; I don't understand. But why did you come to me?"

"This I can answer. Your name is Tobe, but it will be changed to Zeb and you shall become king of Ontelles. It will not be an easy road but I have something that will help you," said Vertunda. Then, like magic, a sword inside a golden sheath appeared in his hands. He handed it to me and with both hands I reached for the gift.

"Pull the sword from its sheath," ordered Vertunda. I placed my right hand on it and noticed the beautiful red and blue jewels embedded in the hilt. The length of the sheath was that of my forearm.

"Draw the sword," repeated Vertunda.

I looked up at his face and he nodded toward the sword. It was then that I pulled the sword out for the first time and what I saw in my hand put shivers down my back and made the hair on my neck and arms stand up. The sword doubled in length and the blade leapt with burning flames of fire.

"It is a flaming sword," explained Vertunda. "There is none like it in the universe. You are the only one to possess it. Now pass the blade through that tree." I turned at his command and with feather lightness I swung the sword toward the thick trunk. The frozen limbs cracked and snapped as the upper portion of the tree fell back into the forest.

Vertunda just stood there and smiled. "There is nothing on this planet that can withstand it. But there is one thing you need to know before I must go. The flaming sword will only burn if you use it in truth. If it is used for a wrong or wicked purpose it will be a plain, steel sword and there will be no flame. You will not know if it will flame until you pull it from its sheath. Now be strong, be brave and courageous, and love the one who has chosen you to be his servant." With those words Vertunda began to fade away like a dying ember pulled from the fire.

"You forgot my elb robe! Don't you want it?" I yelled into the night as he vanished. "I guess he's gone." I looked to the sword in my hand and saw that flames were still leaping wildly off the blade. I put it back into the golden sheath and the flames disappeared. Standing in the shadows of night, I could still see the dark spot in the snow where my head had lain earlier and as I turned, there stood the smoldering stump as witness that I hadn't been dreaming.

Chapter Two

The morning after I received the flaming sword, I stumbled onto something quite unusual. I would later realize that it was fate and that I was predestined to arrive at that place; on that certain day; at that exact time.

The place I fell upon was the ancient city of Rift, whose location is unknown except to a very few outsiders and the inhabitants of the city. Those living there are holy men, priests, virgins and any who are seekers of the living truth. The warriors from Petrapolis have been seeking Rift for ages in order to destroy it. According to an ancient legend, the city is hidden except to those who are meant to find it.

When I accidentally found the entrance into Rift, I was resting next to a large stink tree looking at a rock up-crop wall type formation that was only a few bodies from where I sat. (A body being the length of a human man; one way of measuring distance on Ontelles.) The wall towered high above the trees of the forest and was glassy smooth, which would prevent anyone from climbing it. I had to look twice before I realized that there was a narrow vertical crack running down the face of the rock-wall. First glance made the crack look like a long, dark shadow but after a more careful look, it revealed an opening that a human could squeeze through. I wondered why I had such a desire to explore it, until I left the protection of the stink tree and squeezed through. On the other side of the wall stood a beautiful young girl about Desiree's age and behind her a magnificent walled city of white marble. The girl was wearing a blue elb robe and she had fair skin and long, honey-brown hair flowing from under her elb hat of the same color as her robe.

"What is your name, young warrior?" She inquired innocently.

"I'm not a warrior, I'm just a herder of elbs," I answered, mesmerized by her beauty and still believing my story to the giant.

"No, you're a warrior, but a good one, not like the ones from Petrapolis. Besides, that sword in your hand is beautiful and only a good warrior would have such a sword."

"Come now, if I were a good warrior, would I be wearing such a wretched elb robe that's stained with blood?"

"A true statement, but here at Rift we are taught to look to one's eyes, not to one's outward appearance. Your heart is clean and good. Truly your elb robe doesn't agree with your eyes but there must be an explanation," she said with a charming little smile.

"You are right, my name is Tobe. A warrior in the mountains, about a day's walk from here, took my robe and broke my sword. The sword you see in my hand was given to me last night by a man, or something like a man, who called himself Vertunda. It is a special sword full of magic."

"You met Vertunda?"

"Yes, last night in the forest."

"Then that isn't a magical sword. It is a sword of truth; maybe it is the legendary Flaming Sword."

"Yes, you know about the sword?" I asked, grabbing her blue robe unaware of what I was doing.

"Of course, everyone here at Rift knows of the Flaming Sword, but no one has ever seen it. I must take you to my father. He is waiting for you. My name is Lindas and I am the guardian virgin of the wall for this day. It is my job to meet and greet any visitors, though we receive very few. But today is very special since you have arrived. Now come with me and I will introduce you to my father," Lindas took my hand and led me to the main gate of the city. The doors were made of thick lowben wood and probably took twenty strong men to open or close. They were open that morning and inside the city I noticed houses made of marble with golden roofs and silver doors. There were people in the streets all wearing beautiful elb robes of blues, whites, and light browns. Many said hello to me and smiled at Lindas as we walked to a large marble building that looked like some type of temple. At the gate of this temple I met Lindas' father.

"Father, this is Tobe. He has just come to our city and he carries the Flaming Sword." When Lindas' father heard this, his eyes seemed to light up. I looked past him to the other older men surrounding him and saw that they too were smiling radiantly at the news she'd brought. With a word of thanks from her father, Lindas was dismissed. She smiled at me and then skipped down the street back the way we had come.

Once she'd left, her father addressed me, the light never leaving his eyes. He was wise and old looking with a wide face and long cheekbones. "Tobe, my name is Topaz and I'm the High Priest of Rift. Today is a very special day for our city. A very special day for Ontelles," and all the old men nodded in agreement. "There is an ancient prophecy that on the day a man comes to the Holy Temple of Ontelles bearing the Flaming Sword of Truth, then he will be our king. Now please join me and my colleagues for breakfast and tell us how you came to possess the Flaming Sword."

After eating, I spent the rest of that day speaking to the elders of the city about myself, the giant in the mountain pass, and Vertunda in the forest. Some of them cried like babies when I told how my wound was healed and others

23

cheered when I told of cutting the tree in half. That evening there was a great feast in the huge hall. Lindas sat at my right and Topaz to my left. Topaz was wearing a white robe that had blue trim around the edges. Lindas had given me a blue and red tunic to wear for the dinner and she was dressed in a simple white gown similar to the other virgins in the hall. All of the citizens of Rift were present. I estimated over two thousand men and women of all ages seated at the long wooden tables.

Once everyone had eaten, Topaz rose from his stone chair and lifted his hands to quiet everyone. A hush fell on the hall and everyone's eyes focused on Topaz.

"Brethren and beloved ones of the holy city of Rift," began Topaz in a loud voice. "Today we have been blessed with a special visitor. Sitting to my right is Tobe, the long awaited King of Ontelles." There was a moment of silence as Topaz's arm swept towards me and his words sank into their hearts and minds. Then the hall filled with cheers as most stood and yelled praises to the Creator of all things. I began to feel important and exalted. Here I was, one day a herder of elbs and the next, a king. Life was strange and bizarre.

"Please, everyone quiet!" shouted Topaz, who was still standing next to me. He held up his arms and everyone quieted down. When there was silence again, Topaz spoke. "Tonight we will anoint Tobe as King of Ontelles. Tomorrow evening Tobe and my daughter will be wed as man and wife."

This time, only the other virgins stood and yelled praises to Lindas. All I could do was turn to Lindas in amazement that she was to be my wife. I leaned over to her and whispered, "Explain to me why you are to be my wife?" She smiled and grasped my hand under the table and whispered in my ear that she would explain later after the banquet.

Topaz raised his hands again to quiet the virgins. "Bring the oil and we will now anoint our king," said Topaz looking to one of his fellow priests at the other end of the huge hall. The priest, holding a little glass vessel in his hands, began to walk toward the front of the hall. There was a heavy silence in the hall, except for the sound of the priest's leather shoes against the stone floor. Finally the priest reached Topaz and handed him the vessel. Topaz lifted the blue-green glass container above his head and asked everyone to bow while he blessed the oil. Everyone lowered their eyes except one old man with a long white beard. He stood at his table and began to speak. "No! I have one question before the blessing begins."

"Speak, and ask your question," replied Topaz in a slightly angered voice.

"How do we know this young man is the promised King of Ontelles?"

"The prophecy says that the day the Flaming Sword is seen flaming at the Gate of the Virgins and at the Temple, then this shall be the one who will hold the scepter of Ontelles! And this morning my daughter saw the Flaming Sword in this man's hand," said Topaz, pointing to me.

"No Father," said Lindas, cutting her father off. "I did not actually see the Flaming Sword flame. Tobe only told me it was the Flaming Sword."

"You didn't see the flame of the sword?" asked Topaz now looking very sternly toward his daughter. She lowered her eyes and shook her head no.

"Did you see the sword flame at the Temple today?" asked the old man with a skeptical sneer. Topaz slowly shook his head and the crowd began to murmur. "Let's see the sword now!" yelled the old man as he theatrically waved his arm towards me and then others began to chant, "Let's see it! Let's see the Flaming Sword flame!"

I was now angered and confused. I was told I was to marry a girl I only met that morning and now that poor girl was humiliated in front of everyone. My eyes surveyed the hall and the looks on the people's faces stirred by this old, ancient man disturbed my spirit. *I will show them*, I thought. "Don't worry Lindas," I said, standing with my right hand grabbing the jeweled handle. In anger I pulled the sword to prove who I was. But to my surprise only a cold, blue steel blade appeared from the golden sheath. I hit the blade against the top of the wooden table to get it to flame, but nothing happened.

"Fraud, he's a fraud!" yelled the old man. "Kill him, he's nothing but a fraud!" The crowd in the hall began to rush forward. Topaz threw the vessel of oil to the ground before the feet of the old man who jumped back refusing to step on the holy oil. With Topaz raising his arms and the breaking of the vessel of holy oil, this was enough to quiet the almost berserk crowd.

"No one is going to be killed. But I have made a mistake, and I will pay the price. This young man has lied to us but he is not to be blamed. He came to us from the world outside Rift and lies are the way of that world. He will not be killed but he will be taken and locked out of the city."

"He will bring warriors back to destroy us if we don't kill him!" screamed the old man in the crowd standing before the holy oil that was beginning to seep into the stone cracks of the floor.

"No, it isn't written in his eyes. I believe he will repent by morning and become one of us. But, if he does not, then the Holy Council of Priests and Elders will judge his case tomorrow. So be it. The high priest has spoken!" Topaz signaled to several young priests to escort me to the city gate. I put the sword back into the golden sheath remembering the words of Vertunda about the sword: "If it is used for a wrong or wicked purpose..."

"What about your daughter ?" called out one of the virgins.

Topaz said, "She goes back to the wall in the morning and stays until the next male passes through its portals and that

one will become her mate. This is according to our laws."
I turned to Lindas and asked, "What does this mean?
Explain quickly!"
She looked up at me and said, "At Rift, the women
choose their mates, not the men like at Petrapolis. And each
virgin takes turns waiting at the wall and marries the first
male she sees pass through the wall. You were the first I saw
but now that has been changed."
Two priests grabbed my arms to escort me out of the hall
and to the city gate. I stood and left peacefully. At the door
of the great hall a servant handed me the blood-stained elb
robe and I was taken to the city gate and the giant lowben
wood doors were locked behind me. Once again I'd had
everything and in a moment of time it was taken from me.
"Life at times seems unjust," I told myself as the wind began
to blow like an angry soul along the flat meadow between
the city and where I first met Lindas. To my right I noticed
a heard of elbs grazing and a large fire surrounded by several herders. I decided to walk over and see if I could join in
their talk and spend the night with them. I wanted to leave
the city of Rift but I needed to stay until morning and talk to
Lindas before I left. I just couldn't leave without explaining
to her about the sword.
The elb men welcomed me as a fellow herder and I
stayed by their fire listening to their stories most of the
night. A few hours before daybreak, I rolled up in the filthy
elb robe and slept until a hand poked me to wake up. The
hand belonged to a priest from the city and he asked if I was
ready to repent from my lies and wickedness.
"Answer me, do you repent from your wrongness?"
implored the priest again.
"No I don't," I finally answered in anger. "Tell Topaz I'm
not guilty, even though the sword didn't flame. There is a
reason why it didn't flame."
"Is there anything else you wish to tell the high priest?"

"Yes, tell him I will not stand trial and if anyone tries to force me I will use my sword."

"Very well, you foolish youth. I will tell him and he will send the soldier priests to bring you before trial," said the messenger priest angrily. He turned and marched away in a quick step.

It was a cold, overcast morning and all the elb herders were out tending their animals. The herds scattered all over the fields outside the marble white walls would have been a beautiful sight to enjoy had the circumstances been different.

"What are you going to do now, Tobe?" I asked myself. "Maybe I should leave before the soldier priests come. But I need to speak with Lindas and explain. She must be at the entrance of the rock wall." I began to walk stiffly in that direction as a herd of elbs blocked the way but quickly divided making a passage for me.

"You are scaring my elbs!" yelled one of the herders, but I paid no attention, noticing a group of priests with what looked like clubs in their hands coming out of the city gate. I quickened my pace towards the rock entrance realizing I might not have time to speak with Lindas, even if she was at the entrance this early in the morning. I quickened my step and made a certain click noise that elbs do not like and the herd stampeded towards the city and blocked the priests momentarily. When I was about forty bodies from the rock wall entrance I saw something on the ground in front of the entrance that has remained in my memory ever since. What I saw first looked like a wild animal on top of another in the final act of killing its prey. The animal was a beautiful white furry creature moving almost in a rhythmic motion. With a burning sensation in my stomach I recognized that this was not an animal but someone wearing an elb robe; my elb robe that was stolen from me by the red-bearded giant. To confirm my suspicion the giant looked up at me from his prone position and with the instincts of a warrior I began charging with my full power. He stood throwing my elb robe to the snowy ground grabbing his sword all in one motion. Between his legs lay the limp body of a female with honey-brown hair on top of a blue elb robe.

"You filthy stinking animal!" I yelled after I stopped only three bodies from the giant.

"We meet again and you have a new sword," observed the giant with a grin.

"Yes, you evil beast! And I'm also a nugget and I challenge you to a duel!"

His one eye opened wide and drool rolled from his mouth onto his dirty red beard as a most hideous smile formed on his ugly face. "Take off your robe and unsheathe your sword," spat the giant. I quickly stepped back to protect myself as I dropped the blood-stained robe and drew the sword from the golden bejeweled sheath. With great surprise to both the giant and myself the sword blade doubled in size and leaped with flames. The giant stepped back tripping over Lindas inert body as I quickly moved toward him swinging the sword wildly. The giant gained his feet and held his sword in front of himself to block my sword. I stepped into range and swung my sword parallel to the ground not worried about his blocking action. To my surprise my sword cut through his iron weapon and continued through his waist right through the hips. Smoke and steam poured from the burnt parts as the two halves of his body fell into the snow. The smell of charred flesh stung my nostrils as the most awful scream pierced my ears from the giant's mouth even though his upper body fell away from his legs. The snow hissed and steamed when the still hot parts hit the snow, as I looked back over to the girl on the blue elb robe. She wasn't moving and lay very still.

"He really is the king. He has the Flaming Sword!" came the voice of one priest who arrived in time to witness the fight between me and the giant. I paid no attention to the spectators, but instead sheathed the burning sword and bent over the girl, now confirming that it was Lindas. Her neck was beginning to bruise blue in the cold morning from where the giant had choked her with his huge hands. Her eyes were glazed the same as a dead elb. I put my head to her chest to listen for a heartbeat but I found none.

"Is she dead?" asked one of the priests.

"Yes, and you people killed her because of your unbelief!" I yelled back with great hatred in my voice. I realized that if I stood and pulled the sword now, it once again would be just a cold steel sword. I said no more and covered her body with her blue elb robe and picked up her broken form in my arms. "Take her to Topaz and tell him he can take his holy oil and do whatever he wants with it, but never will he come near me with it!" The priest who had awakened me this morning stood among his soldier priests with a club in his hand and his mouth hanging agape. I walked toward him and handed him Lindas' lifeless body and the group of priests dropped their clubs, turned, and walked slowly back to the marble city. A cold wind cut through the blue and red tunic given me by Lindas for the banquet, awakening me to the reality of what had just transpired. Then in a state of anger I picked up the giant's severed sword and shoved the seared end into his throat, listening to the snap as the sword split bone and muscle. His one good eye opened as I finished the death sentence. With two more wild hacks his head was severed from his body and I lifted it up looking for the name on the back of the neck. *ZEBULUM* was his name and from that day forward my name was no longer Tobe but Zeb. I made the decision I would live by the evil law of Petrapolis and not the holy mandates of Rift. I picked my white elb robe from the snow and covered myself. Then with my sword in its golden sheath and the giant's head dangling from my left hand I squeezed back through the Gate of Virgins leaving the city of Rift.

On the other side of the wall stood a black shaggy beast feeding on the leaves of the stink tree that stood before the cliff. The dark creature didn't notice me and since beasts usually won't allow strangers on their backs, I decided to sneak up and mount him before he realized I wasn't the giant. My plan worked and I was able to grab the edge of the beast's leather saddle and throw my right leg over and mount him before he noticed who I was. With a loud snort and a hiss, the beast must have recognized my weight was less than the giant's. He gave out a loud snort and a hiss as he turned his head showing his razor sharp teeth. I held up the giant's head by its red hair for the beast to see and smell. His nostrils opened and closed a few times before he turned his head waiting for his new master to give him his orders. It was a mystery to me why he didn't snort and buck. I took the reins and turned the beast away from the wall to continue my journey to the city of Petrapolis.

Chapter Three

During that day as I traveled from the city of Rift, a blizzard developed in the mountains. The beast carried me through the blinding wind and snow until I realized we would both perish if we continued. My only hope of survival would be to return to Rift and find shelter. Deciding on this course, I turned the beast around and made my way back, arriving by nightfall. At the wall I strapped the giant's head to the saddle and left the shaggy creature to care for himself while I took the Flaming Sword and pressed through the Gate of Virgins once again. On the other side there was no maiden waiting, which would have caused me some obvious problems. I crossed the open fields to the marble walls and luckily the lowben wood gates were not completely shut, but still ajar for the elb herders who were trying to guide their flocks into the city for shelter from the blizzard. I acted as if I were one of the herders and passed into the city unnoticed.

I walked down a side street covering my face with my elb robe and looking for a barn or some stable for shelter. After searching several streets, I became convinced I wasn't going to find anything suitable. I turned down another street and was met by a small group of men and women going in the opposite direction. I tried to let the group pass but one woman turned to me and asked, "Why aren't you going to the funeral?"

"Oh! I am going, but I forgot something and was only returning home to get it," I said, hoping not to arouse suspicion.

"Well you better hurry for even we are late." I nodded and the group passed on. I waited until they were some distance away and began to follow them. They turned onto another street and when I reached the corner I discovered where they were going. The entire population had gathered at the massive temple in the center of the city, and there in the middle of the crowd was an awesome sight. Lying very beautifully on top of the temple altar was the body of Lindas. Topaz was standing at the altar base with a torch in his hand. During a long prayer, I moved to the edge of the crowd while everyone's eyes were closed. I stood and stared at Lindas' body upon the altar, her blue elb robe wrapped around her slight body. Snow was still falling but the wind had died down. All was motionless except for the torch in Topaz's hand as the flames leaped like mad tree elves. The torch reminded me of my sword and my hand touched my side. I had taken a cord of leather from my new beast earlier and tied it around the sword in order to hang it over my shoulder under my elb robe.

The crowd hushed as Topaz waited to speak before he lit the pile of wood neatly stacked under Lindas' body.

"My friends and fellow citizens of Rift. I grieve tonight in a way that is beyond my understanding. My eldest daughter is dead and I am the cause. I knew in my heart that the strange visitor was truly the one sent by the Most High to be our king. It was written in his eyes. Now tonight I pay the heavy wages for my unbelief." Topaz lowered his head and his left hand reached to cover the contractions of anguish overtaking his face. The crowd murmured their solace to their high priest, and Topaz, after a long pause, controlled himself and began to speak again. "The prophecy came true this morning as everyone now knows. The Flaming Sword was seen at the Gate of Virgins this morning, shortly before this wretched storm struck our city. We were encroached by a giant from the outer world and now my daughter..." and Topaz broke down in uncontrollable tears. The city empathized with their leader as many held cloths to their eyes and wept. Finally Topaz lifted the torch to the wood on the altar and yelled to the heavens as the pyre began to kindle.

"If we would have only believed and accepted I would not have lost my daughter. Forgive us God. Accept Lindas into your kingdom and please bring back our king!"

The flames under Lindas' body began to blaze with great intensity and the face and features of Topaz were lit showing his grief. The light blue elb robe caught fire and the flames engulfed Lindas' peaceful body. I stood paralyzed feeling very distant, almost invisible and detached from what was happening. I felt like screaming and tearing my hair and at the same time alone and uncaring. I began to push through the crowd and to lose my thoughts as I looked at the faces of the people thronging around the altar. Their faces were illuminated by the flames that were now consuming Lindas. The faces were sad and full of pain. Many were weeping and others were just standing very still and in silence.

I found myself at the temple entrance that stood majestically behind the altar. Many of the spectators were beginning to leave because the funeral was almost complete. My original thought of seeking shelter entered my mind again as I was watching the people leave for their warm homes. It was at that time I thought of going inside the temple. The door was open and it appeared to be empty.

I glanced quickly around to see if anyone was watching me and then stepped into the open door and found myself in a huge vaulted room. There was a large oil lamp burning which cast an eerie light within the room. A second source of light came from a small altar where incense was burning.

The only other article was a table across the room from the oil lamp. I walked towards the table to examine the objects that were sitting on top of it. To my surprise I found freshly baked loaves of bread. I didn't hesitate to break a loaf and began to eat realizing now how starved I was.

After I had consumed one loaf, I took two more and sat down against the wall next to the table. "What a strange yet curious world. One moment I'm starving and the next I'm looking at a table full of bread that is there for the taking," I said to myself. I ate and ate until my stomach was aching. I slid down the wall and stretched out on the floor to sleep. The stone floor was hard but I told myself at least I was out of the wind and snow.

I remained on the stone floor for over an hour without moving or closing my eyes. Out in the wilderness as an elb herder, I learned to lie still for one hour watching and listening before I went to sleep. Most wild predators in the wilderness will not usually wait more than an hour after all is still to make their attack. Humans are the most unpredictable of all creatures yet there are some predictable behaviors that do occur.

In the temple all was quiet and still after the first hour and no one had entered the lofty room. I couldn't remember a time when there was such silence as the thick stonewalls kept out all sounds from outside. Not feeling very comfortable, I stood up and quietly walked to the door of the temple and looked out. The snow had stopped, and stars were sparkling in the heavens. All the inhabitants of Rift had departed from the square. The remains on the altar were nothing more than red coals now. Feeling more secure knowing everyone had gone home, I went back to lie down, grabbing another loaf of bread on the way. After I took a bite out of it, I heard something that almost stopped my heart.

"It's the death penalty if you are caught eating the Bread of Presence."

In a fraction of a moment I turned on the voice behind me and pulled my sword from its sheath. The blade leaped with flames. As I began a stroke to cut the intruder in half I recognized Vertunda.

"Put the sword away before someone from outside sees the flame," said Vertunda. I obeyed and put it back into the golden sheath.

"Why did it flame?" I asked.

"Why did your sword flame, is that what you are asking?"

"Yes, in the dinner hall last night it didn't flame but now I was going to kill you and it flamed."

Vertunda smiled, then as he pointed to my sword he began to explain. "Remember the sword is the Sword of Truth. Your heart at the dinner last night was lifted up in conceit after everyone cheered you as their king. And when you drew the sword you drew it in pride. Therefore it didn't flame. You can't put the Sword of Truth to a test and provoke it. Now, just a moment ago you pulled it out to protect yourself and your heart didn't know it was me standing behind you. Ignorance is bliss. Remember that."

"Ignorance is bliss?" I asked.

"Children are ignorant in a way; therefore they are in a state of happiness and bliss. True? If you act out of innocence you are innocent, for you know no better."

"Yes, I understand. Tell me, why did the sword flame when I faced the giant?" I asked bubbling with questions.

"That should be obvious. It was pulled out in a righteous act of retribution. The bearded one committed a wicked act in the presence of the Sword of Truth and suffered the consequences. In your heart you wanted to save the girl."

"Tell me why Lindas had to die, the girl I loved; why did she have to die?"

"First I must tell you that you didn't love Lindas. You were fond of her, but you didn't love her."

I was jarred by Vertunda's words but as I looked down

into my heart I knew his words were true. When I stared into her eyes, it was Desiree I was thinking about, not Lindas. "You speak truthfully, I didn't even know who she was other than her name."

"The girl you love is Desiree, and someday she shall be your wife. Remember these words for there will be a day when you will doubt."

Again I was jolted by Vertunda's words. To marry Desiree was always my dream, as far back as I could remember. But to think about the possibilities of that happening was futile, considering the ways and customs of Ontelles. As I mentioned earlier, once a girl reached the age of twenty, she was taken to Petrapolis and there she became public property for anyone's want. A warrior at the age of thirty was the only one who could choose a woman as his mate and then she left with him to return to their new village. According to my calculations it would be about three years before she arrived at Petrapolis. Then I would have to wait a good six years until my thirtieth birth date in order to choose her as my wife. Desiree during that time could be subject to any number of unbelievable and wretched acts by any warrior. To protect her, even if I could, I would have to fight almost every warrior in the city. Just considering her physical beauty, I knew she would probably be selected as someone's wife in her first year at the city. To think and plan my future with Desiree was ridiculous considering the laws of Ontelles.

"How do I know she will be my wife? This is a hard thing to believe." I admitted to Vertunda.

"It will come to pass. You must understand that the creator of all things is the creator of time. You must understand He does not dwell in time but is outside of the dimension of what you consider as time. From His kingdom everything has already occurred even though it has not for those inside of time. He is not manipulating events as much as He knows the outcome and declares it to His chosen ones, such as yourself at this instant. Your job is to have faith in His words. Now it is almost time for me to go."

"You can't go yet, you didn't answer my first question. Why did Lindas have to die?"

"I will answer your question if you can answer mine. Why didn't you present yourself to Topaz at the altar when he asked the Holy One to send back their king?"

"I don't know if I can answer that," realizing that I had spoken the truth.

"Then I cannot answer you either. Now, two things I must tell you before I leave. Depart from this temple before dawn or you will be discovered and killed. King or not you would be put to a quick death. And secondly, unless you think you would make a wise king now, you had better prepare and prove yourself before you present yourself as king." I agreed and Vertunda melted away leaving me once again in the dim light of the empty temple.

I slept well that night. Before dawn I left the city, carrying six loaves of bread. If I were going to die for eating one loaf I might as well take all I wanted, for the punishment would be the same. Outside the Gate of Virgins I marveled when I found the shaggy beast. He had wandered off but hadn't gone very far. The giant's head was frozen to the saddle and I had to break it loose in order to sit comfortably.

I rode for the next ninety days towards the city of Petrapolis, not really understanding why I was going there. Maybe it was the ways of Ontelles that had been taught to me since I was young, or maybe I had to go there to prove myself, in order to be prepared for the kingship of Ontelles. But truthfully, I wasn't sure what the real reason was.

During those days of traveling I encountered no one, and it was a period full of thought and reflection on the events that had happened to me since I left my village. I also thought of Desiree and wondered why I had hardened my heart towards her, knowing now I truly loved her and wanted her. When I was younger and only a herder of elbs, during the spring and summer months, Desiree would come and visit me in the foothills of the wilderness. She would always bring a basket of fruit and we would lie in the tall grass, talking, embracing and at times kissing. She filled my life with pleasures beyond explanation. All the other herders and boys from my village knew Desiree was my girl, but several were jealous because they also loved her for her beauty. Two days before I left my village as a nugget, one boy who wanted Desiree as his told me he would now have her since I was leaving. I struck the boy with my fist and told him to keep his hands off Desiree. With blood dripping from his mouth he laughed and asked me if I was going to kill all the warriors in Petrapolis when Desiree arrived there. On the final day of my travels towards Petrapolis, I recalled the boy's words, for he was right, that was what I was going to do.

That afternoon I saw the city for the first time off in the distance. It had huge walls that rose out of the snowy plain. I then did something very strange, something I had never done before. I stopped my beast and with hands raised toward heaven, like Topaz did at the funeral, I spoke out loud to the Most High. "Oh Heavenly Creator; God of Vertunda; God of the Temple of Rift; the one Topaz speaks to and believes in. You who gave me the Sword of Truth, I need to speak to you. I do not know who I am, even though I'm told I will be the king of Ontelles someday. I have also been told that the girl Desiree will be my wife and I don't understand even this. You know and understand all, therefore protect and guide me. I know nothing about you, except what I know of your creation. The trees, the snow, the clouds, the wind, the animals, the birds, and the flowers in the springtime; this is all I know of you. From this I know you must care about them and therefore you must care about me. This I believe."

After I prayed I decided to camp where I was and enter the city in the morning. I built a fire out of beast dung and ate some berries gathered a few days back. After I had finished eating I heard the hoof beats of a beast. Looking towards the sound, I saw a man riding toward me. He was moving slowly and very cautiously. When he was about thirty bodies away I called out to him to name himself. It was strange to see another person, for it had been over ninety days since I had encountered anyone.

"Tomorrow my name shall be Joba," said the stranger, then he held up a warrior's head by its hair. "I'm a nugget from a village on the side of the mountains boarding the Lepis Ocean."

"I'm also a nugget from a village on the side of the Lepis. You may join me tonight. I have a bag of berries."

"Thank you," said Joba. He rode into my camp and my fire lit up his features. He wore a black elb robe and had dark hair under his elb hat and dark, heavy brows. His eyes were likewise dark but intelligent looking. Then after I saw his large nose and full lips, I recognized him. He was a friend from my village. He was about half a year older than I, and he had left in the summer before me.

"Pomo, it's me, Tobe!" I finally said. He looked down from his beast then he smiled and jumped from his saddle and embraced me.

"Tobe! I don't believe it. And do you also have a warrior's head?"

"Yes," and I went to my beast's saddle, laying next to the fire and untied the red bearded head and showed Pomo. "Here you go Pomo, look at the size of this frozen head," I said, tossing the giant's remains to him.

"Call me Joba," he said, catching the frozen head with both hands, then turning the grisly trophy over in his hands, he continued. "This must have been a giant of a man... and your new name is.... Zeb. Well tomorrow we will be warriors of Petrapolis with our new names and we will have all our desires fulfilled."

I didn't know about that but I answered by saying, "Tonight we are still Tobe and Pomo; let's have it that way."

Chapter Four

That night Joba and I talked and laughed about the days of being herders of elbs. If there had been an observer listening to our childish talk and laughter he never would have guessed that we each had a man's head tied to our saddles and that we were going to be Ontelles warriors in the morning.

When morning came and we both rode off towards Petrapolis, one in black and the other in white, I pondered about the shortness of life and how as a child I never believed the day would come when I would ride to Petrapolis to become a warrior. But here I was, and a good friend rode beside me. Our beasts ran through the hard packed snow throwing their heads up and down with the knowledge that behind the huge walls up ahead they would receive plenty of grain and a padded stall in some stable. I looked over to Joba and he placed his right hand on the warrior's head bouncing next to his thigh. I reached under my robes for my sword and a feeling of security filled me after my hand caressed the golden sheath. I looked over to Joba again but he was now staring towards Petrapolis, deep in thought. I smiled to myself realizing he knew nothing about my sword or the prophecy of my becoming a king.

It was mid-morning by the time we reached the city gate. Four warriors standing guard asked us if we were nuggets.

We gave them the heads and one of the four recorded the names, villages, and birth dates from each head in a large black book that was lying on a wooden table.

"Today your names will become Zeb and Joba," said the man who wrote our names in the book. "Now wait here and I will see if the Council of Warriors will be able to see you." The soldier saluted to the other soldiers and then he passed into the city.

"That's a nice elb robe you have there," said one of the soldiers to me. I smiled and then he asked how long we had been in the mountains.

"Since summer for my friend," I answered. "Myself since the middle of the winter."

"That's quite a feat. Not many nuggets make it through the winter. Quite a feat it is," said the soldier with obvious admiration.

"What happens at the Council of Warriors?" I asked, but before we received an answer, the soldier who had gone to inform the council had returned.

"You two men dismount and follow me. Your beasts will be cared for," said the soldier. He then slipped back into the city. Joba and I dismounted and followed the soldier. Once in the city I noticed that it wasn't as glorious as I first thought it might be. There weren't any gold or silver houses; not even marble could be seen in any of the structures. The houses along the main street were made only of mud and straw and the streets were nothing but hard packed snow and frozen earth. The houses (they seemed more like huts) looked like they were built on a grand-accident type of plan. We didn't see any public buildings or temples until we reached the center of the city. There we saw three large buildings made of wood and black fieldstones.

"The middle building up ahead is the Warrior Council Building," said the soldier leading us. "The two smaller buildings flanking the council headquarters are the Temple of War and the Temple of Love." The Temple of War was guarded by four warriors who stood at attention by its open doors. To the right of us at the Temple of Love, we saw only females wearing beautiful elb robes, loitering around its doors. I counted over twenty beautiful women around its entrance. Then one of the girls began to walk down the steps towards us. Our guide, not wanting to step into the mud street where we were walking, paid no attention to the girl who was waving at us from the stone steps. Joba waved back and she asked if we were new warriors. Joba nodded yes and she said her name was Leas. "Come to the Temple of Love after you finish at the council and my friends and I will welcome you to Petrapolis."

"Spring is near; it's in the wind," said the soldier talking to himself, not noticing Leas. Joba on the other hand surely noticed her and the other women up at the top of the stairs. He was licking his lips and bobbing his head as he waved at the girls who waved back. Three men exposed to the same stimulus and all three were in different realms, none touching or connecting. One was thinking about the weather, the other listening to the lusts of his heart, and myself caught in confusion: trying to understand and make sense out of what was happening.

"The council chambers are through those doors and the members of the council are waiting for you," said the soldier. He turned and went down the stone stairs we had just climbed. Another soldier appeared from the dark recesses of the council building and motioned us to follow him. We obeyed and entered the open doors and walked down a long eerie hallway, which was lined with spears and ancient shields. Torches lit the way, filling the hallway with black soot and smoke.

"Take off your hats," ordered the soldier after we came to a wooden door at the end of the hallway. We removed our fur caps and our dirty, greasy hair fell to our shoulders. Our faces were likewise dirty, bearded, and weather beaten. "Be prepared to defend yourselves," warned the soldier before the door was opened and two soldiers came out from the chambers, dragging a warrior out by his feet. The man being dragged was mutilated and covered in blood. "If you make it through here you shall be Ontelles Warriors," said the soldier before he entered the council chambers and announced our presence using our new names. We entered the chamber together, shoulder-to-shoulder. The soldier who announced us moved behind us and went out closing the wooden door. I opened my robe and felt for my sword, for what I saw was the most frightful scene I had ever witnessed. The chamber was approximately twenty bodies square and lit only by torches. There were no windows and the ceiling and walls were permanently blackened by smoke. In front of us sat ten warriors between the ages of twenty and twenty-nine. They all wore elb robes, but not as beautiful as mine. They also wore helmets of different styles, from a bowl shape to elaborate versions with golden bird wings, antlers or horns. I then noticed an eleventh man sitting alone against the wall to my right. He wore a golden crown and a long purple elb robe, bordered in white. He was also much older than any of the ten warriors, maybe in his early fifties.

"What's that smell?" asked Joba in a whisper.

"I don't know," I answered out of the side of my mouth. Then I noticed all the warriors were smoking pipes. "Whatever it is, it's in those pipes."

Then the fourth man from the right stood from his stone chair. "We are the Council of Warriors. What you are about to learn is confidential and never to be repeated to anyone who isn't a warrior. My name is Castor, warrior sixth class and sixth member of the council. The other members are representatives from each age of warriors in Petrapolis. You two are warriors of the first class since you both are still twenty years of age. On your next birthday you will be made warriors second-class and so on until you became warriors tenth class and eligible to choose a mate. All warriors have the freedom of Petrapolis along with all its female population. It is your city, supported by the people of Ontelles. The only orders that you must follow are the orders of class. You must be subservient to a warrior of a higher class than you and obey any order given. You will be able to recognize a warrior's class by his helmet, as you both probably noticed each of us on the council wears a different one. If you do not like an order given by a higher class, you may challenge the warrior who gave the order. If you win the challenge you obviously won't have to obey. After you leave our chamber you will be assigned to a legion of warriors for the next four years. After your fourth year you will spend the following three in the mountains challenging nuggets. On your eighth year you may return to Petrapolis and live off the fat of the city until your tenth year when you must choose your mate and leave for your new village. Any questions?" We both stood in silence.

"Good," said Castor. "Now both of you must move to your right, bow your heads and our king will dub you as warriors." Both Joba and I looked at each other for we knew of no king of Ontelles. The older man with the gold crown stood and we complied. With a golden sword in his hand he touched each of our bowed heads with the tip of the blade.

"You are now warriors of the first class. Obey the laws of Ontelles and you will receive all the blessings and privileges of being warriors," said the king in a raspy voice.

The king sat down on his throne that was slightly elevated above the warrior council.

"Now for your first test, before you leave the chambers!" called out Castor, standing before his sixth class chair. He threw off his elb robe and unsheathed a large sword. He wore a beautiful leather breastplate and very elegant leather pants and shirt underneath his breastplate. "I order the one wearing the white elb robe to give it to me."

I froze not knowing what to say or do. My mind flashed back to the red bearded giant in the mountains and I knew I would lose more than my elb robe if I handed it to him, so I stood firm and said, "No!"

Castor stepped down from his chair and said with a grin, "It's a challenge then."

I quickly removed my elb robe and handed it to Joba. As soon as my robe was removed the warriors all began to murmur among themselves until the king stood and spoke. "You wear royal garments from the city of Rift. You have been there?"

"No!" I lied. "I stole the garments from a man I came across in the mountains."

The king sat down obviously believing my story and Castor stood waiting for me to take hold of my sword. Joba moved back towards the door and I went to pull my sword, but as my hand touched the jeweled handle I hesitated, not wanting to reveal the Flaming Sword. I quickly turned to Joba, "Give me your sword!" Castor waited for Joba to obey my request. With a questioning look on his face, Joba pulled his sword and tossed it to me. I caught it in the air by the hilt. Castor slowly stalked towards me, crouched and floating his sword slowly in small circles with the tip pointed at my face. I just stood where I was and prayed silently for the second time to the God of Vertunda. "I need you now Holy One. I should not have lied about knowing about Rift and with your help if I get out of this mess I will never lie again, so please guide me to victory."

I blocked his first thrust and stepped backwards as Castor circled with the precision of experience. I somehow blocked every assault as sparks and metal flew from the clashing blades. Without realizing it I slammed up against the wall opposite the king's throne. Castor had me now. I was breathing hard and my reflexes were slowing. Since the fight began I had been on the defensive and I now had to try an offensive attack to get away from the wall. I swung for his legs, since they were unprotected, but Castor's sword blocked swiftly. He slid his blade in an expertly handled technique, laying it into my right hip, cutting me to the bone. Blood began to flow and all my wind was almost lost as he pulled his sword out and aimed for my chest. I dropped Joba's sword to the stone floor clutching my wound and flew back into the wall barely missing the tip of his blade.

Castor stepped back to regain his balance and during that moment my eyes focused on a torch flickering across the room and my mind thought of the Flaming Sword. Castor had now lifted his sword above his head and was ready to bring it down into the center of my skull. My blood covered hand wrenched the sword out of the golden scabbard with lightening speed and it was still leaping in length as I cut Castor's sword arm off, just below the elbow, while he still held the sword above his head. I had the Flaming Sword back into my scabbard before Castor's sword and hand hit the floor. To the warriors and Joba it looked like only a flash of light struck between Castor and me, not realizing what really happened. Castor grabbed his cauterized arm and ran out of the council chambers wailing. The other warriors stood and slowly walked over to examine Castor's arm and sword lying on the floor still smoldering. Joba picked up his sword and I slid to the floor not knowing what was going to happen to me. I pressed my hand once again to the wound, desperately trying to stop the bleeding. The last thing I remember in the council chambers was the pool of blood I was sitting in and the surprised looks on the faces of the warriors looking at Castor's severed arm.

Chapter Five

W hen I came back to consciousness I found myself lying on a leather cot in a cold, stonewalled room. A torch burning on the wall across from me was the only source of light and heat. I tried to sit up but found my injured hip tightly bound with white bandages. I couldn't move. It was several hours, looking up from the cot at the walls and the flame of the torch dancing its twisted jig, before anyone entered the room. A wooden door opened and in stepped the man who had dubbed Joba and myself as warriors.

"Good, you are awake!" said the king and he disappeared out the door. Within a few moments he came back carrying a tray full of food and drink. "Don't try to get up. I will feed you."

"Aren't you the king?" I asked while he placed the tray on a wooden table next to the cot.

"My name is Topo, King of Ontelles. You probably know my brother. He is Topaz, the High Priest of Rift."

"Yes, I know him," I said before I realized what I had said; yet I had made a promise not to lie. Topo put a spoon full of bread pudding into my mouth without any expression on his face.

"My brother Topaz chose the righteous path and I was destined to walk the evil way. At the age of eighteen I was accused of lying and stealing. The council of elders at the city of Rift ordered me to be blindfolded and removed from the city. They told me never to return."

"Have you ever tried to return?" I asked after I swallowed a mouthful of the pudding.

"I've tried many times, but the way is lost to me. No one can find the crack in the rock except by accident. Even you who have been there probably can't find your way back."

"That may be true. However, I did find the crack in the wall twice, both by accident."

"I believe you, and that is why you are still alive," said King Topo as he wiped the edge of my mouth with a white cloth. "Some of the council didn't believe your lie about your garments."

"Where am I, and what is going to happen to me?" I asked, realizing my serious situation.

"You are safe for now. You are in a back room underneath the temple of Love. Only the high Priestess knows you are here. After you cut Castor's arm off the other warriors left you to die in the council chamber. I had your friend Joba carry you here and Leas, the high Priestess, sewed and bandaged your wound. You will live and become King of Ontelles just like the ancient prophecy says."

"Prophecy, what prophecy?" I asked trying to appear not to understand.

"The prophecy concerning the Flaming Sword, which states, 'The day the Flaming Sword is seen in the council chambers of Petrapolis, your king has arrived and a new order will be established.'"

"But you are the king, not I."

"No, I am the king only by falsehood. You are the true king and that is why I didn't let you die. I don't want to be king. It's a horrible job, believe me. What I want more than anything else is to return to Rift and repent of my wicked ways and you can help me." Topo then lifted a vial of black liquid and he ordered me to drink all of it. After a few moments all my limbs began to tingle and sleepiness invaded my body. As I fought to keep awake I felt for my sword but it wasn't at my side. "Where is my sword?" I asked with slurred words.

"It's in a safe place," replied Topo before I fell asleep.

How long I was asleep I don't know. When finally awakening, I found myself drifting in and out of delirium. Three figures were standing over me talking in whispers, unaware that I was conscious. Listening to their voices, I recognized Topo, Joba and the third was a woman.

"There has to be something that we can give him," said Joba.

"He will live, that I know, but how I don't know," said Topo.

"I will offer a sacrifice to the goddess of love," said the woman.

"No, this man serves the God of Rift who is an enemy to your goddess. A sacrifice would only serve to kill him," said Topo in a loud whisper.

"Who is this man?" asked the woman.

"Yes, who is he?" I was surprised to hear Joba ask.

"I can't explain yet, but I know he will live. Let's just leave him to rest," said Topo, and the others followed him out of the room.

I opened my eyes that burned with fever. My hip was also burning as if a hot iron was touching it and my heart was pounding like the hooves of a charging beast. "Holy One of Rift, God of Vertunda, the one I'm called to serve, please help me," I called out before I passed out again.

"Zeb, wake up or you will die," said a voice I couldn't recognize; yet it was familiar in a strange way. I didn't know how much time passed since the three were in my room talk-

ing about my death, but it seemed like days. I opened my
eyes and there stood Vertunda, filling the room with a brilliant light. He reached over and with his finger, touched my
hip and the burning pain left. "I would have come sooner
after you called for help but the spirit of Petrapolis held me
back these two days. There was a great spiritual battle and I
can't stay much longer, for my forces are temporarily being
beaten back. Listen to Topo for he shall instruct you, and
Joba shall be your right hand and commander. I'm sorry but
I must now leave. Peace be upon you." Vertunda melted
away and at the same moment the wooden door to my room
opened and Topo and Joba entered.

"Look! I told you he was going to recover!" exclaimed
Topo to a surprised Joba. I sat up and asked Joba to remove
my bandages. He cut them carefully with a sharp dagger and
to the surprise of us all, we found no scar or wound.

"What happened?" asked Joba.

"A miracle took place by the Holy One of the universe,"
I said excitedly. "A miracle took place and you two are wit-
nesses. Topo, you are to instruct me about this God of Rift
and Joba you are to be a great general and commander." Both
men glowed with awe because of my words and the sight of
my healed hip. They both believed and we all grasped hands
in a gesture of commitment to show the Holy One and each
other that we were going to follow his command.

I found out later that the miracle took place in the early
afternoon on the seventh day after I was wounded and that
evening the three of us feasted in King Topo's private chambers, which were part of the council building. After we finished our meal we sat around a large fire pit built in the
center of the floor. A small hole in the blackened ceiling
allowed most of the smoke to escape. Each of us had a
creamy drink in our hands and we relaxed on large cushions.

"Well Zeb," said Topo. "Tell me what you want to know
and I will try to explain."

"First I want my sword," I said, trying to be polite but forceful at the same time. Topo stood and went to a wall and removed a loose stone. He reached in an arm's length and pulled out my sword in its golden sheath, handing it to me as he settled again by the fire pit.

"Does he know about the sword?" asked Topo pointing to Joba.

"No he doesn't, unless you told him."

"Told me what?" asked Joba, with confusion written in every line of his face.

"Remember the flash of light in the council chambers during the fight?" queried Topo. When Joba nodded, Topo continued. "Well that was Zeb's sword. It's the legendary Flaming Sword, also called the Sword of Truth."

"Can I see it?" asked Joba. I looked to Topo and he nodded yes. I stood from my comfortable position and removed the blade from its scabbard and the room lit up as the blade ignited in blazing flames. Joba's eyes almost fell out of his head as he watched me pass the sword through the air above our heads. "I'll be the dung of an elb, I've never seen anything like this before," blurted out Joba in his awed excitement. "Well, except a week ago."

"And there isn't anything it won't cut through," I stated after I slid it back into its scabbard.

"Please sit Zeb," said Topo. "I must tell you both something. According to the ancient prophecy, you Zeb, are the rightful King of Ontelles, but as you both know, I'm the acting king. I told you Zeb that I became king by deception and this is true. At the age of thirty I was to choose my mate and leave Petrapolis but I wanted to stay. That's when I devised a plan, which would allow me to do so. The plan worked and it convinced the council of warriors that I was the long awaited king and they enthroned me. That took place twenty-three years ago."

"Well how did you convince the council of warriors?"

asked Joba, angered by Topo's wrong doing.

"Please don't be angered at me, though I deserve death. I carved a wooden sword and soaked it in fish oil. On my thirtieth birthday I went into the council chambers and announced myself as king according to prophecy. I drew the wooden sword, igniting the oiled wood with a hot coal that was secretly placed at the top of the sheath. I waved it several times and then placed it back in the sheath. They wanted to see the trick a second time and fortunately for me it worked. They all believed and I was made the first king of Ontelles. Now you both see that if anyone sees the real Flaming Sword in Zeb's hand, they will either make Zeb king and kill me, or kill Zeb for stealing my sword."

Joba and I both looked at each other realizing the words of Topo were true.

"What do you suggest?" asked Joba.

"This might be hard to understand, but I suggest that Zeb leave the sword in the wall until I'm dead or an emergency dictates otherwise. No one on the council realizes what they saw when you cut Castor's arm, just like Joba didn't know. The only reason that I knew was because I've dreaded the day ever since I proclaimed myself as king. But please remember this, I've changed since those days and I've prayed to the Holy God of Rift and asked for forgiveness; but that doesn't mean I will escape the rewards of my evil deed. I need time to work out an escape and you, Zeb, need to learn many things only I can teach you, and I do need you Zeb."

"Alright, I will hide the sword in the wall, but it comes out when I say so." I demanded.

"Agreed," replied Topo with a great sigh of relief. "Besides, if I were trying to deceive you Zeb, I would have let you die in the council chambers. Secondly, I wouldn't have given the sword back to you, true?" And I believed his words were true enough.

The next morning when the three of us awoke from our beds of cushions, spread out around the dead coals of the fire pit, Topo called to one of the many girls that ministered to him. She entered carrying a tray of fruits and cooked fish. After we had eaten, Topo revealed his proposed plan for Joba and myself. He said that Castor thought I was dead and it was best to leave it that way. Therefore it was necessary to place Joba and myself in a legion that would be leaving that day to collect the sixty-percent tax imposed on the villages beyond the mountains. We would be away for a few years and when we returned we would be men educated in the arts of war. Castor would either be dead or gone from Petrapolis with his mate. Finding no fault in Topo's plan, Joba and I quickly agreed.

Before we left the council building, King Topo took the Flaming Sword and placed it in the wall. He also wanted me to put my white elb robe in the wall with the sword, since that was a giveaway to Castor. Topo offered an ordinary tan elb robe in exchange. I saw the wisdom in his words, but I had lost my robe and sword once again even though only until returning to Petrapolis.

Joba and I were signed out to the Vth Legion of Petrapolis by special orders from the king. We were given leather breastplates, and leather uniforms, along with the simple metal helmet of a warrior first class. The Vth Legion left that night on beasts and war wagons. These wagons were large two-wheeled carts pulled by six beasts that carried supplies and the taxes we collected. In all, six thousand warriors and beasts marched through the city gates at dusk. Joba and I saw nothing of Castor and hopefully would never see him again.

Outside the city walls the moonlight washed the snowy plain and I knew my warrior education was well under way. My impressions of Petrapolis, though unable to see much of it, told me it was dull and disheartening. The walls and buildings didn't compare to the hidden city of Rift. I later asked Joba about his thoughts of the city and he said he had seen nothing to compare to it. He pointed out that he had spent seven days guarding the door to the room where I lay wounded, even though he was tempted many times to go upstairs to the Temple of Love and engage in the activities that went on there continuously.

Chapter Six

During those years of collecting taxes, neither Joba nor
I asked to escort loaded war wagons back to
Petrapolis. Many of the soldiers in the legion found this a little strange but I always joked saying I would probably get
lost if I were to escort wagons back to Petrapolis. By the end
of the third year with the Vth Legion, an incident occurred
that seemed designed to set my heart totally against the
ways of Ontelles. It was the middle of summer during that
rare time of the year when one didn't even need to wear an
elb robe. The Vth Legion camped in the Lepis Wilderness
outside a small village, but to Joba and I it wasn't just any
small village, it was our village. The commander of the
legion ordered my patrol and two others to enter the village
and collect the taxes while the main body of the legion
waited in camp for our return.

When I learned of my orders I went to the commander
and told him that Joba and I were from this village.
According to Ontelles' law, we were released from our
orders. That afternoon, being disturbed by many thoughts, I
took a walk by myself and went to the spot where Desiree
and I had last kissed and parted when I left to be a warrior.
I sat on the grassy plain looking at the dust cloud hanging
over my village, as people such as my parents were turning
their hard-earned profits over to the soldiers of Petrapolis.

As I watched the village I reminisced about my life there. I also began to think about Desiree and for some reason had a burning desire to speak with her, although it was the death penalty to enter the village and seek her out. She had to be about nineteen now and fully developed in her womanhood. I tried to bury my thoughts about her and the love we had for each other. I was about to leave when I heard my name called, and I turned my head to find Joba walking towards me. I stayed seated and waited for him.

"Zeb, what are you doing way out here? I've spent most of the day looking for you."

"Why have you been looking for me?" I asked, not looking at him but instead staring off towards our village.

"Because I know what you're thinking about."

This statement caught me by surprise and I looked up at Joba feeling the guilt that had to be written all over my face. "What was I thinking about?" I asked, trying to hide behind an uncaring bluff.

"You're still a nugget," Joba jested. "You want and you are probably planning on talking to Desiree." I didn't say anything but looked back at the village. "Wait a year and you can see her in Petrapolis."

"Do you realized what will happen to her after she enters Petrapolis? And I can't stand at the city gate everyday waiting for her," I said, realizing he had guessed my thoughts accurately.

"Oh, but you can ride into our village and go knocking on her door and tell her parents that Zeb, formerly Tobe, wants to see Desiree for just a moment."

"Funny my friend, but I need to see her. I don't know how to explain this but I am sick of spirit and feel like I am dying unless I can just see her and speak with her."

Joba said nothing and sat next to me. "Look at the tree elves!" exclaimed Joba breaking our long silence. He pointed off to our left to a small family of three animals running through the short grass, heading towards a large low-ben tree. I knew Joba was trying to change the subject but I didn't want to.

"I love her and I need to tell her not to come to Petrapolis. I need to tell her she can find sanctuary at Rift and that's where I will meet her someday. Do you understand Joba?"

"I understand that this is love sickness, but it is forbidden for you to enter the village!"

"Say's who? The God of the universe? No, it is not His law, it's man's law and it is a wicked law!"

"But it's a law that is punishable by death just in case you forgot."

"Well if they catch me, they will have to kill me!"

At the moment I finished my last word, Joba was on his feet behind me, pulling his sword. He swung the flat of the blade against the side of my helmeted head before I knew what was happening. I tumbled over to my side, not unconscious but dazed. I lost the power in my limbs to lift my body off the ground. I felt Joba tying my feet and then my hands. After this I became very sleepy and my thoughts went into blackness.

When I came awake I found my head in great pain and lying next to the lowben tree that the family of tree elves had run to earlier. The suns had just gone down and there was a warm breeze blowing. My hands were bound tightly behind my back and my feet had been hobbled with my very own hobbles that I always carried on my belt. "That Joba is going to pay a heavy price for this," I swore to myself. The sunsets were bright crimson and it nicely matched the anger I felt boiling inside towards Joba. When I saw my dented helmet it set me off like a spark in dry tinder.

"That son of a beast! Joba, you no good piece of wet elb dung!" I yelled, as I struggled against my bonds. My outburst seemed to double the intensity of the already violent throbbing in my head. My shouts were also enough to star-tle the elves in the branches above me into dropping samples of what I'd just called Joba.

It was too painful to struggle with the hobbles. I tried to remain still and for several hours I sat leaning against the lowben tree watching all of the animals come out and play when they normally hide when a human is present. After a while it became almost surreal and pleasant being forced to sit still. The two moons of Ontelles, Lepis and Venu, were full and illuminated the wilderness in a basking light of blue. There weren't any clouds in the sky and I stared off into the heavens watching for falling stars. A huge piece of space rock came arching in, pulling a bright red and blue tail behind it. The star burned out before it reached the planet surface and I took this for a good sign. Then I believed for some reason that this was superstitious and the one God of Rift didn't want his people believing in such falsities. I began to think about Vertunda and wondered why he hadn't visited me since he had healed my hip in Petrapolis. I hoped he wasn't angered with me for leaving the Flaming Sword with Topo, even though he did tell me to listen to Topo's instructions.

As I was thinking about these things a ground hog ran through the grass into some thick bush off to my right. I listened for what might have caused his breakaway, since they were only afraid of either a beast or humans. I heard footsteps and could tell that whoever it was, was coming towards the lowben tree. I tried one last time to free my hands but it was to no avail. Whispered curses began to cross my lips, but then I heard a familiar voice call my old name.

"Tobe, are you there, Tobe? It's me, Desiree."

"I'm behind the lowben tree!" I answered with shocked excitement. The footsteps quickened and I rolled over to get a glimpse of the girl I had longed for years to see. When I saw her, I realized she had developed into a beautiful woman, beyond what she had been. When she reached the lowben tree she stopped and cocked her head to the side like she always did and smiled her sweet smile.

"Desiree, you are a sight I have longed to see." Her smile broadened and she bent down cutting my hands and feet free with a sharp knife.

"How did you know I was here?" I asked, rubbing my ankles and wrists.

"Pomo, I mean Joba, found me going to the village well. He told me where you were and said I had to come."

I stood up and looked around the lowben tree squinting towards the village trying to spot his worthless hide. "Where is he now?"

"He said you both could square things tomorrow but he told me to tell you that he had to do what he did in order to protect you, and that is his purpose in life. He said you would understand."

"Well he has a strange way of protecting me."

"He really loves you Tobe, I mean Zeb."

"And I love you Desiree," I said, noticing how beautiful she was under the light of Lepis and Venu.

"I have never stopped loving you either."

We stood looking into each other's eyes as I waited for that twinkle that she had when she wanted to be kissed. She smiled and my hands held her head as our mouths softly came together. After a long while we went to our knees and rolled onto the soft grass and there we stayed all night in each other's arms. It was one of those rare nights on Ontelles when a southerly wind blows from the equator keeping the night pleasantly warm.

When the first rays of light appeared in the morning I discovered that we had both fallen asleep sometime in the night between kisses. Desiree's mouth was only a breath away and her soft, tender face was radiantly beautiful. Her long blond hair was cascading in layers that framed her high cheekbones and delicate jaw and chin. I carefully pulled my arm free, which she had been sleeping on all night. I discovered that my hand had fallen asleep and my fingers were stinging. I sat up and began to stroke her soft hair until she opened her eyes and looked up at me smiling.

"Good morning my love," I spoke in a whisper.

"You haven't changed; strong on the outside but gentle on the inside."

"Well if you, my dear, don't learn to harden yourself you will never make it, especially if you end up in Petrapolis."

"Tell me about Petrapolis. Is it a beautiful city?"

"It's a very ugly city actually, but don't worry, you won't ever have to see it."

Desiree now pulled her head back, sat up and looked me in the eyes. Then she slowly moved her head towards mine and kissed me. "Now tell me what you mean by what you just said or I shall never kiss you again."

I kissed her back and took her hands and began to explain my plan. "You aren't going to Petrapolis. You're going to the ancient city of Rift instead: the city I told you about last night. There I will meet you and we will be married and live out our lives."

"No, this cannot be. My father takes me in two weeks to cross the mountains in order to reach Petrapolis by the first snowfall. Besides, what do you propose? Do you want me to run away and try to find a city that cannot be found? Or do you ride into our village to kidnap me and sentence yourself to death?

"I don't know what, but you can't go to Petrapolis. Do you know what happens to women at that city?"

"I think so, but it really doesn't matter. I have no free choice in the matter. I'm locked in just as you were locked into becoming a warrior."

I stood and leaned my head against the lowben tree as I stared blankly towards my village. "It's a wicked world we live in. I'm sorry I didn't forget who you were when I left this village.

A hand touched my shoulder and I smelled the sweet fragrance of Desiree's hair as her lips whispered into my ear. "I'm yours and no one can take me from you. I'll wait for you at Petrapolis."

I pulled away from her and angrily screamed the horrible truth to her face. "You don't understand, all women in Petrapolis are nothing more than physical objects to anyone who wants them! You will be used and then cast aside for someone else! If you don't do what someone wants you will be killed! It is an evil place! Do you understand? You must listen to me and go to the city of Rift. You will be able to find it, I will tell you what to look for."

"You know the law, if a father doesn't deliver his daughter on her twentieth year he is cut and scattered on the four winds. I can't kill my own father by running away!"

"Oh! Then you will save your father by killing yourself!"

"I love you Zeb, but I do not know how to destroy the ways of Ontelles."

"Everyone in the villages is a slave to the wicked system of Ontelles, yet no one can tell me who made the laws. Well I know who made the laws. They are man made! And only man can change them."

Desiree stood, looking at me as if I had gone mad, but my eyes were opened to the truth and I felt like screaming, but said it only to myself. "Go to Petrapolis if you must. But this I know, you shall be my wife someday. How, I don't know, but it will happen as Vertunda promised." I kissed Desire on the mouth and told her I had to get back to my legion before roll call. I told her I loved her and she cried out the same words in a voice that was choked with grief. I turned and ran towards the camp as the red suns began to break over the flat plains of the wilderness, eating up the landscape in its generating warmth.

By the time I reached camp, roll had been taken and I

was counted as missing without permission. During time of war this crime was punishable by death, but in peacetime it was to be answered by forty lashes from a leather whip. Even though morality and discipline in Petrapolis were very lax, it was quite a different story in the legions. The commander of the Vth Legion, a tenth class warrior, asked no questions when I reported to him, but instead ordered his staff to take care of my punishment. Word spread like a wilderness fire in a dry summer that someone was going to get forty lashes. Boredom was the plague of the life in the legions and the news that someone was going to get the lash became a treat indeed to the time-hating soldiers.

Six warriors of the commander's staff led me to the wheel of a huge war wagon, where I was to be scourged. A seventh class warrior unfolded a long whip and snapped it in the air several times in order to limber up both his arms and the leather. Many of the warriors of the legion began to buzz like insects; all calling out odds and wagers on how many blows it would take before I cried out in pain. On Ontelles it was a sign of weakness if a man ever cried out when he was in pain. I was stripped to my waist and asked if I had anything to say before I was tied and lashed. I turned and searched for Joba in the crowded mass of excited men. I saw him with a very dejected look on his face. "Yes, I want a second with that soldier," I said, pointing to Joba.

"Make it quick," commanded the warrior with the whip.

I walked into the empty space between the gathered soldiers and the war wagon and stopped in the middle. I signaled Joba to join me, pretending I had something to tell him. He reluctantly stepped out of the crowd and cautiously walked up to me. I knew I didn't have much time so I had to work fast. Joba gave me an apologetic smile and a moment later my right fist connected with his stomach. As he doubled over I said, "That's for hitting me with your sword." My left hand crashed into his chin straightening him back up. "That's for tying my feet." Joba was too stunned to respond as my last strike tumbled him onto the grass like a heavy bag of seeds. "That's for tying my hands." I went behind him, dusted his back off and grabbed him under the arms, lifting him to his feet and whispered into his ear. "And this is for risking your life and finding Desiree for me." I left him standing there in a daze and walked back toward the war wagon as the soldiers began to cheer the small display of the one sided fight. What they didn't realize was the fight they could have seen if Joba had fought back.

Then something happened as the crowd quieted and I reached the war wagon wheel. It was a glimmering thought that entered my mind as if someone had whispered in my ear. It entered my mind again as my hands were being tied to the huge spokes of the wheel. When the leather thong of the whip began to rip into my back I barely felt a sting, for my mind was lost in the realization of a horrible and grue-some truth. How I learned this truth I'm not sure, but I wanted to believe Vertunda had something to do with it. After I was cut down from the wheel of the war wagon I was something different, something to be feared because of what I had realized. If a man constructed the system under which man was now enslaved, why does man continue under this oppressive system? That was the question. The next logical step was: if someone was to come along and try to change the system, how could it be done? I asked these questions over and over. First man had to comprehend his need for change and then only could change take place.

The burning touch of the whip fueled my hate for Petrapolis and all her evil ways and as far as I was con-cerned finalized her destruction. After the last stroke of the lash came down upon my shredded back I had the answer on how to change the ways of Ontelles. With the power of the Flaming Sword I could free the people from bondage by destroying Petrapolis, the source of all the evilness that existed. Vertunda gave me the sword and with the sword I could destroy the city and I was sure the God of Rift was planning this. There seemed to be no other way than to destroy this city and those who would not change from the brainwashing of duty to the ancient ways and laws. It would be costly yet it had to be done and this was my conclusion. It was the only way to free all victims such as Desiree and myself.

Chapter Seven

The morning after I had been flogged, the Vth Legion broke camp and headed out to the next village. The commander gave orders for Joba to stay to care for me since I was unable to travel because of my scourging. Two war wagons containing our village's taxes were also left with Joba and he and I were to deliver the wagons to Petrapolis as soon as I was able to travel.

Joba erected a tent of leather tarps stretched between the two war wagons and I spent the next two weeks recovering. During that time, we ate like kings since we had access to all the supplies in the wagons, but the boredom was killing Joba. During the first week he disappeared in the afternoons and it wasn't until the end of the week I found out where he had been going. He told me after a huge meal of roasted pig and several cups of cream juice that he had been waiting at the well outside our village, hoping to speak with Desiree. He said he wanted to make up for hitting me so hard and thought that by bringing Desiree to me one more time would make his atonement complete.

"You fool, what am I going to do if you get yourself killed?" I yelled after he spoke. It had been seven days since I was scourged and my back was a mass of long black scabs. My anger was about to explode so I left the fire and lay down on my bed of elb robes. The suns were about to set as

Joba remained at the fire not returning my verbal attacks. After darkness began to blanket the wilderness Joba finally got up from the fire and walked over to me.

"All right, King of Ontelles, tell me what is so important about my life that I can't have a little adventure to break the boredom of waiting for you to heal?"

"After I heal! Do you have any idea what we are going to do?" I asked rolling over on my side in order to look at Joba as I talked.

"Return to Petrapolis, what else!"

"That's very good, but we return to Petrapolis only to get the Flaming Sword. Then we leave to gather an army."

"Have you gone insane? What do we need an army for?"

"We are going to take Petrapolis and level it to the ground, that's what we need an army for."

"Now I know that whip affected your brain, or I did more damage than I realized when I hit you with the flat of my sword."

"And you, Joba, will be my general and together we will free all the villages from their bondage."

"Are you serious?"

"Never have been more serious. I've been lying here for the last seven days working out all the details and it's going to work." Joba sat down beside me and I began to reveal the knowledge that came to me when I was being whipped. After I had finished he believed it could all work. He then broke out a case of cream juice and we drank ourselves to oblivion, toasting to our new purpose in life.

In the morning, after we had washed and eaten, I asked about Desiree, and whether he had seen her or spoken to her at the well. He said he hadn't seen her at all and this news worried me. Later in the day I realized since Desiree was going to be my wife according to the words of Vertunda, I needed to talk to her once again. When I asked Joba to get her that evening he acted very smug trying to hide his joy in my asking him to do this task.

For the next seven days Joba hid at the well, but each day he reported back the news that he hadn't seen her. I began to fear that her father may have punished her for being out all night with me and had her locked in her room, or something even more terrible. The laws on Ontelles allowed a girl's father the right to even cut an arm or hand off if he thought it was deserved.

By the end of the second week my back was almost mended and I made the decision to sneak into the village at night, find Desiree and kidnap her. Joba insisted that he was coming along. That night we sat around our dinner fire sharpening our swords. We had our beasts packed with enough provisions to get us to Petrapolis and we were just waiting till the middle of the night to make our move. About two hours after sunset Joba noticed movement between us and the village. We sat frozen, as we watched what looked like two men walking towards us. Only Venu was full, but there was enough illumination to recognize the two men. They were Benda and Tetu, twins from our village. Joba and I knew them well. They were fellow elb herders and the pride of our village. They were about four years younger than us but they both had huge hands and limbs along with a fierce nature that gave them the nickname *twins of thunder*.

"Greetings Benda and Tetu," I said when we were close enough to talk. "Is that you, Tobe and Pomo?" Asked Benda.

"We are now known as Zeb and Joba," answered Joba.

"Then you are both warriors and today is our birth date and we are both now twenty," said Tetu.

"So you are both now nuggets looking for two heads," I said with my stomach tightening, as I understood what this meant.

"Are you challenging us?" asked Joba as he already was gripping the hilt of his sword.

"Of course," answered Tetu with a self-assured chuckle.

"Come now, we are from your own village, you must find some other warriors to fight," I said trying to dissuade them.

"We can, but we have already decided on you two."

"You can't fight us, we are all from the same village. Don't you understand? If you both are able to kill Joba and myself you will have no village to return to, since the law says a man child can never return to his own village after he turns twenty."

"We will deal with that problem when we reach thirty," said Tetu mockingly. "Besides, you should have listened to that law. Joba has been seen at the well and there is an order out for his death. Your father, Tobe, is at this moment gathering the men of our village to hunt Joba down. So now you see that we have an obligation to our village to challenge you both. It is the law of Ontelles."

"Very well you cursed pups!" breathed Joba and his grim expression even scared me when I looked into the dark recesses of his face.

"We will fight, but understand we gave you the opportunity to pass on," I said.

"We will not pass on," stated Tetu as he paired off with me and Benda with Joba.

"Before we begin I want to know how Desiree is." I surprised myself with the request, for I had been suppressing it since the twins entered our camp.

"And they let you become a warrior at Petrapolis? He still thinks he owns Desiree," laughed Tetu. "Now I know why Joba was at the well: very clever, and such camaraderie. Well since you both are about to die it won't hurt to know that Desiree left with her father for Petrapolis two weeks ago. And you know what happens to girls at Petrapolis."

Tetu laughed hysterically when he realized he had struck me deeper than he ever could with his sword. But his laughter left as I took the offensive and systematically slashed and thrust with my sharpened steel. With daily practice for the past three years I had become an expert with a sword. Joba and I worked together for hours each day, developing new and different techniques. Most warriors in the legion fought with brute strength and hoped for luck. Joba and I on the other hand had developed sword fighting into an art that could be mastered only with intelligence and constant practice. Within the first few seconds I realized Tetu knew nothing of sword fighting. I had opened a large line on his right cheek and blood was staining his leather shirt. Fear began to burn in his eyes as he faced his death and there wasn't much he was going to do to alter that. I intuitively found an opening and my sword thrust deep into his stomach. With a twist of my wrist the blade did lethal damage to his intestines. I removed the cold steel as fast as it went in.

"You are a master with the sword," were his words before he dropped to his knees clutching his stomach to keep his innards from falling out. From the corner of my eye I saw that Joba had wounded Benda in both arms and was only toying with him like a pet ash lizard toys with a cornered tree elf.

"Kill me Tobe, please, the pain is too much," begged Tetu. I shook my head and picked up his sword and tossed it in order that he couldn't inflict his own death.

"No, you are going to die a slow, painful death and you have only yourself to blame. And when my father gets here, you tell him how you feel. Tell him that's how I feel about the ways of Ontelles and where you are headed is where this world is going." Tetu fell to his side and rolled up in the fetus position after he heard my words. I turned to Joba and Benda at the moment Joba thrust his sword into the other twin. Joba gave me a smile as he cleaned his sword on Benda's shirt.

"Let's get out of here before we have to take on our entire village," I barked to Joba.

"Aren't you going to finish Tetu?"

"He has a message to deliver before he dies," I replied.

"Well, we better move fast; there is a cloud of dust heading this way," said Joba pointing with his chin towards our village. A growing cloud of moonlit dust was lifting high into the night sky. Joba and I mounted our beasts and left our camp, but not before we had set the two war wagons ablaze with burning sticks from our fire. We headed west towards the mountains at a three-beat gallop and when we looked over our shoulders, the two war wagons were burning like twisted souls in the night. I thought of the funeral of Lindas and a sadness filled me and kept me from looking back again.

Chapter Eight

By morning when we had reached the mountain pass where I first met the red-bearded giant, Joba's beast collapsed in a sweat soaked death. My beast was also close to an exhaustive death and while I watched Joba cutting his bags of supplies from his silent beast, I felt a strange sadness for the death of the animal. I turned for the second time since we began our escape that night and the cloud of dust was still following. It had to be at least fifty riders and they hadn't slowed since we left the burning war wagons.

"Your beast is going to die from exhaustion just like mine if he doesn't get rest," stated Joba matter-of-factly to keep me from suggesting that he mount my beast and ride double.

"Both of us are going to have to run alongside my beast. We will hold onto him from either side and he will help sustain us as we run. Otherwise we stay here and take on my father and the others."

Joba dropped his bags of food and grabbed the right side of the saddle. I dismounted and held the left side and we began to run along beside the beast for what seemed to be an eternity. After the first hour my body was covered in sweat and the muscles in my legs began to grow numb. The momentum of the beast carried us twice as fast as a man could normally run. My stomach ached with the heat of fear. I hated and cursed this weakness.

During the fourth hour of the morning Joba lost his hold and tumbled, gashing his right knee on a sharp rock. I was able to stop my beast by yelling halt several times and ran back to see how badly he was hurt. When I reached his side he was just sitting there waiting for the blood to begin pouring from the long, open lips of his cut. Finally the rich, red liquid began to flow and I tore a long strip from my shirt and wrapped it around his knee, slowing the bleeding. "What do you suggest now, my wise commander?" I queried as I looked for any sign of our pursuers. "Well, I don't see any sign of them, but it is hard to see through trees," I said jokingly hoping this would lift Joba's spirits.

"Will you look at that? I've never seen anything like this before," cried Joba pointing to the stump of a tree that had been burned in half. "That tree wasn't cut down, something burned it in half."

I comprehended at once where we were and I was about to explain when the trumpet of a hunting horn pierced the silence of the valley floor. I recognized the sound instantly as that of my father's bull-delf hunting horn. "They are still on our trail and they can't be more than an hour behind us. We have to keep moving or we will die." I said, helping Joba stand. I helped him to my exhausted and froth-covered beast. The beast was having muscle spasms in his legs and coughing blood in large wads from his throat. Another hour of running and he would die but we had no choice except to mount and ride double until he collapsed. Joba sat in the saddle and I rode behind him and the beast hissed and snorted his own frothy blood at the unbearable weight of two grown men. At every step of the beast I felt the agonizing torture it was experiencing as he was kicked to run to his death.

By early afternoon the beast died and we all came crashing to the soft-needled floor of the forest. Joba let out a scream of pain as he landed on his cut knee, with me on top of him. I cupped my hand over his mouth to silence his screams after I heard the bull delf horn for the second time. I turned towards the sound of the horn and through the trees of the forest I counted twenty riders moving towards us, each with a fresh beast running alongside. "That's how they have kept up with us."

"This is the end, old friend," moaned Joba.

"No it's not!" I exclaimed after seeing the surprise of my life. "Joba, do you see that rock-face wall over there?"

"Yes," he answered indifferently.

"Come on, it's our escape!" I bellowed, pulling Joba to his feet. I literally dragged him to the glassy wall that towered about thirty bodies above the forest floor. When we reached the familiar crack in the wall I looked back and was relieved to find that the riders were now out of our sight because of the trees.

"You squeeze through first," I demanded, remembering the custom of the guardian virgin at the other side of the wall. I followed through the crack, just in time to hear the pounding sound of forty beasts charging towards my fallen mount.

When I reached the other side of the wall, Joba was lying in the arms of a beautiful girl from Rift. I stood for a moment, not looking at Joba and the girl, but stared at the magnificent city of blinding white marble and gold, reveling in its beauty. Before, the sky had been overcast and I didn't notice how it was nestled in among the towering peaks and walls of pink and purple rocks. I now understood why the warriors from Petrapolis had never found the city before. The meadow between the crack and the city gates was alive with thousands of elbs feeding on the green lush grass, still wet with dew and colorful summer flowers. While I watched this beautiful and living painting I remembered those long summer days in the wilderness with Desiree. My thoughts intensified when I looked again at Joba and the young virgin.

"Your friend has a high fever and needs help," stated the

blue-eyed blond virgin with authority. She looked like the girl I found here on my twentieth year.

"Run to the city and get some priests to help carry my friend and I will stay here with him until you get back." The virgin looked at me with a start knowing I had been here before.

"Do you know the Creator and are you one of His?" asked the girl after she stood up from Joba's side. I now noticed that she was more beautiful than I first thought. I also realized she possessed a sharp mind.

"I'm a servant to the God of Vertunda if that answers your question." She said it did and smiled down to Joba. I could see that she had developed an attraction for my friend. She then turned and began to run toward the city for help.

"She is beautiful, who is she and where are we?" asked Joba, still lying on the damp grass where the girl had left him.

"That girl is going to be your wife and this is the ancient city of Rift." I explained watching the comical expression come to Joba's face.

"She's what and we are where?"

"You heard me, she is your future wife and this is Rift. Here at Rift when a virgin sees a man come through the wall over there he is to be her husband. That's why I sent you through first," I said with a laugh.

"Thanks a lot, but on the other hand she really isn't bad looking."

"The next thing you'll be asking me to do is hide at the city well to tell her you want to see her." We both began to laugh releasing all the stress and tension of the chase and pain we had endured since our fight at the war wagons.

The young virgin hastened in her return and four young priests carried Joba to a large white building in the city that stood next to the large dining hall I remembered so well. The eldest of the four priests told me Joba would be cared for and I was to be escorted to the Holy Temple and be interviewed by the high priest.

"Is the high priest still Topaz?" I asked, surprising all the priests that heard me.

"Of course, a high priest remains so until he dies. And who might you be?" asked the same priest.

"I'll explain to the high priest who I am."

"Very well, follow me."

We walked down several narrow streets until we reached the Holy Temple of Rift. The city looked completely different without its snow cover, but still a magnificent city from a structural standpoint. Gold and silver were used abundantly in door hinges, window frames and roof tiles. Snow-white marble seemed to be the common building blocks for houses, buildings and the temple. My escort led me into the large compound where the huge altar stood, the same one Lindas was cremated on. Behind the altar was the huge temple and I looked at the open doors and a feeling of awe struck me when I remembered my night spent in there and the visit from Vertunda.

To the left of the altar a group of twenty elderly men in priestly robes stood engaged in what seemed to be a heated debate.

"High Priest Topaz is with that group of men," indicated my escort. I followed him to the gathering of elders and I immediately recognized Topaz. He hadn't changed terribly much in the three and a half years I'd been away. There may have been a few more lines around his eyes, but it was hard to tell.

I had only studied Topaz's face a moment before his gaze fell upon me. There wasn't a smile or a twinkle in his eyes to show me that he remembered who I was. There was only a look of indifference.

"This is the man, the other is with your daughter at the infirmary," reported my escort.

"Which one did my daughter first lay her eyes on?" asked Topaz in a cold voice.

"The other one, your holiness."

"Very well, I will speak with this man in my study chamber." Topaz turned back to his colleagues as I was led away towards a marble building that was adjacent to the temple. I was told to wait inside a large room that had a fire pit in the center and soft cushions were scattered around the fire pit, almost like the pit in King Topo's chamber in Petrapolis. The only difference was this room was more ornate with gold and silver and the ceiling wasn't blackened by smoke. On all four walls were wooden shelves that contained hundreds of scrolls: all rolled and tied with different colored ribbons. There were long narrow slits at the top of the scroll shelves that provided natural light to read by and allowed the smoke from the fire pit to escape without blackening the ceiling. At the far end of the room was a long lowben wood table that had two long matching benches on either side. The table was half a body wide and about three bodies long, big enough to spread out a couple of the scrolls.

I was curious about the contents of the scrolls. As a boy I was taught to read and write and I read every scroll in our village bibleous, which was a building about the size of this room but contained maybe half the scrolls that this one did.

"Take your hands off those scrolls!" came the rebuke of a deep-voiced man who had entered the study chambers without my hearing. I put back the scroll that I had in my hands. "They are holy writings and you are unfit to read them." I turned and the man speaking was Topaz.

"Then if I am unfit for the holy writings, why did I hear the words of Vertunda who was sent from the Holy One to speak with me?" I asked recklessly, considering my exhaustion and the strain I'd been under the last few hours.

"Then you have returned. I thought you were one of the outsiders." I now realized my warrior's uniform and the growth of my beard hid my appearance to Topaz. "Please forgive me," and Topaz fell to his knees before me in a posture of repentance.

"You needn't bow before me and I haven't returned to become your king either."

"What! But why are you here?" he asked, still on his knees but now looking at my eyes.

"First what did you mean by one of the outsiders?" I asked moving over to the cushions and sat down on a large, blue silk covered one. Topaz stood and joined me on the cushions.

"Answer my questions first, it is of most importance," stated Topaz.

"I think we are both talking about the same thing," I said. "My friend and I were chased by evil men and we found sanctuary by entering the Gate of Virgins."

"Were these warriors from Petrapolis that chased you?"

"No, ex-warriors and dedicated villagers. Now tell me, are you hiding something from me?"

"Shortly after you and your friend entered the city gates the elb herders reported about twenty warriors from the outside world came through the Gate of Virgins. As soon as they saw the walls of Rift they began to yell and jump for joy in their discovery. They then left, no doubt to take this information to Petrapolis."

"They found Rift only because the Holy One allowed it for some reason."

"These men found our city because you wanted to save your life. Had you sacrificed your life instead of leading the evil ones to our city, then thousands wouldn't now be in danger!"

Anger began to fill my heart and I clenched my fists. "Listen Topaz, how dare you hang this wickedness on me. You want me to die for a bunch of people who wanted to kill me because my sword didn't flame. Besides, how long did you think you could keep this city a secret, and doesn't the legend say no one finds Rift unless they were meant to? Well is this true or not?" I yelled and stood to leave.

"Stop, please forgive me again. I'm worried and I'm responsible for the inhabitants of Rift. I do believe you were sent here by the Holy One with the Flaming Sword to protect us and to be our king."

"No!" I barked from the doorway as I was about to leave, but turning, I told him very calmly, "I told you a moment ago I'm not here as your king and secondly I don't have the Flaming Sword with me."

"Where is it?" asked Topaz now standing.

"It's at Petrapolis and your brother has it."

"My God in heaven! Topo has the Flaming Sword?" Topaz grabbed his robes and ripped them and then he fell to the floor pulling his hair and beating his chest. I couldn't believe what I was seeing. A man who was under control of himself when he turned his daughter into ashes on the funeral pyre, but who lost all control knowing that his brother had the Flaming Sword.

"Your brother wants to repent and return to Rift. He's not who you think he is," I said hoping he heard me above his cries.

"You young fool! He is evil! An anti-god, and he tricked you into leaving the Flaming Sword with him. Don't you understand! He'll give it to the Prince of Darkness!"

I left the room and its smell of old parchment, blocking my ears to his rebuke. The square in front of Topaz's study chamber was filled with what looked like the gathering of the entire city. Every eye was on me as I passed through the sea of people, a sea that opened up to allow my passage outside the temple compound. Several of them spit on me and yelled ugly curses. I kept my eyes forward and passed the wet and verbal gauntlet out into the deserted city streets and headed towards the infirmary.

Inside the room where I left Joba, the same young girl at the wall was spooning soup to Joba's waiting mouth. The room was whitewashed and simple in decor. There were no windows, only air and light slits along the junctures of the ceiling and the walls.

"Lift yourself out of that bed, we are getting out of here," I demanded after I picked up Joba's sword that was laying next to his wooden and corded cot.

"Have you gone mad?" the girl yelled out. "He's not going anywhere. Just look at his knee."

My eyes saw what her hand was pointing to and I noticed Joba's knee had swollen to four times its normal size and the skin was red and purple from the wound and bruising. "Get out of that bed Joba," I now ordered. The young virgin put her slim body between Joba's and mine in order to prevent me from pulling Joba to his feet. My chest brushed up against her small but supple body. With surprising strength she pushed me off to keep me away from Joba.

"Help! Help!" yelled the girl, hurting my ears. I backed off and noticed Joba was grinning pleasantly at the girl's patronizing protection. Behind me I heard the door open and as I pivoted I saw two young boys dressed in white tunics standing at the door.

"Quick! Get my father; tell him to hurry!" called out the girl.

One of the boys left on the run and the other stood at the door with a threatening but almost humorous look on his face. I turned to the virgin, barely able to hold back my anger. "And who is your father?" I finally blurted out.

"Topaz, the High Priest," she replied with an impish look on her face. Now I knew why she reminded me of Lindas and I also remembered Topaz asking about his daughter at the temple compound.

"Did you once have a sister named Lindas?" I asked. The fire in her eyes cooled quickly.

"Yes, and who are you?"

"I'm the one named Tobe who was to marry Lindas, who killed the giant at the Gate of Virgins, and who is the rightful King of Ontelles." The girl stepped aside and the joyful smile on Joba was now gone. I looked to Joba and began to speak again. "Commander Joba, you are going to stay here and when your knee is well, I want you to organize an army to defend Rift. My father and the others from our village have discovered Rift and are most likely headed this moment towards Petrapolis to deliver their prized discovery. By the time they arrive at Petrapolis it will be the middle of winter. Couriers will be dispatched to all the legions to return and organize a march on Rift. This will not take place until spring, so we have some time to prepare."

"And you, what are you going to do?" asked Joba, now sitting up on his cot.

"I'm leaving for Petrapolis to recover my sword and elb robe and then I will return to help defend Rift. The Flaming Sword is the only thing that will be able to save this city, because I doubt the inhabitants will take up arms to defend themselves. But remember it's your job to recruit and train them."

As I pronounced the last sentence I gave a cutting stare to Lindas' sister. "And what is your name?"

"Lydia," she replied in a soft voice.

I then turned towards the door and saluted Joba from the threshold with a clenched fist against my leather breastplate. "May the Most High be with you my friend and you, Lydia. And Lydia, be a good wife to him."

Turning to the boy who had moved into the hall to allow me to pass, I sent him to secure an elb robe and a bag full of dried fruit and seeds and then meet me at the Gate of Virgins. He looked at Lydia and she gave her approval to my order. The boy left and I followed him out of the building and made my way down alleys and back streets until I reached the city gate. I crossed the flowered meadow between the city and the Gate of Virgins. There wasn't a virgin at the wall and I waited only a short time before the boy arrived with an old gray elb robe and a white cloth bag full of dried fruit and seeds.

"What's your name boy?" I asked as I took the bag from him.

"Neco, son of Tampalas," he replied very proudly.

"Bow your head," I commanded and he obeyed. "With my sword I dub you a warrior of Ontelles under the true king. You are now second in command under Joba my commander. Tell him what I said and follow his orders. I will try and return before spring."

"May the Holy One be with you, King of Ontelles," called out Neco as I squeezed through the crack in the wall.

Chapter Nine

On the other side of the rock-face wall I saw the spoor of many beasts and men. I followed the trail and discovered that it was heading west towards Petrapolis, except for a single beast that turned around and went east. I wondered about this until I figured one of the men must have returned to the village to inform all the men's wives and families what they discovered and that their men would be away for quite some time. I didn't encounter the lone rider as I followed the main body and decided he must have turned long before I began to follow the spoor.

By late afternoon I wanted to stop and sleep. I hadn't had any rest since Joba and I encountered Tetu and Benda. However, those that I was now following hadn't rested either. They would soon be stopping for the night and if I could reach them while they slept, I could steal a beast and reach Petrapolis before them. This possibility drove me on and I even found myself jogging at times realizing that once the suns were down it would be harder to follow the spoor.

It was the middle of the night before I overtook the band of riders and beasts. They were all rolled out sleeping around a dying fire. The beasts were hobbled in an open meadow not far from their camp. There was a fast moving stream and a waterfall between the camp and the meadow. I sat quietly next to a tree for about an hour resting, eating handfuls of dried fruit and studying the camp. I couldn't see any guards and I wondered about this. My father taught me to set guards when others slept. If you were alone you had to take chances and try to sleep lightly. Secondly, he taught me never to camp near fast moving water or brush that could blow in the wind, because this gave a predator or a man the extra cover of noise to sneak up on you. I couldn't understand why my father would make two major errors such as this, but I finally buried the thought and accepted my good fortune.

After a quiet hour, my plan was made and ready to be executed. I knew I couldn't kill all nineteen men lying about the fire before they awoke and killed me. My only option was to ford the stream and hamstring all the beasts except the one I chose to steal.

I circled around the sleeping men and crossed upstream above the waterfall. When I reached the meadow I quietly came down upon the first beast. He was big and black and thorns and twigs knotted his shaggy fur. I already had my sword out of its scabbard as not to frighten the beasts when I removed it. I took careful aim and with a quick and calculated stroke I cut the large sinew in the back of the hock crippling the animal. The beast barely knew what hit him. Then to the second, third and on down the line of sleeping beasts until there were only four left. I selected the best of the remaining four to be my mount, the second best to be a spare and to carry my food bag and elb robe. I made fast the bag and robe to his back with several hobbles tied together. All the saddles were stacked next to the fire where the riders slept. I was going to have to ride bareback but as a boy that was how I first learned to ride. Removing the hobbles from the two beasts I went back to the last two in order to finish my work and saw the carnage in the meadow as I approached the last beasts. Six of the hamstrung beasts were down in the dew-covered grass and the rest were limping with blackish-red blood covering the lower joint of the hind legs. The men in the camp still slept.

It seemed to be getting darker and I realized the morning suns would be rising within the hour. I knelt behind the second-to-last beast to cut and I swung my sword for the hock. The blade cut cleanly but smashed into the joint and on through. I had swung too hard. The beast let out a horrifying shriek and stumbled forward in its hobbles, crashing to the ground. I looked over and saw that I had frightened the two beasts I had freed. I ran to them and quieted them before they ran away. By the time I had calmed them I heard the cries of the men crossing the stream. Still one more beast needed to be hamstrung but I knew I had no time to do it. I reached over the shoulder of the beast without the food bag and pulled myself up on his back, took the length of hobbles I had tied around the second beast's neck and drove my heels deep into my mount's ribs. He gave a snort and hissed as he bolted across the open meadow and into the woods. The pack beast ran alongside, obeying the lead of the hobble halter. Just as I reached the woods, I heard another outburst from the villagers behind me. The clamor of blade against stone, as the ex-warriors, finding no enemy, battered their swords in frustrated anger against the rocks and ground of the mountain meadow.

I rode at a steady pace until morning, and then slowed to a canter. By the middle of the day I realized I had a follower. The lone beast that I had failed to cripple was behind me with a rider. He was perhaps an hour behind but no more. I found a stream and watered my beasts, giving them some seeds from my bag before I changed mounts. The rest shortened the distance of my follower, but I would be able to lengthen it in the long run, considering that I had two mounts and could maintain a stronger pace.

I pulled myself up onto the second beast and began riding at a gallop. Within a half hour I discovered my lost time had cost me too much. I had just passed a large flat rock and on top were two nuggets. I didn't see them until it was too late. One of them had thrown a corded rope expertly over my head and it tightened around my chest, pinning my arms to my side. I was pulled off my beast and landed flat on my back. The two nuggets jumped down from the top of the rock with swords drawn and pointing at me.

"We are nuggets from the Topan Wilderness and we need your head."

"Only one of you can use it," I replied and then both of the nuggets began squabbling on who was going to challenge me first. They still hadn't decided when the rider following me rode up on his beast. I recognized the rider to be a friend of Tetu. His name was Veatus, son of the founder of my village. His father had helped me make my first sword in the village foundry. He was the boy I hit the day before I left as a nugget, the one who made the comment about Desiree now being his because I was leaving.

"I see that you have the warrior I've been following for several days now," said Veatus, who wore the brown cloth tunic of an ironworker.

"He is ours, unless you are a warrior, then one of us will challenge you," said one of the nuggets.

"I'm a nugget just as you two, for today is my twentieth birthday, but this warrior is more than just a head. He knows about the city Rift and he left my best friend to die a slow and painful death." Veatus then looked down upon me with piercing eyes and said, "Isn't that right Tobe?"

"Did your friend deliver my message?" I asked brazenly and Veatus jumped from his beast and put the heel of his leather boot into the side of my head.

"You son of an ash lizard!" he screamed, then looked to the two nuggets. "He's mine and I will kill you two nuggets if I must!"

I tasted blood in my mouth as I watched the other

nuggets struggle with Veatus and knock him to the ground. I stood up and slipped the rope off my shoulders while they held Veatus down. "I don't have all day, so let's get this over with." I stated, surprising myself with my own courage.

"He is a son of an ash lizard, isn't he?" said the smaller of the two nuggets, who was holding Veatus' legs while the other nugget was lying across his chest.

"Go by birth dates. Oldest to youngest, and the one that wins, gets my head." My reasoning being that it was better to go one at a time than all at once. The three of them looked at each other and Veatus asked for their birth dates. My idea worked and they all compared each other's dates and checked the brands on the back of each other's necks to see if any were lying. As I stated earlier on the eight day after birth our birth names and date of birth was burned onto the back of each persons neck. It turned out to be the small nugget that got to go first, then the other nugget and Veatus last.

I didn't want to tire myself as I was going to have to take chances and finish each one quickly. The first one handled his sword like a child and as I went for a kill I wondered how Petrapolis ever received any nuggets with warriors' heads. It seemed to me the population was deci- mated very quickly, considering there were probably twenty dead nuggets for every nugget that reached Petrapolis' walls with a head. But of course this system did weed out the weak ones.

The second nugget was just as unskilled as the first, but he was able to inflict a cut on my left arm as I gored him to the hilt of my sword. After I pulled my sword out and watched the life of the nugget come out with it, I felt tired and weak. I had only an hour's rest in the forest and the few hours in Rift since this ordeal began over a day and half ago. It was the hottest part of the day and the faistrags were already swarming and settling on the eyes and wounds of the two dead nuggets.

"You are as good as Tetu said," confessed Veatus as he stepped out for his turn with me. "He said you were a master with the sword after he repeated your grisly message; just before he died."

"And my father, did he hear the message?"

"You hate your father don't you?"

"I hate the ways of Ontelles. Two young lives are now wasted and yours too because of this wicked world and its ways. I hate this planet and what it stands for. Now did my father hear the message?"

"Yes, you sick creature, he heard it."

"You are the one that is sick. You are going to die for no reason other than your hope of becoming an Ontelles warrior."

"No, that is where you are wrong. Ever since the day you bloodied my mouth before you left as a nugget, I swore to pay you back," he breathed and then spat a wad of mucus that splattered on my leather breastplate. "And before I kill you, I want you to know that I desecrated Desiree, just like she is being desecrated with some soldier in Petrapolis right this moment!" And with that statement I lunged out for his throat with my sword, but he was ready for me and he caught me with a staggering blow across the chest. I was knocked off my feet and all the wind was thrown out of me. I quickly looked down at my chest to see how much damage was instilled. All I saw was a shallow slash through my leather breastplate right across the wet spot where he had spit on me. I looked up in time to see Veatus preparing to lop my head off with a well-rounded swing, both hands on the sword hilt. I ducked and placed my shoulder into his off balanced legs. He fell with a thud and I scrambled to my feet still trying to get my wind back. Veatus rolled back to his feet and was now crouching and waiting for me to make my next move.

I came at him with a feigned thrust and as he went to

block it, I pulled back and thrust the tip into his throat while he was recovering from his useless block. Blood gushed out of his throat and mouth as he fell to the ground, kicking his feet in a spastic dance. I turned away not wanting to watch.

I left the three bodies to the insects and the predator birds. I took Veatus' saddle and supplies, put them on my beast and left the spot of death and blood. As I turned around to take one last look, I thought of the horrible truth, 'Ontelles sons were nothing more than food for birds and insects.'

Chapter Ten

The first storms of winter began to release their burdens of snow as I left the mountains and entered the Plain of Blood. It would still be several months before I reached Petrapolis, but it would be close to spring before the men from my village reached the capital city by foot.

During the long cold days of riding towards Petrapolis I encountered no one. I used the same landmarks I had followed on my first trip. Many of the same thoughts from those days still filled my mind, along with the burdens and guilt that seemed to be weighing me down. My own hands had killed five men: the two unnamed nuggets, Veatus, Tetu and the red giant. There was also the cutting off of Castor's arm, and two of the dead men were once playmates from my own village. Then there was the death of Lindas that I witnessed and Desiree, a true love who seemed gone forever. Vertunda's words seemed so far away that I doubted even them. He told me Desiree was someday to be my wife, yet how was this to be?

What was I to do when I reached Petrapolis? Was I to get the Flaming Sword then go and hunt down the remaining men from my village and kill them before they were able to deliver their message of discovery? If I were to do that I would have to most likely kill my own father. Or was I to find Desiree and escape with her to the mountains and fulfill

Vetunda's prophecy? What was I to do? Proclaim myself as king and watch Topo killed for his deception? Or go to Rift and protect and defend a city that rejected and spat upon me?

On the evening when I finally reached the city walls of Petrapolis my questions were still unanswered and my hate for this city was glowing like hot embers in a fire. The snow had stopped and all seemed falsely purified by the newly fallen cover of white. The two moons were full as the overcast began to clear and the moonlit darkness covered the sleepy plain. I found the city gates closed with a sign that read, **'Closed at Dusk and Opened at Dawn.'**

A cold wind began to blow and my visions of a warm bed and hot food inside the city quickly vanished. I began to search for shelter for the night and noticed a large mound not far from the city gate next to the wall. The mound would provide protection from the wind but I had failed to gather wood or beast dung during the day, thinking I wouldn't need it. Behind the mound I hobbled the one beast, for the other had been slaughtered about nine days ago and used for meat. I rolled up in the old gray elb robe given to me by the boy, Neco, and fell asleep on an empty, cramping stomach.

When morning finally arrived there was a light cover of frost on my fur robe. I stood very stiffly and stretched my limbs. The beast was digging in the snow for food with his long snout. Like him, I also wished I had some food to eat. The beast was chomping on something but I gave no mind as I stepped out from behind the mound and saw the gates were opening. A great crowd began pouring from the city's throat and was headed towards me. They were all on foot and the ones in the middle were women, flanked on both sides by warriors.

The crowd of seventy or eighty kept coming. As they got closer, I heard the cries of little infants and then I saw them wrapped in cloth and held in many of the women's arms. I wondered about the babies, since the laws of

Petrapolis did not allow anyone below the age of twenty to be inside her walls.

The group was almost beside the mound when I noticed the women in the middle were weeping, some even louder than the wails of infants.

"All un-chosen women turning thirty today against the wall!" ordered a soldier with the helmet of a warrior sixth class. It was the same type of helmet Castor wore four years ago in the council chamber. It was a bowl shaped helmet with golden bird wings protruding from each side. "Soldiers, bind their hands and those on child patrol take the violaters and exterminate."

I stood in shock as warriors grabbed the little, frail infants from the weeping mothers and with the babies dangling from the warrior's huge hands, they swung the living bodies into the wall smashing their heads. The laughing soldiers then threw the lifeless bodies onto the snow covered mound.

"That's what this mound is," I said to myself as one broken body rolled down the mound and stopped short of my leather booted feet. I felt sick but there was nothing in my stomach to disgorge. I lifted my eyes from the infants and watched in frozen horror as the other soldiers took their swords and began to hack the women, who had been bound to keep them from fleeing. Warm blood flowed thickly, forming clouds of steam lifting in the cold air. The carnage was over quickly and I counted over forty babies and thirty women systematically killed. The soldiers finished their gruesome task by quartering each woman. One piece was thrown on the mound with the babies, the remaining were gathered up and I was sure there were three other piles around the city so the letter of the law wouldn't be violated. 'Woman of thirty without mates were to be cut and scattered on the four winds.' I knew nothing about the killing of the newborns but understood what went on inside the city walls;

newborns would be a problem, so this was the outcome.

I followed the group back to the city gate leading my beast behind me, now realizing what he had been feasting on in the snow. I reported at the wooden table with the open death log on top.

"Name and legion?" asked the soldier behind the table.

"Zebulum, warrior fourth class. Vth Legion."

"You will need a new helmet and according to my records you are deceased. Let's see.... you died at the hands of Castor, member of the warrior council four years ago." I now knew my folly at reporting at the gate. I should have tried scaling the walls during the night, found my Flaming Sword and left.

"Now hold it one moment. There is also a Zebulum with the same birth date and village who left with the Vth Legion four years ago."

"That's me, the other must be an error," I said jokingly.

"There are no errors in the death log. You are going to report to the Council of Warriors." Then the soldier behind the table looked over to two guards. "Escort this soldier to the council; fit him in as soon as possible, and watch him closely. I'll submit a written report within the hour."

The two soldiers grabbed my arms and pulled me into the city. I turned to the soldier at the table. "Watch my beast, he has served me well. Feed him and stable him."

"Yes, yes," he said without looking up.

After I turned away from the man at the gate I saw a soldier tenth class and a woman riding towards me on a pair of matching beasts. For some strange reason my eyes fell upon the woman and as I saw who it was the pain was as if a knife had pierced my heart. The woman was Desiree.

"Desiree!" I yelled pulling at the hold of the two soldiers. She looked down as she passed next to me finally recognizing me.

"Zeb!" she cried out as she and the one with her passed

through the city gate. She turned in the saddle keeping her eyes glued to mine, her lower lip trembling. The one with her pulled up on his beast's reins and Desiree jumped from her saddle onto the snow and was about to race towards me when the man she was with jumped down and grabbed her. Then with the back of his hand he slapped her and told her to get back on her beast. After he struck her I immediately recognized him by the missing arm as the man that had fought me for my elb robe in the council chamber.

Castor recognized me as well. "It is you, the one I challenged to a duel. Well this time I will make sure you are dead!" he cried out drawing his sword with his left hand.

"I'll take you on right now!" I replied but the two soldiers held me inside the city.

"You enter the city and it's the death sentence Castor!" cried out the man behind the wooden table. "No one enters Petrapolis after his thirtieth birthday and lives. Besides, this man is going before the Council of Warriors because our books say you killed him over four years ago. If you didn't and this is he then how are you going to answer to that. You better take that pretty girl of yours and keep moving."

Castor spat through the gate towards me, and then breathed a cursed threat. "We will meet again and I'm going to pay you back for this!" And he lifted the leather bound stub that used to be a hand and forearm. Desiree was back on her beast with her face washed in tears. Castor turned away and the two soldiers pulled me away. My mind began to tear like the ripping of a cloth. I turned my head twice in a daze while the soldiers pulled me along the main street to the center of the city. I didn't remember passing the Temple of War or Love but was only awakened to reality by the foul smell of the pipe smoke that drifted as a low hanging cloud within the council chamber.

"What do you have to say for yourself soldier?"

My eyes focused and adjusted to the dark, torch lit room.

The sixth man from the left was standing and speaking. The sixth class warrior on the council must be the spokesman I thought. I looked to my right and sitting very smugly on the elevated throne was Topo. He was wearing my white elb robe and his right index finger was tapping his cheek as if he were in deep thought.

"Answer me, soldier, or you will be flogged!" screamed the sixth class warrior.

"I'm sorry, I didn't hear the question."

"Our books state that Zebulum was killed here in the council chamber almost four years ago. Your name, birth date, and village correspond to be this very man. Also our books state that King Topo gave you a special order to join with the Vth Legion eight days after you were critically wounded. Considering you were dead, would you be kind enough to explain and possibly clear this problem up."

"Ask the king, he gave me the orders and my very presence today suggests that I'm not dead," was my simple reply that I tried to deliver in a non-threatening tone. However, I felt that same recklessness overtaking me as it did in Topaz's study chamber. My mind was three places at once and I wasn't able to keep it all straight. I was watching the women and children being killed; Desiree was calling out to me, and the warrior was questioning me.

"Ask the king? You rebellious youth, who do you think you are?" The warrior sixth class turned to Topo, "What do you suggest, your holiness?"

"Six months in the pit and he will be submissive to the council," said King Topo, with his finger never missing a beat on his cheek.

"Take him away to the pit to return six months from this day," ordered the warrior sixth class to the soldiers standing at the council door. Strong hands grabbed my arms and I wanted to yell out and call Topo a phony and a liar. I wanted to demand to see the Flaming Sword but my voice cracked and tears began to flow from my eyes. I cried like a baby but without the noise. My mind was gone and there was nothing else to do but weep.

Chapter Eleven

The pit was a cylinder-shaped hole, ten bodies deep and a body across. It had been bored into solid rock and the walls were polished smooth as glass. The bottom was solid ice, keeping the pit at unbearable temperatures. The ice was black and deep looking, which sent signals of fear through my mind as I began to consider the length of time I was ordered to stay here. Within six months it would be summer and the ice would surely be melted into water, and I could only imagine what would happen then.

The soldiers who lowered me into the pit left me my sword and elb robe. I understood the reason for the elb robe but I didn't know why they left me my sword until that noon. When the sun was high in the sky, about a dozen warriors appeared at the mouth of the pit all with grins of excitement on their faces. Then one of them tossed in a wild-tish bird. This was a deadly bird with poisoned claws. I killed the bird with one stroke of my sword and the warriors cheered and paid off their bets.

Each day at noon, when the sunlight best filled the pit, some wild or poisonous creature was thrown into the cylinder pit with me. Wild hogs, tish birds, poison shank snakes and ash lizards were some of the common creatures given to me. This carnage became my food, which I had to eat raw, and the only water I received was the amount I could cut and suck out of the icy floor of my imprisonment. At night, I learned to sleep on my elbows and knees because of the cold floor. During the days I paced in circles, never resting except to eat and do my toilet. At evening I would toss the bones, the rotten meat, and my own dung out the top of the pit. The first three months I talked to no one, except the God of Rift. I asked to either be delivered or to receive the strength to survive.

On the ninety-fifth day of my captivity, which I calculated by marks I made on the wall of the pit, the soldiers didn't come to trouble me with an animal at noon. There was great joviality and cheering echoing down to me from the surface. Finally that evening a soldier appeared at the top of the pit and threw a loaf of bread to me.

"This loaf will have to be in place of fresh meat," called down the soldier in a non-mocking compassionate voice.

"What is all the celebration about?" I asked, hoping he would reveal something to me.

"Men from outside Petrapolis have arrived at the gate with knowledge of the ancient city of Rift and its location."

I sank to the floor of the pit as if my knees were made of water. My father and his men had finally arrived. All my plans of getting the Flaming Sword and protecting Rift had gone awry. "When do the armies of Petrapolis leave?" I found myself asking the soldier.

"The first sign of spring we march, that's the unofficial word."

That night another unusual event occurred. Several celestial bodies in the heavens came together and produced a brilliant star that lit the city of Petrapolis and even the bottom of my pit with a glorious light. The cheers in the city continued into morning, as everyone viewed the star as a great sign from the god of war to destroy Rift, and I felt like the only human in deep despair. I wondered about Joba and if he had been able to persuade the citizens of Rift to stand up and prepare for the protection of their city. I also thought of Desiree and Castor. How could something like this happen to me? The girl I loved taken by a man that I hated. Vertunda had revealed to me in the Temple of Rift that Desiree was to be my wife. My faith was already waning long ago but on this night I tried to sleep in order to be rid of the unfaithful thoughts; but the star over the city coupled with the noise kept me awake.

Fourteen more nights and days passed from the night the great star appeared, which vanished after the night it first appeared. Since then, the joviality of the city returned to its normal hum of boredom. But I realized the thoughts of marching on Rift filled the warriors because since that first night of the star no one came and threw any more wild or poisonous animal in the pit with me. The same soldier who threw me the loaf of bread was the only one to appear at the mouth of the pit at evening to throw me bread or some scraps of cooked meat. This small act of kindness caused me to ask the God of Rift to bless the man who gave me the bread and meat.

On the one hundred ninth day of my imprisonment I fell into a deep state of depression. My mind was still injured by all that I had witnessed the morning I returned to Petrapolis. It was still such a mental shock to stand and watch the killing of the babies and the innocent women. Then, seeing Desiree, only to discover she was the mate of Castor and leaving with him forever. Also the change in Topo, this was a mystery beyond any understanding.

The good soldier came that evening and threw me my loaf of bread and after I ate and sucked on a chip of ice I slid down the side of the wall and pointed the tip of my sword to my chest, fitting the tip between two ribs. I placed my hands on the hilt and was taking a deep breath before jerking the sword into myself. I held in the breath as I felt the sharp point began to cut into my flesh.

"Put down the sword Zeb." My hands fell from the hilt and standing at the end of my feet was Vertunda. It had been over four years since I saw him last. He hadn't changed a day since then and I felt very foolish because of my loss of faith.

"I don't have much time, since the forces of darkness are battling this very moment for the city. Had I not arrived when I did they would have had a great victory over you." I was speechless and just sat with my mouth agape and eyes staring into Vertunda's brilliant face. For the first time I noticed he had a large nose with a bird-beak look to it. "Listen carefully now for great things you shall be required to do. Tonight you will go to Topo's chamber and recover the Flaming Sword he holds; then you are to go and secure two beasts. One for you and the other for two other travelers who will accompany you."

"Shouldn't I get three beasts if there will be three of us?" I asked, speaking for the first time.

"Silence! I told you what to do; now I must go." He vanished and again I found myself in darkness. I drew myself up from the icy floor, sheathed my sword and began pacing in circles as a fierce wind began to howl at the mouth of the pit. Within an hour after Vertunda's visit it began to snow.

"I really don't understand, Vertunda!" I finally yelled up into the falling snow. "How am I to get the Flaming Sword while I'm down in this pit?"

"Please be quiet," said a voice from the entrance. A man's head was hanging over the edge of the pit and he was holding a rope. He dropped one end to me, "Take hold of the rope."

I did as he instructed and with the excitement that only freedom can bring to a caged man, I climbed the side of the glassy pit. When I reached the top the soldier who had thrown me the rope began to untie the end that was looped around a stake he had driven into the ground for an anchor.

"You're the soldier who has been throwing me the bread, aren't you?"

"Don't you recognize me, Tobe?" asked the soldier and I studied his face but it was dark and the snow was falling heavily. "I'm your brother, Jeeba. But my warrior name is Deeobulus or just Dee."

"Jeeba? It is you, isn't it?" He smiled so broadly that I thought his mouth would split and we embraced. Jeeba was four years older than I and we were the best of friends until he had to leave and become a warrior. "How did you know I was in the pit?"

"I saw you when you entered the city. I also saw your encounter with Desiree and Castor."

"What do you know of Castor?" I asked impatiently shaking him with my hands on his shoulders.

"He's only the most feared warrior Petrapolis has ever produced. He's killed over two hundred warriors and nuggets in personal hand-to-hand combat. He never lost a fight except when he fought a pelot in the council chamber and lost his hand and forearm. But anyway, the man is to be feared and not challenged by the likes of you. Besides, don't you recognize his name?"

"No I don't," I said as I was trying to remember what a pelot was.

"Castor was our eldest brother, the one who stole your beast when he became a nugget, he was the one-armed man's first kill. Now he is living out our dead brother's life in our village with your girl and under the approval of our mother and father."

"Do you hate the ways of Ontelles, my brother?" I asked trying to discover his loyalties.

"Yes, sorely do I hate this world, and I know father would kill me for saying this."

"Then we shall change it. Secure three, no only two beasts and provisions. Meet me near the city gate at dawn.

We will be leaving this place, and when we return we will destroy it."

"My little brother, the one with all the brains."

"And now the muscle to go with it. Hurry and remember to only get two beasts. I have some business to attend to and I will meet you at first light." My brother saluted me and ran off into the falling curtain of snow.

I couldn't believe that I was free just as Vertunda had said. I made my way to a wide street and recognized the temples of Love and War with the Warrior Council building nestled between. I climbed the steps to the council chambers and made my way to King Topo's private chamber. A warrior second class was guarding the entrance; or supposed to be guarding it. He was sitting with his legs outstretched, crossed and snoring like an old man. I stepped over his legs and found the door unlocked. Inside there was a fire blazing in the pit but I saw no one in the room. I walked quietly over to the wall where Topo had placed the sword in the presence of Joba and myself. I found the loose stone and removed it. I reached into the dark hole and my hand felt nothing. "That lying beast!" I cursed in a low voice.

"You speak highly of me," said a voice that I recognized to be Topo's. I turned with my sword drawn in the time it took me to pivot. From behind a red embroidered curtain stepped Topo laughing hysterically, wearing my white elb robe. Dangling from his arm was the woman I remembered to be Leas, the high priestess from the Temple of Love. She wore a diaphanous, green silk gown that hid very little of her female shape. Gold and jewels glistened from her hands, neck and hair as she began to snicker along with her lover. "Did you really think I would leave the sword in there for you to take back at any time?"

"The man who told me to leave the sword in the wall was not the same man I see today."

"True enough. You see the difference? I have changed;

since our last encounter I have given myself to the Dark Prince in exchange for the Flaming Sword. When you gave up the sword you lost your right to be King of Ontelles. You have lost everything. You've lost Joba your commander, you've lost the woman you love, and now you are going to lose your life.

"How do you know all this?"

"I know everything. I knew you were coming here tonight, that is why I drugged the guard outside my door."

"In exchange for my sword, the Dark Prince gave you special powers?"

"Very perceptive, but your observations will not save you."

"Alright Topo, the game is over. I'm hungry, I'm tired and I want answers. Now where is the sword?"

"I told you, the Dark Prince has it. Didn't you read the holy scrolls when you were at Rift? Why do you think the Dark Prince wants Rift destroyed so badly? It's not because they haven't paid their taxes, but because it is there that the only copies of the holy writings are located. You fool; I can see your ignorance now. You know nothing of this world or of the spiritual."

I was once told that ignorance was bliss, but I was hurt by the words of Topo. I prepared to kill him with my sword when he pushed Leas aside, and dragged a black handled sword that hung at his side from its scabbard under the white elb robe. Dropping the elb robe from his shoulders he pulled the sword and it lit with flames and I stepped back in fear.

"I know what you are thinking, but I'm not the Dark Prince and this is not your Flaming Sword."

"What is it then?"

"This is the Sword of Guile," said Topo waving the sword over his head in a circle. "Your sword was the Sword of Truth. There are two flaming swords, not one."

"But Vertunda told me there was no other sword like the

Sword of Truth," I said very confused now.

"True enough. The Sword of Guile can cut through anything except the Sword of Truth. But now the Prince of Darkness is possessor of the Sword of Truth and the universe is his. I have possession of the Sword of Guile and now I am the true king of Ontelles, since the prophecy states, the one who has the Flaming Sword in the council chambers is the king. And as you can see, this sword is flaming," he laughed.

Topo came toward me and I tried to block the burning blade, but his sword passed through mine leaving only a handle and a third of my blade remaining. I stepped back after his first attack and dropped my gray elb robe to the floor as it was on fire. I now felt it was all over but tried to vanquish the thought. I fell to one knee and grabbed the edge of the elb robe I had just dropped and threw it at Topo's legs hoping to trip him up. He struck at the gray fur with his sword cutting a smoking trench in the stone floor. The robe tangled his feet and as he tried to regain his balance. I drove a shoulder into him, knocking him off his feet. The sword flew from his hand sliding, without flames, along the floor. Topo tried to stand but I swung what was left of my sword into the side of his head knocking him over into what looked like a dead heap. I removed his scabbard and hurried to the Sword of Guile. Leas was trying to recover it but I beat her to it. I snatched up the sword and sheathed it in its scabbard.

"You malignant beast, the building is going to burn!" yelled Leas, and I noticed that the embroidered curtains had been set aflame during our fight by my burning gray elb robe.

"I hope it does with you and him in it!" I shouted back. With the Sword of Guile and my white elb robe I left the council chambers burning behind me.

Chapter Twelve

I huddled under my white elb robe in an alley behind a pile of garbage, near the city gate. The snow continued to fall all night and the sky over Petrapolis was lit from the flames that ate at the council chambers, the Temple of War and the Temple of Love. Warriors and women alike fought the flames with bucket lines and cross fires. Before the first light of morning the three structures and adjacent dwellings were piles of smoldering ashes. Many of the warriors, blackened by smoke and soot, were weeping for the loss of their holy places.

The suns had been up for over two hours and I wondered if the city gates would ever open, and I was also concerned about Dee's rendezvous with the two beasts. I didn't want to stand in the open in case Topo hadn't been killed in the fire and was now looking for me. I kept peering out of the alley until I saw a group of about eighty women being escorted by warriors. I heard the wail of babies and it registered immediately what this group was. I couldn't believe that even after Petrapolis' very heart was burned out it still continued its evil ways without rest.

As the company of doomed women and children drew closer to me I began to feel a compelling urge to step out of my hiding spot and save them. I was feeling for the sword that hung at my side when a hand from behind touched my shoulder.

"Zeb, it's me, Dee," whispered my brother as I turned on him.

"You spotted elb; you gave me the shock of my life, sneaking up on me like that," I rebuked as he smiled in delight. As children he always had the ability to sneak up on me in our village or out in the wilderness. Behind my brother were two white shaggy beasts.

"Here are your beasts," he said as he handed me the reins. "Do you recognize Peton?"

My eyes squinted in the early light looking at the two beasts until I recognized my first wild beast that I caught and trained as a teenager. The one my brother Castor stole when he became a nugget. There was no greater friend that Peton my old white shaggy beast. "Come here boy," I said, moving carefully to him to see if he remembered me, and he began to whine and whimper his recognition. I buried my head into his neck and hugged him. Just in a few moments a healing occurred in my soul and spirit by being recognized by my old beast.

"I don't see your other traveler," commented Dee trying to break up the reunion and probably feeling a little uncomfortable with my show of affection.

"I don't know who it is yet."

"Well I guess there will have to be two, because I'm not going with you, Zeb."

"What!" I shouted, as the deafening cries of the passing women filled the alley.

"It is best if I stay. I will gather an army of dissatisfied soldiers, for I know many. We will wait for your return or your word, then we will overthrow the Warriors Council and King Topo."

I didn't know what to say or think. The snow was still falling in huge flakes that gave everything a mysterious and eerie indifference. I turned and watched the mass of women lost in confusion. When Dee's hand pulled at my shoulder to bring me back to reality I turned on him and shouted, "What about these women and children that are slaughtered everyday, you can't help them by staying!"

"And I can't help them by leaving either. Now follow the women out the gate and make your escape. By the time the warriors reach Rift this summer I will have an army ready from within to strike at your word."

Dee pushed me out into the snow-covered street as the company of women passed. I looked to my brother still in the alley and he saluted me with a reassuring look of success and self-confidence. I accepted his plan and led the two beasts behind me as I followed the victims out the now open gates. I passed through the gate unchallenged, maybe because of the heavy snow or the memory of events in the night on the minds of the guards at the gate.

The condemned group was being guided to the left of the gate and towards the gruesome mound. I followed in a daze wanting to free all the women in front of me. A lone woman with a child wrapped in a blanket turned to me and cried for mercy, thinking I was one of the warrior guards. My eyes fell upon her tear-streaked face and my heart melted. She had long black hair flowing onto a white elb robe almost as beautiful as mine. Her face was extremely attractive and her eyes were dark and full of innocence and kindness. Her appearance was striking, and as I reached out to her, the trembling in her lower lip stopped.

"Just save my child, please save him," she pleaded. I looked to the warriors flanking the crowd. All had their eyes forward; I pulled the unusual woman out of the crowd, and we just stood there as the weeping mass moved away into the falling cover of snow. All was now surprisingly quiet. I lifted the woman and her child onto one of the beasts and mounted the other. The three of us then moved at a slow walk east, toward the mountains. The snow kept falling, and the white beasts and our white elb robes hid us to the eyes of soldiers on the walls.

It was the first time the wounds in my mind began to heal. I was riding Peton after so many years and I was now able to help save someone from the horrible ways of Ontelles. The woman kept turning to me and thanking me over and over. I said nothing to her but just tried to smile, not letting her know that she was actually applying ointment to my mental wounds each time she thanked me.

The distance covered on that first day was small because of the deep snow. Before the suns began to set that evening I hobbled the two beasts and dug a snow cave for the woman, her child and myself. Inside I gave the woman some cooked meat my brother had provided in the bags of provisions. The woman and I ate as her child suckled under her elb robe.

"We will not have a fire tonight since it wouldn't be safe, and there isn't any wood or beast dung to be found. It will be cold but if we huddle together under our elb robes we will keep warm."

"Did the Holy One send you to save me?" asked the woman.

When she asked me that, I recalled Vertunda and his instructions. I hadn't imagined that one of the travelers would be an infant. "My name is Zeb, and what is yours and the child's?" I asked, not trying to evade her question, but wanting more information from her before I shared anything about Vertunda.

"My name is Eviea and my son is Theo."

"I will answer your question, but please tell me of yourself first."

"Permit me to ask you a question first," said Eviea with all her womanly charm. "I saw in your eyes this morning that you are a man who has once been to the city of Rift. Is this true?"

"True, I've been there three times."

"And you are not one of those who reported its locations?"

"No!"

"The reason I ask is that I'm from Rift, and I was afraid to tell you this in case you decided to turn back and give me over to the warriors at Petrapolis."

"Never would I do such an evil thing, or why would I have saved you and your child this morning?"

"True enough, and I'm sorry to have feared you. I will tell you my story. I was born at Rift and was raised there until I was twenty. On my twentieth birthday I had a visit from a pelot."

There it was again, that word *pelot*. Eviea must have sensed my ignorance in the snow cave for she stopped her story, and asked if I knew what a pelot was.

"I'm not sure, I only heard the word for the first time last night from my brother."

"You haven't read any of the holy writings at Rift?" she asked.

"I tried but didn't get very far," remembering Topaz telling me to put down the holy scrolls that day in his study.

"Well, the word 'pelot' comes from the scrolls and it is the name of a spiritual creature sent from the Holy One. There are virtuous pelots and pelots of guile. The name of the leader of the evil pelots is called Leatos, now called in the holy scrolls the 'Dark Prince.' Then there is the leader of the virtuous pelots who appeared to me."

"Vertunda is his name; isn't it?" I interrupted.

"Yes, you have seen him?"

"Several times in the past four years."

"You know what a pelot is then, you just didn't know the word for it," she laughed for the first time that day and it was a lovely laugh that was contagious. I began to laugh with her. Then Theo started and it was no stopping us as we all laughed and laughed grabbing our sides and whipping away the tears that came because of the deep releasing of pent up emotions. After we finally stopped Eviea started again along with Theo joining in. I tried my best not to laugh, which caused them to guffaw even harder than they had before. Finally I gave in and embraced this most healing moment in my life.

The next morning I dug my way out of the snow cave and discovered that the storm had passed in the night. The walls of Petrapolis were still in sight far in the distance, and the morning suns were lighting up their dirty brown color against the plain of white.

"Good morning Zeb," called out Eviea as I was looking out of the cave.

"The same to you. We must be leaving soon for we have overslept. The suns are already up, and the walls of Petrapolis are still in sight."

After eating some dried seeds, I recovered the hobbled beasts. Within the hour we were riding east again, and it was noon before the walls of Petrapolis disappeared and we stopped for rest and food. Eviea nursed her child on top of a large flat rock that I had cleared of snow. We ate dried fruit and drank beast milk that my brother Dee had put into a dried elb skin. During lunch I found myself staring at this lovely woman as she watched her child.

"You never finished your story last night, and I also want to learn more about pelots and the Dark Prince," I said, hoping she wouldn't mind.

"Where do you want me to start?" she asked with a lovely smile beaming from her face.

"Your first visit from Vertunda," I answered.

"I have had only one visit. I was standing at the Gate of Virgins when he appeared and said he was a messenger from the Holy One and that I was blessed from above. He told me I was going to have a son and I was to name him Theo. He said my son would serve the king of Ontelles and the Holy

One in a very special way; then he vanished. That evening I went to the boy I loved and told him what had happened at the Gate of Virgins. Afterwards we were overcome by our passions.... well, we did something we shouldn't have done. Three months later my mother found me weeping on my bed and asked what was the matter. I just needed someone to talk to, since I feared to tell Neco, who was the boy I was in love with. That night my mother turned me over to the elders and I was called before their holy council. I was asked who the father was, and I told them nothing. I was escorted to the Gate of Virgins and told to leave and never return or I would be killed, because of my fornication. I was fortunate that it was late summer and the snow hadn't begun. I wandered in the forest for several days until a villager and his daughter met me. The man asked who I was, and I told him nothing except my name and age. He said I was to go with him and he would take me to **Petrapolis** with his daughter who was the same age as me."

"What happened when **you re**ached Petrapolis?" I asked wanting her to continue.

"When we reached the city I was six months pregnant, and it was obvious that I was with child. No warriors touched me while I was at **Petrapolis** because of my condition. The girl that I traveled with was very kind to me and found a small mud hut for us to live in that was located near the Temple of Love. This girl was also with child, but it was only three months along. Then two weeks after we arrived, a warrior who had made her his mate took her and they left the city. I was all alone for the last three months of my pregnancy. I had my child alone in the hut on the night the star appeared in the sky, the night the villagers arrived with the news of Rift's discovery."

I now understood that this woman was truly chosen by the God of Rift and this child of hers was very special. I felt privileged to be the woman's and the child's guardian, and pondered what this child would become. "Two weeks later the great fire broke out and I had to escape with my child, and that was when I was discovered and herded with other mothers and un-chosen women to be slaughtered outside the city."

"The rest of the story I know. Now we must be on our way again," I said as I jumped from the rock. "Spring is near, it's in the wind," and I remembered that these were the very words the soldier used at the Temple of Love on my first visit to Petrapolis.

"Where are we going, Zeb?" asked Eviea as she pulled little Theo from her breast. His little hands began to wave in protest to the end of his feeding.

"We go to Rift, where else?"

"I can't go there, they will kill me and Theo! Please Zeb, don't take me back there! I can't go! Please!" I stood at the bottom of the rock and watched her break down into tears and trembling in the same fashion as when she had begged me to save her child outside the walls of Petrapolis.

"Alright, I won't take you there," I said as my mind began to search for a place of refuge. "Somewhere in the mountains, we will find a sanctuary."

We traveled east, towards the rise of the suns and it was the middle of summer before we finally reached the mountains. The snow had all melted and we didn't need our elb robes. We traveled long hours and encountered no one during those days of travel. At night we never spoke of Petrapolis, Rift or the Holy Scrolls. We only talked of the weather, our experiences as children and other non-essential matters. My affections for the woman were strong but my heart was still knitted to Desiree's. I spent hours each day thinking of her while riding on my beast, and especially that night we spent together outside our village.

On the one hundred twentieth day after we left Petrapolis we found a U-shaped, glacier-cut valley high in the mountains. We rode up the valley until we came to a wall of rock forming a dead end. Above the rock face, near the pinnacle in front of us, was a hanging valley or cirque that had a magnificent waterfall cascading down over the vertical cliff of stone to where we stood in the lower valley.

"There has to be a fairly good size lake up there to produce such a waterfall," I observed. "And that cirque would be a perfect place to hide out."

"It looks like the magical valley of Farella," whispered Eviea very softly not meaning for me to hear.

"Are you talking about something?" I asked teasingly, for she was consistently talking to herself.

"I just said, Farella, it looks like Farella."

"What's Farella?" I asked mockingly.

"No, it's pronounced *Fa-rell-a,* with the same sound as in father. It's a cirque situated at the end of a steep valley. Long ago in the hanging valley of Farella the evil pelot, Leatos, fought with Vertunda. It will also be the location of the last battle Leatos will have with Vertunda, but that won't be until the last days, shortly before the true kingdom begins."

I found her story interesting, yet my mind was thinking about our immediate problem: such as how to get up there and if wood gathering would be easy, since it looked like the cirque was just at the edge of timberline.

"Zeb, did you listen to what I just said?"

I took my eyes off the falling water and looked at Eviea. "I heard you and as soon as we can find a way up there we will name it Fa-rell-a," I said pronouncing the name very slowly and correctly.

She laughed with that contagious laugh of hers after I pronounced Farella and touched my arm with her hand. I also began to laugh as I dismounted and Eviea did the same. As she held her side from the pain her laughter caused, she said she was going to feed Theo and went to lean against a rock. While she was busy with Theo, I went to search for a way to reach the cirque. I walked around the large misty spray of water that was continuously filling the air from the pounding water of the fall. When I walked back towards Eviea I had concluded that it was going to be impossible to reach the cirque. The vertical wall of stone that was at least one hundred bodies high where the water fell over the top edge prevented any human access to the upper valley.

"I can see no way we are going to reach it!" I called out when I was in hearing range to Eviea.

"It must really be Farella if it is so well protected from intruders!" she yelled back over the roar of the falling water.

I turned back scratching my head looking up at the point where the water began its descent. I hated the idea of turning back out of this valley, but it was a dead end if we couldn't reach the cirque. Then I saw something white and shaggy at the top of the cascade. It only appeared for a short time and I wondered if I had seen something or not. As I looked around for the beasts that I had forgotten to hobble, I realized it was Peton that I had seen. "Eviea, there is a way to Farella!" I shouted. She just sat next to her rock and smiled. "Aren't you excited to know there is a way up?" I asked, curious at her lack of surprise. As I waited for her reply, it came to me. Of course, the Holy One would not have brought us here if there was not a way.

I turned and picked up the spoor of the two missing beasts and followed it into the wet spray of the waterfall until it disappeared under the pounding water. I walked underneath the waterfall; and behind the cover of the cascading water I saw what the beasts had discovered, a natural tunnel formed by what must have been a small underground river at one time flowing from the lake above. It rose at a steep grade and I saw daylight at the entrance in the valley above. I ran up the tunnel and found myself in the back of a small hollow with green meadows surrounding turquoise waters of a glacier lake. The two white beasts were frolicking through the meadows of dwarf mountain flowers and grass.

"Zeb, are you up there?" came the voice of Eviea echoing up the tunnel. She had seen me pass under the waterfall and had followed after me, carrying little Theo in her arms.

"Yes, come on up, the view is spectacular!"

When Eviea emerged from the underground passageway, she looked in awe at her new home. "It's exactly like the description given in the scrolls. We have found the ancient valley of Farella!"

After the first night in Eviea's new haven I began to build a rock house, close to the waterfall, that would provide shelter throughout the winter. By the time fall arrived I had constructed a magnificent two-room abode of white and gray stones. I had also hunted and frozen enough meat in a glacier above the house to last several long winters. Eviea worked hard curing the animal skins and fished in the lake when she wasn't making pottery or baskets.

Fall is a short season on Ontelles and before it was over I had decided to leave the hanging valley and ride to Rift to see if Joba had raised an army capable of defending the city. I saddled Peton and packed the spare with provisions; then went to tell Eviea. She was busy washing some of her pottery dishes in the stream that emptied from the lake at the lip that hung over the valley. Little Theo was asleep in the shade of a rock on some animal skins.

"Are you going hunting Zeb?" she asked as I walked up behind her.

"Not the type of hunting you think," I said seriously. After a long pause I asked, "Tell me, Eviea, before I go, do you love me?"

Eviea turned and looked at me with her striking eyes for the longest time, which made me feel embarrassed for even asking. "I think I might, but I have promised my heart to Neco, the father of my child. And I know I love him. Do you love me Zeb?" she asked almost hesitating in her question.

"I think so, but once when I thought I loved another girl who was also from Rift, I found out later that I was only fond of her and it wasn't love. Maybe we are just fond of each other and we should always just remain friends."

"Zeb, why didn't we meet when you were in Rift?" asked Eviea.

"I wasn't there that long, but you probably remember me. My name was Tobe and I was thrown out of the city because my sword didn't flame."

"Yes, now I remember. You killed the giant the next day with the Flaming Sword; you are the King of Ontelles!"

I didn't say yes or no. "I know Neco, and I will try and bring him back to you."

Eviea stood and took my hands in hers. I looked away from her and stared blankly down into the beautiful colors in the valley below. "I will always be eternally grateful to you even if you never return." She then released my hands, kissed her finger and placed it very gently on my mouth. "Go in peace, and may the God of Rift go with you."

I turned and walked the two beasts to the tunnel and left the obscured valley in the peaks that were now swathed in clouds. I rode the next four days towards Rift and late on the fourth day I found the crack in the wall along with two-dozen warriors from Petrapolis guarding the entrance. I felt saddened at the sight knowing that Rift had most likely fallen into the hands of the soldiers of Petrapolis.

As I turned around without being noticed, I rode quietly into the dark. Suddenly three men jumped out in front of me with swords ready to cut me down. "Are you Zeb?' asked one of the men who wore the armor of Petrapolis. The other two only wore elb robes with white tunics underneath.

"Yes. How did you know my name?"

"We were sent here by our commanders, Joba and Deeobulus, to wait close to the crack in the wall until a warrior appeared riding a white beast."

"Joba and Dee?" I asked. "Are they in Rift?"

"No, a day and night's ride north of here."

"Good, then let's be on our way."

The three men had beasts hobbled not far from where we stood. We traveled the distance without stopping until we reached a stronghold in the rocky parts of the mountains where the renegade army of deserters from Petrapolis and remaining men of Rift had chosen to hold out. I found Joba and Dee in a makeshift tent of animal skins eating cooked meat and drinking cream juice. It was late evening and I was tired and the sight and smell of food made me realize how hungry I was.

"Hail the king!" called out Joba as I dismounted my white beast. I embraced Joba then Dee.

"Well I'm glad you two found each other and these three soldiers found me or I never would have found your fortress in these rocks."

"It's not a bad hiding spot, do you think?" said Dee with a proud wave of his hand.

"How many men do you have?" I asked Joba.

"About five thousand men and a thousand women..."

"And a lot of children," said Dee cutting Joba off. We all laughed and Joba offered me a place next to the fire with some meat and drink.

"Where did you get such provisions and the cream juice?" I inquired as I sat to partake.

It was Dee who answered with obviously good natured pride, "We captured some war wagons going to Petrapolis but what they didn't know is that there isn't any Petrapolis anymore."

"What do you mean, no Petrapolis?" I asked.

It was Dee who answered again. "A week after you left Petrapolis, all the legions in the city were preparing to march on Rift, and I with the aid of about twenty others set

the city aflame from every quarter. King Topo ordered all
the soldiers out of the city and then he had all the women
locked in. For eight days and nights the city burned with all
the women inside. King Topo sent the word around the
legions that there was now no coming back. We had to take
Rift and make it our new capital, and if anyone wanted
women they would get all the virgins they wanted at Rift.
The only woman to survive was Leas, the high priestess."

Dread entered my heart after I learned of the evil of Topo
and that he was still alive. I felt guilty that I hadn't killed
him when I had the chance and saved over a hundred thousand from a fiery death. "What happened at Rift?" I asked
Joba almost in tears.

"Topaz refused to protect his city and said it was God's
will whatever happened. All he did was crate up the scrolls
from his study and had them hidden under the Temple floor.
I secretly gathered about a thousand men with the help of
Neco to defend the crack and when the legions arrived we
held for about two weeks. But they finally overwhelmed us.
I tried to evacuate the city, but what we have here are all that
made it along with the deserters Dee brought with him after
Rift was taken.

"And Topaz, what happened to him?" I implored.

"He died holding onto the altar along with all the other
old priests. Only the young who were able to climb out by
the high cliffs were able to escape. Most of Rift's women
were captured."

"What is the size of force that Topo has at Rift?" was my
final question.

"At least sixteen legions," reported Dee. "Our army is
outnumbered at least twenty to one."

"You hailed me as king when I arrived. Do you both
swear allegiance to me as the chief commander of this renegade army?" I asked looking both men in the eyes.

"We do," said Joba and my brother held up a cup of

cream juice in salute to their new commander and king.

"All right then, this is what we are going to do. We need to build and train this army into a fighting power. Winter is going to be upon us soon and we should be ready to attack in the spring if we are lucky. We will make this place our winter quarters and train our men all winter." Joba and Dee smiled broadly at my firmness in taking command. We ate and drank into the night planning how we were going to train the men into what we wanted, and we also drew up various master plans of attack that would commence in the spring.

Chapter Thirteen

I woke late the next morning and ate a good breakfast. Joba and Dee gave me a personal tour afterwards of the camp and by noon we had surveyed it all and saw that this rocky fortress would do well for winter quarters. I told Joba we needed scouts watching Rift at all times and we needed more men guarding the outer rock fortress. "We also should send men to the villages in the wilderness and try to recruit ex-warriors to join us," I said. "Is Neco in camp here?"

"Yes," replied Joba. "He's my aide and a good one at that."

"Good, I want him to go with me."

"Go with you; where are you going?" asked Joba in a surprised voice.

"I'm taking Neco and a small patrol to the Lepis Wilderness to get them started on their recruiting." I then turned to my brother. "Dee, I want them all to be high ranking warriors from the bunch that defected with you, and have them ready by morning." Dee saluted and left to begin picking the men. "Joba take me to Neco, then you have work to do in setting up more guards and scouts."

We found Neco counting supplies from the captured war wagons. After introducing us, Joba left to do his work.

"I heard you were in camp but I was afraid you had forgotten me," said Neco.

"I haven't forgotten your help and I'm going to pay you

back in a very special way. But I want you to be ready to leave with me in the morning."

"Yes sir, but may I ask where we are going?"

"Recruiting work in the Lepis Wilderness, and I'm going to need an aide. You're it." He smiled and bowed his head in subservience.

The next morning I shook hands with Joba and Dee. All the troops were gathered to see their king and it felt very odd that so many men put their faith and confidence in me. The soldiers Dee selected were all mounted on their beasts and ready to travel. I turned to Joba and asked about Lydia and if she was in camp, since I hadn't seen her.

"She is with the women working at our infirmary."

"You did marry her?" I asked with a smile.

"We were married a few days after you left Rift and I have you to thank for sending me through the crack first," he said as he waved his hand towards me.

"Well, I'll get these recruiters started and I'll get back to you in a few months." We all saluted and I mounted my beast and headed out of the rocky fortress and rode east towards the Lepis Wilderness.

Five and half days later our small company of warriors reined in our beasts next to a giant lowben tree, the one Desiree and I had spent the night under. My eyes surveyed the ground that was now covered by red and yellow leaves that had fallen from the branches above.

"Neco, I want you to wait here by this lowben tree until I return." Then turning to the eldest warrior of the group I told him he was now the officer in charge. "There will be no recruits from this village; that I am sure of. You will find the next village half a day's ride to the east. Send two men into the village to work it. Have them tell the inhabitants that he is a messenger from Petrapolis and tell them of its destruction. If they see anyone smile or who seems pleased to hear this bad report, those will be the ones to seek out later and to tell of our true mission. Two soldiers to each village, then after each team works a village have one soldier return to the mountains with whomever they get. The remaining soldier will go on to the next village." Turning to the others I called out to them, "Good success men and I'll see you all in the spring if not sooner." The group of twenty riders rode off in a cloud of dust leaving Neco and myself in the shade of the tall, branch-laden tree. The noon suns were bearing down, but a westerly wind from the mountains kept the temperature refreshingly cool. I still had Eviea's white beast on a lead and saddled. I handed Neco the leather lead-shank and told him to be on the alert, for when I came out of the village it might be at a full gallop with riders following me.

I turned my beast towards the familiar village and tapped my heels gently into his ribs. I was hoping this would be the last time I'd ever see this village under the sentence of the ancient laws of Ontelles. I thought to myself, what a criminal and evil law that said a son could never return to his home after his twentieth year. Hopefully this law will be done away with after all the Petrapolis warriors are defeated in the spring. But today the law was still in effect along with all it consequences. My beast picked each step carefully along the stone and shrub-covered ground. As we got closer my eyes looked to the lowben tree where Desiree stood and called out to me when I left as a nugget. My heart was pounding in my chest. I wore no armor or leather breastplate and I felt very un-kingly dressed as I was except for my white elb robe. I found the black hilt of the evil sword that hung at my side and I wondered if it would flame or not if I had to use it. For what I was doing, I did not know if it was evil or true.

No one was in sight as I entered the wide, dirt covered street. I remembered in the fall most of the men were away with the elb herds and only the women remained in the village. But there would be some men in the village such as

Veatus' father, the founder, and other domestic laborers.

No one had yet spotted me when I dismounted at my parent's humble hut of stone and wood. I knocked on the door and stepped back with my elb robe open, in case I had to draw my sword. My mother opened the wood door and her eyes went wide and her mouth fell open in horror at my sight. She had aged and her health looked poor.

"Hello, Mother," I said very calmly.

"You are no son of mine. You're a dead man for being here and now you have disgraced your father and me."

"Where does Castor live; that is all I want to know Mother?"

"His hut is next door," she answered pointing in the direction with her head. "I hope he kills you."

I wanted to scream out and remind her whom Castor had killed and whose name he now bore, but I knew it would do no good to say anymore. I had obtained the information I wanted and I was turning to leave when I turned back to her. "I loved you and Father when I was younger; and I'm sorry..." The door slammed in my face before I was able to finish.

I cautiously looked up and down the street and there were several women carrying clay jars to the well outside the village. My presence went unnoticed. I led my beast to the hut next to my parents and took a deep breath as I knocked on the wooden door. Inside I heard the crying of a child and the voice of Desiree call from within. "Come in Mother, I'm feeding little Tobe!"

I didn't enter for I wanted to stay in the street and keep watch. I also didn't want to leave Peton unattended. I knocked again but much harder this time. Finally the door was opened and there stood the young girl I saw so many times in my dreams and imagination. Her beauty took my breath away as she stood looking at my cleanly shaven face and washed hair that I had specially taken care of before the other men woke on this morning. Her blond hair was still long and flowing down over her shoulders. All was the same or better as I remembered, except the little child in her arms, who was about the same age as Theo.

"I see that you named him after me," were my first words as my eyes fell upon the small child.

"Why did you come here? This is dangerous," she said as her smile left and her expression turned to that of concern.

"Aren't you glad to see me?" I jested.

"This isn't the time or the place to make jokes," she rebuked. "Does your mother know you are here?"

"Yes, I had to find you somehow and I'm not joking; aren't you glad to see me?" I said very seriously feeling the power of my question attacking through her concern for my safety.

"Oh Zeb, you know I've longed to be with you and that I've always loved you," and she reached up with her free arm and placed her hand on my neck, drawing me down to her lips. Our mouths came together and her lips parted under mine as waves of warmth and love flowed from my inner being, through my lips into her. I also felt the total giving of Desiree to me and a peaceful glow lit my heart as I received her love. After a long moment we parted and our foreheads touched, as we looked each other in the eyes.

"I love you Des, and I've never ceased thinking of you."

"I love you too, but both our lives are in danger now that you have come here."

"I've come for you; now get your things and let's get moving."

Desiree stepped away and placed little Tobe on the dirt floor that was covered with animal skins. The little child began to crawl away as the girl I was mesmerized with placed her head on the door jam looking blankly at the hand-carved wood. I stepped next to her and placed my arms around her slender waist and whispered into her ear, "What is wrong?"

"I should have left with you when you asked me under the lowben tree, the night Tobe was conceived."

"Tobe is my child?" and I looked over her shoulder and watched the happy child playing with some wooden blocks. I began to calculate in my mind the days and months and when I understood the truth, I took Desiree's head and we stood in the open doorway kissing passionately as we held each other. Finally I pulled away and I ordered her to fetch her elb robe and hat, along with a good blanket for little Tobe. As she scurried in the house I walked in and took my son in my arms. I could now see my eyes and my curly auburn hair on Tobe. He was a strong, healthy-looking lad and I felt proud holding him in my arms.

"Hurry Desiree," I called before I walked back to the door to see if anyone was coming.

When she had her things she ran to me and we embraced again before I walked her to Peton, my faithful beast, and lifted her to the saddle. I handed her our child and pulled myself up behind her. I walked Peton out of the village and saw no one except an old woman who looked like my mother walking out into the wilderness, most likely to inform the men of my visit.

We found Neco waiting at the lowben tree and I changed mounts, and the three of us, along with little Tobe rode west toward the mountains. That evening we camped in the mountain pass where I first encountered the Red Giant. Desiree and I spent the night in each other's arms. When I awoke in the morning I felt like a man who was now complete. I had my white elb robe, the woman I loved, and a son who bore my birth name. While everyone was still asleep, I reached down and picked up the bundle of blanket and flesh and carried my son to the top of the pass. As the suns of Ontelles finally broke over the Lepis Coast, which I could barely see far on the horizon I lifted my son up to heaven and prayed, "Oh God of the universe, may your eyes be upon this child all his days. May he grow up in a world that will not take away his birth name and give him a new name from the man he has to kill."

Four days later we arrived at the end of the valley where Farella was majestically situated at the top of the cascade. We saw no sign of being followed by the villagers.

"Your new home is up in that cirque," I said to Desiree pointing up the mountain with my arm.

"How will we ever climb up there?" asked Desiree.

"The way up is easy but you will get wet. But it is worth it for it's the most beautiful spot on this old world, especially in the spring and summer."

"And the clouds probably choke your breath and freeze your bones in the winter," said Neco jokingly.

"I wouldn't be too critical, for you may be spending a lot of your time up there," I retorted with a smile.

"What do you mean, my king?" replied Neco with a funny look. Desiree glanced over at me in a quizzical manner after she heard what Neco called me.

"You will understand once we reach the valley," I said as I patted him on the back, and then began to lead the way towards the waterfall evading any questions from Desiree. Desiree followed me with Neco at the rear and little Tobe tied securely on Desiree's saddle. My son gurgled and laughed as he looked out over the valley and peaks. I knew that the tunnel was large enough to ride through on our beast. When Desiree exited the tunnel I turned and watched her face to catch the first expression when she saw her new home: the home I fell in love with when Eviea and I arrived here. Her eyes opened in wonderment and her mouth formed a cute smile as she cocked her head to the side like she always did when she was pleased.

"This place is really something and the house, who built the house?" she asked as she jumped from her beast with the lightness of a bird in flight and ran to kiss me. I dismounted in order to hold the woman I had longed to love and be with. Neco was still in the tunnel and didn't see what occurred next. Desiree held me tightly then whispered she wanted to see the house. She released me and took a few steps when Eviea came out with Theo in her arms and waved to me. Desiree turned on me in time to see my return wave. Her mouth was open in shock, and then she charged towards me and began beating me on the chest with her fists.

"It isn't what you think!" I yelled above her crying, as I tried to hold her arms.

"Don't lie, I have eyes you deceiver. I left my husband for you and now you expect me to..." and she broke into sobs as her knees gave way and fell to the ground. Neco reached the top of the tunnel as Desiree fell to the ground weeping. With my head I directed his attention towards the stone house and Eviea. His puzzled look disappeared when he recognized the woman he knew from Rift and loved. He dropped the reins of his beast and ran towards the house reaching out and hugging Eviea as they came together.

"Desiree, I want you to see something!" I said, turning her head towards the house. As she saw the man and woman embracing, her sobbing ceased.

"Then she isn't your...and that isn't your...oh Zeb, I feel so foolish."

"I should have warned you before we arrived," I said lifting her to her feet. I wiped her tears with my hand and held her tightly and kissed her still trembling lips. And I suppose there was no one on Planet Ontelles at that moment that was happier and felt more complete than those of us in Farella.

Chapter Fourteen

I took Desiree by the hand and with little Tobe still strapped to the beast, we walked around the edge of the lake up to the stone house. Eviea and Neco saw us coming and met us halfway. It was at that moment that Desiree and Eviea saw each other and they both let out a cry of joy and ran to each other embracing as they met. Neco and I just stood and looked at one another somewhat bewildered. Neco was holding little Theo and I went to unstrap Tobe from his hanging perch on the side of the beast's saddle while the two women held each other, talking at the top of their voices with excitement.

"Zeb, this is the one!" cried out Eviea. She then pulled Desiree by the hand over to the beast in order for me to see. "She is the one I traveled with to Petrapolis. The one with her father."

I handed little Tobe to Desiree, "Eviea, this is my son." Desiree took Tobe and he began to laugh in her arms as if he understood all that was happening.

That night the four of us, along with the two infants playing together, had a huge feast and sat at the edge of the lake drinking fermented berry juice that Eviea had made and stored in large pottery jugs. We sang old village songs and I told the story of how I found Neco counting supplies at the war wagon. Eviea shared with Desiree and Neco about her and myself leaving Petrapolis, the months we spent together, and how we built the stone house. It was late in the night before we all went to bed.

Three days of warm delightfulness passed before the first snows of winter began to fall and the temperature dropped. They were three of the most beautiful and happy days as we all frolicked and picnicked in the most beautiful setting I could ever remember. On the third day I asked Desiree to climb the peak above the house with me. The wind howled and I knew the weather was going to change when I saw a dark band in the western sky. When we reached the summit we had the view from the top of the world. It was clear and we could almost see the stone fortress, which was about two days by beast south of us. We also could almost see Rift, which was two days beyond Stone Fortress. There were several tish birds gliding and riding the wind above us. We had left Tobe with Eviea and Neco back at the house and we used our freedom to be together and alone as much as possible. On this last day before the storm hit we sat on a ledge on the top of the rocky peak embracing and looking out at the wonderful creation. When we weren't staring into each other's eyes there were long silences as we treasured the moments of being together. I had my arm around her and when I turned to her and kissed her, she would smile and give a sigh of contentment and tranquility.

After about an hour of silence I finally broke the hard news to her and she took it harder than I expected. Yet maybe I did predict her behavior correctly, for why would I have taken her to the top of the peak, away from everybody and everything to tell her.

"Desiree, I have something to share with you," I began very cautiously.

"You look so sad, what's wrong?" she whispered with her head cocked to the side with concern.

"I have to leave tomorrow, and I don't know when I will

be back."

"What did you say?" she asked, leaning away from me.

"Please, this isn't easy, but I do have to go."

"I don't believe this. I left everything to come with you, and now you're leaving me. Who do you think you are?"

"There are a lot of things you don't know or understand. And first of all, Castor isn't your husband, I am."

"According to the legal laws of Ontelles, he is my husband. And he is going to be looking for me, and he will try to kill you." She looked away and covered her face with her hands and her body began to shake.

"The old laws are about to be done away with. And the Holy One from heaven has united you and me from the beginning of time. You are the mother of my child, and we loved each other from childhood. We are husband and wife in the eyes of God."

"But he holds us accountable to the laws of the world," she said through her hands.

"And that is about to be changed; that is why I have to leave. Believe me I would give anything to stay, but I must go. I love you, and I can hardly live a moment without you on my mind. Since I've been separated from you it has been tortuous, and I really don't know how I will survive being away from you again. But I have to go, and you have to accept this. You will be with Eviea."

"Does Neco have to leave also?"

"I haven't decided yet."

"Does this leaving have anything to do with what Neco called you before we entered the tunnel?"

"I am the King of Ontelles. That is why I have to leave. I have to go fight for my kingdom and destroy the evil one that now exists."

"But I don't want to be married to a king. I want to live like a normal person. If you leave I will take my child and go back to Castor."

My anger began to glow because she named the man I hated with all my heart and I couldn't understand why she didn't also hate him. I saw him hit her at the gate of Petrapolis and then it finally came to me. "Whose child does Castor think Tobe is?"

"He thinks Tobe was born prematurely. He thinks he is his," answered Desiree almost in tears.

"Do you love him?" I found myself asking.

"He isn't as bad as everyone says. He is good to me."

"That isn't what I asked," I said thinking of the strike Castor made upon her at the gate of Petrapolis but bit back that sight. "Do you love him?"

"I don't know. Why do you ask me this?" she screamed.

I stood up and began to climb down from the pinnacle. Desiree called after me that she loved me, but I didn't answer. I climbed down to the stone house by myself. That night the snow began to fall. Desiree and I didn't talk much, and the next morning before sunrise I saddled Peton and began to lead him towards the tunnel.

"Zeb, please wait."

I turned around hoping it was Desiree but I saw Neco running towards me instead. "Where are you going?" he asked puffing out clouds of breath.

"I'm going to the stone fortress and start acting like a king."

"Does your quarrel with Desiree have anything to do with your leaving?"

"No, it doesn't, and we really didn't have a fight. We had a taste of truth and that caused the silence between us."

"Well, wait for me and I will join you."

"I've decided to leave you here. The women and children need you, and the task you have here is more important than coming with me. Watch and protect them. And don't let Desiree leave and that's an order." I turned away with a horrible bile taste in my mouth and an uneasy feeling in my stomach. Ordering someone to be held captive against his or her will was a wrong and evil thing to do. Didn't I learn anything while I was in the pit? With that thought, I turned to Neco still standing there like a lost elb in a winter storm. "Forget that last order. Tell Desiree if she wants to return to her village, she may go. And if she does decide to go, I would want you to escort her."

I left Neco and Farella, and my heart was crushed. My hope of a wonderful life with Desiree was only a short dream. My passion felt like rottenness to the bones, and my love for her would always be with me to eat away at my heart.

Within two days, I found myself back at the stone fortress. The first storm of winter had blanketed everything in white and once again the beautiful world of Ontelles took on its natural colors. I found the troop's morale very high, and Dee and Joba wanted to attack now and not wait till spring.

"There has never been a successful military campaign conducted in the winter," I stated as a solid fact to Dee and Joba as we sat in council around the pit fire in the makeshift tent.

"He is right, that is what our father always taught us when we were boys," said my brother to Joba, supporting my statement.

"But don't you both see, that is exactly what the warriors at Rift believe. They won't be expecting it and we will take the city by surprise," explained Joba almost in a passionate rage.

We both looked at Joba, and we knew he had the conviction that it could work. Finally I stood up from the fire and pointed down to Joba to make my point as powerful and direct as possible. "You give me a plan in twenty-four hours on how to get our men through the crack in the wall and through the marble walls, and we will do it." I then turned to Dee, "And you work out all the details of how to move our armies from here to Rift without detection; and also work out all our supply problems."

Both men smiled and moved their heads in agreement that it all could be done. I turned and found a spot to roll up in my elb robe and tried to find sleep, but found only thoughts of Desiree and my desires for her. All I wanted to do was saddle Peton and ride to her at Farella and tell her I loved her. But I knew no one could buy someone's love, even if he was the King of Ontelles. After many hours of questions and no answers, I found sleep only to wake to a world without joy or desire to live. Dee and Joba were busy with their planning, and I sat drinking cream juice at the tent entrance watching the snowfall and still thinking of Desiree.

"Zeb, what's wrong?" came the question from behind me. I turned my head and there stood a young girl. She wore a soft blue elb robe and her blonde hair fell to her shoulders, framing the face I recognized to be the wife of Joba.

"You are Lydia, aren't you?" I asked still seated at the tent entrance. She nodded and smiled.

"I'm sorry I startled you. I came in by the back flap. Joba asked me to check on you, for he said you weren't acting normal."

"He did, did he? Well Joba is always worried about me, and I'm glad he sent you. You're better looking than him."

"Don't say such things about my husband," she said jokingly. "His features are dark and fearsome, but his heart is kind and soft."

"I thought you came to cheer me up," I returned in my levity. She put her hand on the top of my head and smiled down at me. "Would you care for some cream juice?" I asked holding my cup up to her.

She sat next to me and took my cup from my hand and sipped on the juice.

"This is all I want," she replied and handed it back to me. "Now tell me, is my husband correct; are you not acting normal?"

I looked away from her penetrating eyes and stared out at the slowly falling flakes of snow and soldiers who were working on their sword fighting skills. I noticed the same tricks Joba and I developed back in the Vth Legion. "Joba's a good commander. He hasn't left a stone unturned. Vertunda called it correctly when he told me about Joba."

"You have spoken with Vertunda? It has been hundreds of years since Vertunda or any pelot has appeared to any human."

"You are kidding of course?" I said jokingly holding her shoulder with my hand.

"Of course not; that's what the holy scrolls say," she replied in deep seriousness.

"You have read the scrolls?"

"My father was the keeper of the scrolls, you knew that. He always read them to me when I was a little girl."

"Tell me what you know about Leatos, the dark pelot?"

She looked at me, contemplating deeply behind her blue eyes probably wondering how much I knew about Leatos. "All right, I will tell you all you want to know, but first you must tell me what you know."

"I know nothing, only that Leatos was once a good pelot but chose not to follow the Holy One. And he is now battling against the good pelots and the universe is the battlefield."

"Then you know all there is, except Leatos also tries to hurt the Holy One by attacking us, those that choose to follow the Creator."

"In what ways does he attack?"

"He attacks our minds...by throwing in evil thoughts; he can also enter willing ones and control from within, giving them supernatural strength."

"Can other pelots enter living beings besides Leatos?"

"Oh yes, and actually only the pelots that follow Leatos are the ones who enter living souls. The good pelots have never done such a thing and that is something you should not forget."

I stood from the cold ground and stretched my legs. I stepped out of the tent and pulled my elb robe around my neck. Joba was walking towards the tent and waved to me. I returned his greeting before I turned back to Lydia. "Your father was able to hide all the holy scrolls in the temple floor?"

"Yes."

"I appreciate your coming and sharing with me."

As Lydia looked at me my mind flashed back to the beauty of Lindas.

"Commander in Chief, I have good news," Joba said slapping me on the back.

"Let's take a walk, and you can tell me the good news," I returned, as I looked my commander in his dark enigmatic eyes. He smiled at his wife who was still sitting at the entrance of the tent as he turned to follow me. We passed the soldiers who were training. "You have taught these men well," I complimented.

"Yes, they are all good soldiers."

"Tell me, does the good news have anything to do with Rift?"

"Yes; Dee and I have worked out everything. I'll explain over in that tent," as Joba pointed to a supply tent staked out next to two war wagons. Once inside I found the tent empty except for a large leather tarp that was covering something that protruded up in different bulges. I looked to Joba but he seemed to be controlling his excitement.

"Dee will be here shortly, and then we will explain."

I stood looking at the tarp wondering what was under it, while Joba looked out the tent flap for Dee. I felt for my sword instinctively touching the hilt. I hadn't removed the sword from its sheath since I placed it there the night Topo and I fought in his chambers. I thought that this was mysterious and couldn't understand the reason.

"Here he comes, now we shall see if you approve of our plan."

My brother stepped into the tent glowing with excitement. He told Joba to bring three cups, while he removed the full elb skin from under his fur robe. When Joba returned with the cups, Dee filled them with cream juice from the juice-skin and offered a toast to our plans and success. We all emptied our cups and had refills before Joba officially began our meeting. My senses were relaxed by the cream juice, but the object under the tarp was stirring my curiosity. My eyes watched the hand of Joba grab one corner of the tarp and with the snap of his wrist the tarp flew off its hidden treasure with the ease of a floating feather. As the tarp uncovered the object, my eyes opened in amazement. I was looking at Rift. "It's a scale model of Rift with the mountains and valleys surrounding it," said Joba.

"This is incredible," I remarked. "It's a bird's eye view, and it's a perfect representation. All that is missing are little people."

"The men from Rift are all highly skilled and educated. Artisans and geographers who escaped with us made this model," said Joba very proudly. I walked around the model and couldn't get the feeling out of my mind that I was flying high above Rift on the wings of a giant tish bird. The mountains were painted green and brown, with snowcaps on the peaks. There were trees and buildings of gold, silver, and marble. The huge temple with its altar stood majestically in the center of the city pulling all the lines of the mountains and valley to its center. It was amazing to look at this city that had been hidden for centuries.

"I can't understand it. All the valleys and rivers seem to point to Rift, yet no one found it until now," I said.

"And it was because of you and I that it was found," replied Joba who was following me around the model.

"All right, what's the plan?" I asked changing the subject.

"It is very simple," answered Dee. "Each man in our small army will have a certain assignment to carry out."

"They will all memorize this model," broke in Joba as his hand pointed towards the white temple. "We will take the city in one night, and it will totally be taken by surprise."

"Fine, but how do we get an entire army into the city, considering the mountains are covered with ice and snow," as I countered his enthusiasm.

Joba looked to Dee before he answered my question. "One question Zeb. Could you cross the snow-covered mountains and enter the sleeping city?"

I thought for a moment realizing the trap my commander was laying for me. "Yes, I could do it, but it would be difficult even for one man."

"Rightly said, but isn't an army nothing but individual men, and if one man can do it; a thousand men can do it."

I felt a smile on my face, and I submitted to my generals and asked for the details. Both men worked out an intricate plan that provided for a thousand hand-picked men. The thousand were divided into three groups, which were to be led by Joba, Dee, and myself. Each third would approach Rift by three separate directions, crossing the mountains with ropes and ice-climbing gear. Each group carried the same assignment in case two of the three groups were not able to make it into the city. This also provided a backup of two men to each task. The plan was rather simple if the element of surprise was maintained. Sentries would be eliminated, and then each house in the city would be accounted for and be liquidated of warriors sleeping therein. After this was completed all would converge on the temple compound and await any additional orders. Joba had worked out all the minute details, and Dee had worked out all the supply and deployment problems. The plan seemed to be sound as I watched it enacted in my mind as I stared at the model and listened to my two generals.

"When can you have all the men trained and ready to march?" was my only question.

"Three weeks, provided we have all the information we need concerning sentries and the changing of night guards," answered Joba.

"Begin to train, and I will get the information you need and be back with it in one week," I barked with authority.

"You are our king," Joba said. "You can't risk your life when we have others that can do it."

"Get one of your geographers to draw me a map and I will leave in the morning, and that's an order." I pulled my elb robe together at my throat and walked out of the tent. The snow outside the tent was ankle deep and I turned and circled around the tent. I paused for a moment to pull some snow from the top of my boot. As I was bending over, I heard Dee talking to Joba inside the tent.

"I don't know what's wrong with Zeb, but it bothers me. He isn't the same as he was when he was younger. He never barked orders or tried to dominate anyone. Actually, he was quite the opposite."

"He's been very aloof that's for certain. He's got his mind somewhere else. I suppose when we take Rift and he becomes the king of Ontelles, it will be you and I running his empire, if he doesn't snap out of it."

"Unless it goes to his head and he becomes a power-hungry tyrant. Then we will have to....well I don't know what we will do, but I pray to whatever god is in control of this universe that he watch over our king."

"Well we better get a map made up for him, or the mad king will have our heads," jested Joba and both guffawed together.

I left the side of the tent and asked a soldier guarding the supply wagons where the infirmary was. He pointed me to a long narrow tent. When I entered the front flap I found sick and injured men and women on cots, which lined up in two long rows. I saw Lydia looking at me from the other side of the tent. We met at the center between the two rows of cots.

"What is wrong Zeb?"

"Nothing is bothering me. Why?"

"You just look funny."

"Well I feel fine. I need to know what part of the floor the scrolls are hidden under."

"Why do you ask this?"

"If you don't know just say so, otherwise tell me!" I said almost in a shout and realized my rudeness. "I'm sorry I raised my voice, but it is important that I know."

"The stone under the lamp stand. Under it you will find a room filled with the scrolls; that is, if my father's evil brother hasn't already." I turned to leave, but her hand held my arm. "Zeb, what did Vertunda say about Joba?"

I stared into her eyes and saw that she loved her husband very much. "When I was wounded and about to die in Petrapolis, Vertunda appeared and touched my wound with his finger and the burning pain left. He told me something about your uncle that I don't even understand today. He said I was to listen to Topo for he was to instruct me. Also in the same sentence he said Joba was going to be my right hand and commander."

"Was that all?"

"Yes, that was it. He said he had to leave because there was a great spiritual battle with the spirit of Petrapolis."

"Oh no! Petrapolis is no more; therefore the evil spirit of Petrapolis is now at Rift. Zeb, you must find Farella and seek out the holy prophet who lives there and ask him what we must do."

"The prophet of Farella; what are you talking about?"

"It is all written in the scroll entitled, FARELLA. There

will be a prophet who lives at Farella who will prophesy before the kingdom begins."

A sick man in a cot began to scream as if someone was choking him. Lydia ran to him and began to pull his tongue from his throat. I left the infirmary since we couldn't talk any longer. I went back to the soldier guarding the supply wagons. "I need a chest protector and a helmet. Make the helmet a tenth class helmet. I will also need a rope, fifteen bodies in length, and food for two weeks." I carried all the supplies that I requested and piled it all next to Peton's saddle inside the makeshift tent that had become headquarters for the new army of Ontelles. Joba and Dee were busy handing out orders to men who were their lieutenants and commanders. My two generals worked as a team giving orders and commands to the officers that came and went from the tent. I was impressed with the organization and skill these two men demonstrated as I laid next to my saddle and tried to act as if I were asleep. Joba was handling all the attack problems while Dee was tackling the supply details. Joba instructed his subordinates to begin mountain training at once. He said our entire army was going to enter Rift by way of ropes and every man had to become as agile as a tish bird on the wind currents of the heavens. Rift had to be taken in one night or all would perish.

Early the next morning before daybreak, I saddled Peton and tied my supplies to the back of the saddle. Joba and Dee were still asleep when I left. I dared not stir them since they were up late working out the attack plans. I had discovered a very good map drawn on a thin piece of vellum, rolled up and leaning against my saddle when I awoke. The sentries at the entrance of Stone Fortress saluted me and allowed me to pass into the dark eerie light of morning, an hour before daylight.

The next two days I traveled towards Rift. Late on the

second day I saw the wall with the Gate of Virgins barely visible. Petrapolis warriors were passing in and out of the crack while I watched from the recesses of the forest. After a short rest I walked Peton around the gate towards the south. As the suns of Ontelles began to disappear over the mountain peaks, I hobbled my beast and I took the rope, the helmet, and a small bag of seeds. I then walked towards the rocky, vertical wall that had to be scaled if I were to reach Rift. I remember studying the scale model before I left and knew there was a natural-formed chimney running up the side of the rock-faced mountain in this vicinity.

Darkness was settling quickly, and I spent about an hour looking for the spot. When I found it, I quickly removed my elb robe and rolled my helmet and the sword of guile up inside the robe. I then tied one end of the rope around the bundle and the other end around my waist. My plan was to shimmy up the chimney, and when I reached the top I would retrieve the bundle by pulling on the rope. It was freezing as I braced my back against one side of the crack with my feet and hands on the opposite side. I pushed and pulled my way up the rock chimney until I reached the top of the snow and ice covered mountain wall. At the summit I could see Rift sitting sleepily behind its huge marble walls. The meadow surrounding the city was vacant of elb herders and the city looked pretty much intact. The huge temple in the center of the city still stood and shimmered a whitish-blue from the moons, and I wondered if the scrolls were still under the temple floor.

After I recovered my bundle I quickly covered my frozen body with my elb robe. Hoarfrost was covering my face and hands as I moved my limbs back and forth to warm up. I sat for a long time doing this, and I felt very odd sitting on the mountain ridge that surrounded the meadow and Rift. When my fingers had feeling restored in them, I pulled out a pouch of black powder and when mixed with my saliva it made an ink substance that I used to make marks on the map I had with me. I marked all the sentries I spotted on the walls.

Two hours before daybreak I had all the information I needed. I put the Petrapolis helmet on and with the evil sword at my side I lowered myself down the rock cliff onto the snowy plain of Rift. The rope was tied off at the top of the cliff in order for my exit when I returned. I walked across the snow-covered meadow hoping no one saw me. All was still dark and quiet when I reached the white marble walls. To my left I noticed a snow covered mound. Fortunately the pile was next to the wall and almost reached the top. I walked up to the pile and scaled it. At the top I pulled myself over the wall and dropped inside the city without any of the guards on the wall noticing my entrance.

Once inside the city, I checked the map and made my way to the temple. The city was still asleep. Yet had I been seen I would have been left alone since I wore the helmet of a tenth-class warrior. When I reached the temple compound I found all untouched. If there had been a great battle fought in these streets I saw no sign of it. The giant altar, the compound and the massive majestic temple still stood as before. The compound was vacant of life and I walked around the edge of it keeping myself next to the cloister walls. I ran up the temple stairs to the open door, and inside I found it the same as the compound and city: empty and void of humans. The lamp was standing as before, but it wasn't burning. The table once full of bread was empty, and the small altar of incense was lying on its side, broken in half. Remembering the visit from Vertunda on the night Lindas was cremated caused a strange holy awe to fill me. I walked up to the lamp stand and pulled it away from the large stone, which it stood upon. I didn't know how I was going to pry the stone out of the floor. There were scratches on one side of the stone where it looked as if a pry bar had been used. I opened my elb robe and looked down at the black hilt of the sword. If my motive was wrong then the blade would flame and it would be of no use to me as a tool to pry with. On the other hand, if what I was doing was right it wouldn't flame. Without any more thought I yanked it out of its scabbard and for the first time since I took the sword from Topo's chambers it was bared from its prison of the scabbard. Only a black cold steel blade stared me in the face in the darkness of the temple. I felt relieved as I placed the tip into the crack and pulled back on the hilt. With a loud lurching sound the huge stone that was about half a body square slid under the other stones on what sounded like wheels, leaving a dark hole in the floor. My eyes were acclimated now to the darkness of the temple and I could see stone steps leading down under the temple floor. I replaced the sword in its scabbard and carefully stepped down the stairs. At the bottom of twelve steps I found myself groping in total darkness. I walked forward until I bumped into a wooden table. There was a smell of old parchment mixed with fish oil. On the top of the table I felt for the fish lamp that I smelled. When I found the lamp it was only a matter of lighting it. Tied to my belt was a small pouch filled with sulfur sticks, and I struck one on the cold stone floor and the flash of light almost blinded me as it ignited. The fish oil lamp began to burn brightly. I blinked several times trying to adjust my eyes to its light. The room was about the same size as Topaz's study chamber with wooden shelves filled with the scrolls. The table under the fish oil lamp was long with benches on both sides. A long thick rope hung from the ceiling that was connected to a pulley system, which controlled the opening and closing of the stone at the top of the stairs. I pulled on the rope and the stone slid back into place with the same lurching sound as when it opened.

Chapter Fifteen

A thin curly line of smoke continuously lifted from the fish lamp as I was standing in front of the table staring at the scrolls contemplating where I should begin to read. I slowly moved around the table and chose the last scroll on the bottom shelf on the far right hand side. I removed a soft red ribbon and carefully unrolled the parchment. The title at the top read, FARELLA.

"Don't begin with the last scroll."

I dropped the parchment and had the Sword of Guile out of its scabbard before the scroll hit the floor. I pivoted and saw the black steel of my sword as I was now face-to-face with the being that had just addressed me. It was Vertunda, dressed the same as before.

"Put the sword and its scabbard on the table," Vertunda said as he pointed to the roughly-finished wooden table. I did as he asked. "Now put the scroll back and take the first scroll, which is at the top left end. You shall begin there."

The first scroll had a blue ribbon holding it in its cylinder shape.

"The scroll is entitled, BEGINNINGS," Vertunda said in his deep, but gentle-sounding voice. "You may sit down to read, and I will be here to answer any questions you might have."

"I'm not a swift reader, and it has been awhile since I've

read anything. What I'm saying is, it may take a long time to read all of it. And are you going to stay here that long?"

"Yes. And I will be here until all the scrolls you are to read have been read."

"What? It will take days; weeks!"

"Sit and begin now. When you are finished you will begin with the next scroll and continue reading."

Vertunda smiled at me as if I were some young child excited with a new toy. I sat and began to read and surprisingly my eyes never grew tired, nor did I get hungry. The oil in the lamp never ran out as I read, read and read. When I didn't understand a word or a concept I turned to Vertunda, who sat next to me on my left. He would explain, and my mind began to grow and expand with the information from the scrolls. There were history scrolls and ones of poetry and songs. Others contained proverbial sayings and others with true stories of people long ago and pelots which all had to do with the Holy One who created all. I was amazed at how none contradicted the other concerning the Creator. Days passed into weeks, yet I had no way of telling how many days went by. Finally I reached the last parchment, the prophetic scroll of FARELLA.

"I now know the Holy One," I said to myself as I pulled the last scroll from the shelf.

"You only know what the Holy One has allowed you to know from the writings of his faithful servants. You will never stop learning of Him even as you pass into eternity," Vertunda said still smiling, almost laughing at the banal thought that tumbled off my lips. "Now tell me what you have learned," quizzed Vertunda.

"I understand the history of the people of Ontelles. I comprehend the laws given by the Holy One and what he wants His people to be like. I realize Ontellians have been very wicked at times but also there have been some righteous ones. I understand the evil that is deep within a man's heart, and the truth and goodness that can change and override that wickedness. I believe the Holy One loves His creatures, but they don't seem to love Him, or even care at times. A man can be educated in truth and still not choose to follow the teachings of what he knows. It all seems to be a battle between knowing and believing. But what I know for sure is this...if I share what I have learned, I will be considered mad, and I will be locked away, if not worse. Humans live in the flesh and think only in the flesh. The Holy One is spiritual and thinks in the spirit. The two are against each other, and I don't believe they can be mixed. Maybe I will find the answers in this last scroll."

"No! Time is up. Take the scroll with you and read it later when you are alone at Farella."

"What? What do you mean time is up?"

"Your friends are battling in the city above and they are about to make you the king of Ontelles."

"How long have we been in here?"

"Your friends took you for dead when you didn't return to them. They went ahead according to your orders to take the city."

"What do you mean my friends..." and as I spoke, Vertunda reached for the Sword of Guile that still rested on the table and he disappeared with it. Then a lurching sound above my head brought me back to reality. I looked up and there stood Joba and Dee looking at me with faces and hands covered with blood and sweat.

"By the creator of all, he is alive!" sang out Joba above the opening as joyful cheering began to flood down the stone stairs from the temple.

"Our king is alive and with us everyone!" yelled Dee to the soldiers in the temple. I placed the FARELLA scroll in an inside pocket of my elb robe and walked up the steps into the cheering cries of my soldiers. It was almost dream like and mystical. I was in a euphoric daze as I looked at the faces of boys and young men cheering and singing out praises for their victory and king. All waved swords in the air below a huge beam of sunlight which was pouring into the vaulted temple, and dust motes danced silently, unaware of the victory that was being celebrated by the new army of Ontelles.

"Has the city been taken?" I implored Joba.

"Yes, and you are now the true king of Ontelles!" he shouted back. "We thought you were dead, and we went ahead without you."

"This I know!"

Joba looked at me with a strange expression on his face. "Are you all right Zeb?"

"Get all of these men out of here! This place is holy and it isn't to be defiled by swords of blood! Now do as I say!", which I assumed was my first official order as king of Ontelles.

"All right!" Joba barked back in anger. His eyes glowed with murder and if I hadn't the authority of a king I was certain he would have run me through with his sword. Instead he turned and at the top of his lungs he commanded all the soldiers to leave the temple and gather in the compound. All the soldiers lowered their weapons and slowly flowed through the open door into the early morning light.

When the temple was empty except for Joba, Dee and myself, I turned to my two commanders and addressed them. "I thank you for the work that you have done and you both will be rewarded with the rule of this world. This stone is to be replaced and no one is to go into that room until I say so. Put the city in order and protect it since it still isn't safe from attack."

"How did you know?" asked Dee with a quizzical look.

"It is written in the scrolls that the holy city will not be safe even after the king's army recaptures it."

"That is true," answered Joba. "A legion of warriors is

still out there looking for our stone fortress but we didn't know this until we captured the warrior council's books and read the daily reports."

"I'm hungry and tired, and I'm going to the infirmary to rest. Now replace the stone and put the city in order." I turned and left my generals and walked out into the blinding light of morning. A roar of cheers blasted me as I exited from the temple. I lifted my arms in salute and then passed through the sea of men. Outside the compound I noticed several columns of smoke lifting from different quarters of the city. There were men dragging the dead from different buildings and throwing them on the piles of corpses. I turned down a street and the aroma of the smoke touched off a cold sweat. It was the same smell the night Lindas was cremated, the smell of burning flesh. A soldier came out of a house in front of me pulling a dead warrior by the feet. I stepped into the open door and looked in. The room was covered with blood and two other Petrapolis warriors laid prostrated as if they had been killed in their sleep.

Down a second street I saw the infirmary and the large dining hall. Inside the infirmary I found all the beds filled. The wounded and dying were crowding the hallways. I turned around and walked out into the street. My fatigue and euphoric daze were still with me, and I leaned up against the infirmary wall shoving my hands into the outer pockets of my elb robe. My right hand felt the bag of seeds I had placed there when I left Peton hobbled in the forest. I quickly pulled the bag out and began to counter my fatigue. After the seeds had been consumed, the desire for sleep began to pass. The scroll in my inner pocket along with what Vertunda said about reading it when I was alone at Farella began to gnaw at my mind. "I can't be king until I have read the last scroll," I said to myself. "And Desiree, I need to see Desiree." I dropped the empty seed bag to the slush covered ground and began to walk towards the city gate through the busy streets with its piles of dead.

I left the city gate and walked south through the white-blanketed meadow. The sky was cloudless and the morning suns were beginning to melt the top crust of snow that didn't seem any deeper than when I sneaked into the city weeks ago. The rope was still hanging where I had left it and within an hour I had climbed to the top of the rock mountain. I pulled my elb robe up, which I had tied at the other end of the rope. A warm southerly wind was blowing and the greasy smoke from Rift was hanging low over the city. I felt a strange feeling overcome me as I thought about the success of Joba and Dee's plans. I sat there thinking about my two commanders and the harsh way I had treated them in the temple, when I told them to get the soldiers out.

"What is wrong with you Zeb?" I said to myself disgustedly. "These men offered their lives for you and now you treat them like foolish elbs. I need to find Desiree, that's what's bothering me." I lay down and closed my eyes as my fatigue overtook me.

When I finally awoke it was a miracle I hadn't frozen to death. It was night and I was covered with a thin layer of snow and ice. I sat up and looked towards Rift and all was silent and still, except for the sentries walking along the top of the walls. My limbs were cold and stiff, but I felt rested. After my body was limber I threw the rope down the backside of the vertical mountain.

It was still dark when I reached the forest floor, but I was able to see the shadow of a large animal moving in between the trees.

"Peton! Peton, is that you?" I called out. I heard a snort and a hiss and the white longhaired creature cautiously came towards me. I was totally surprised to see Peton well and alive. His front legs were still hobbled and as I slowly walked towards him I saw all the low tree limbs in the forest stripped past the bark.

"Hey Peton! I see that you have been eating the trees since I've been away." He was still saddled and the bags of food were still over his hindquarters. "You're fortunate a pack of wild hogs didn't find you and rip your guts out." I said as I reached down to un-hobble him. Affectionately he rubbed his long snout along the side of my head. This was the first time I ever witnessed this type of gratitude from a beast. Had I been hobbled for no telling how many weeks and my owner finally arrived, I'm sure my behavior would have been quite the opposite.

I removed the saddle and rubbed his back and sides with a hard cloth. He liked this. Then I allowed him to frolic and run free while I built a fire and cooked the largest breakfast ever. I had six elb steaks, hot bread, berry juice and eight tish eggs that I scrambled on a flat rock that straddled my fire pit. After my breakfast I laid back well satisfied, and watched the snow flakes slowly falling through the still air and melt as they reached the hot coals of my fire pit.

"Are you a warrior from Petrapolis?"

I turned my head towards the voice. Standing in the forest and hidden by the early light of morning, was a young man with a crudely made sword in his hand. He stepped out of the shadows of the trees and I could see the dull edge of his sword. Not wanting to get hacked to death by a dull edge, I slowly moved my hand towards a hot rock that was next to the fire pit in preparation for my defense.

"Answer my question!" he demanded in a deep and intense voice.

"Come sit down and I'll offer you some food."

"After I have your head I'll have all the food I want," he boasted with bravado.

"If you're a nugget you can put down that sword. There isn't any Petrapolis to go to with a warrior's head. Those days are over."

"True, but one still needs a head to get into Rift, the new

capital."

"Well for your information you don't need a head to get into Rift any longer, starting today actually," I said with a chuckle, feeling the fruits of victory just won by the new warriors of Ontelles. "Besides, do you know where Rift is located?"

"No, but I will worry about that after I have your head..."

"Peton! No! That's enough!" The hissing beast had charged out of the forest and knocked the nugget to the ground and was about to take the boy's head into his razor-sharp mouth. My cries stopped the loyal creature from shredding his head like a peeled palma fruit. The beast snorted several times and stomped back as I picked up the dull sword and ordered the shaken nugget to his feet. "You have guts nugget, but you have no brains. I should have let my beast feast on the little you have. But instead I'm going to give you your freedom."

"Why?" he asked in a different sounding voice as we both smelled something foul coming from him.

"Because, I told you the truth and today I am full of mercy."

"I think I believe you. I'm really not as brave as I tried to sound."

"Nobody really is. You see that rope hanging over there?" I said pointing with the nugget's sword. "You climb that rope and at the top you will see Rift. Go into the city and ask for a man named Joba. Tell him what happened here and that you want to be an Ontelles warrior. And you won't need a human head to become one. Also tell him the king of Ontelles has gone to Farella and will return when the Holy One sends him back."

"Yes sir, or your highness. I will do as you say. May I have my sword back, I made it myself."

"I know, and you probably spent an entire summer look-ing for the choicest of iron stones."

"Yes, how did you know?" he asked with a boyish look on his face.

"I will keep the sword and its scabbard."

"I don't have a sheath for my sword."

"I lost my first sword to a red-bearded giant when I was a nugget but I was given a new sword that was much better. When you talk to Joba, ask him for a new sword since the king kept yours."

"You are the king?"

"The rope, climb it and ask me no more questions." He stood and bowed. Then he ran through the hard crusty snow and began to climb the rope. When he was about seven bodies up the chimney, he looked down at me. "My name is Taman, remember when you return to Rift."

"Your new name will be Peton, that will be your warrior name since it was my beast Peton who spared your head."

"Yes sir, remember Peton!" The nugget's voice echoed through the quiet forest as the snow began to fall faster and heavier.

"Well my faithful beast, we'd better be on our way if we're ever to reach Farella."

PART II

THE ORDER OF THE KINGDOM

Chapter Sixteen

A blizzard developed within hours after I had left the nugget whom I had renamed Peton. My beast, Peton, carried me through the blinding wind and snow which was comparable to the storm I encountered the first time I left Rift, shortly after Lindas had been killed. That was five winters ago and I calculated that I was now twenty-five years old.

That seemed young to be a king, but then, what was the right age? The truth was, I couldn't begin to function as king until I reached Farella and finished reading the last scroll. The urge to stop and read it was overwhelming. Had there not been a blinding storm I believe I would have fallen to this temptation.

My faithful beast plowed through the drifting snow, instinctively traveling in a northeasterly direction. There were no stars or landmarks to guide us. Moss on the north side of trees was my only guide. I contemplated turning back as I did winters ago, but the drive to reach Farella and Desiree was pushing me on, no matter what the obstacle.

The killer storm raged on into the night and I kept moving, not wanting to stop and freeze under the blowing drifts. The heat from Peton kept my legs warm which helped warm the rest of my blood and upper extremities. The snow was light and powdery, reaching at times up to Peton's chest. He snorted and used his long snout to plow a trench for his legs. My vision went no further than an arm's length but we kept moving by an intuition that seemed to be guiding through the darkness and blinding snow.

When morning finally arrived it was still hard to tell the difference between day and night. Dark angry clouds hung low over our heads and the snow hadn't let up in over twenty hours.

"Peton, we should be near the waterfall if we have been traveling in the right direction. And if we don't find it soon we will never find it. I will have to spend the winter in a snow cave and you will perish my long-haired friend." I looked up at the gray and ominous clouds and raised my arms up towards heaven.

"Oh God of the universe. You have called me, and now I am lost in this storm. Save us from this wicked situation. Lead me to Farella, I beg you."

I lowered my arms and I waited for God's answer to my prayer. Nothing happened, and the snow just kept falling. Peton couldn't go any further and in my mind I was fighting the horrible sense of panic and devastation, causing a mind to think crazy and irrational things. Then the most mysterious thing happened. It was almost too baffling to even believe. A break in the storm occurred.

The snowing stopped all at once, and the feeling and sensation was unforgettable. The sky above was blue and as calm as the Lepis Ocean during early morning tide. But what was beyond belief was the sight my eyes beheld. There I sat on Peton and we were standing in the lucid light of morning in the middle of the camp of what had to be a legion of Petrapolis warriors. There were hundreds of war wagons and makeshift tents full of snow and stretched over quickly dug snow caves. There were no sentries because of the storm and I saw no one except one soldier about my age who must have realized the snowing had ceased and had pulled himself out of a snow cave. He stood silent and stared at me while I did likewise. Then he spoke.

"Who are you, dressed white and straddling a giant white beast?" he called out in a frivolous manner.

"I'm the King of Ontelles," I answered in the same lightness of speech. We both began to laugh because of the oddity of the situation. While I laughed I looked over my shoulder to see if anyone else was watching, but what I saw stunned me and washed the laughter from my throat. I saw a long frozen waterfall and at the top of the giant icicle was the dish-shaped trough of the hanging valley of Farella.

"Creator of all, we are here," I said out loud. I looked back to the soldier and he was calling to his comrades to come up and see the King of Ontelles. Before any of his comrades climbed out of their warm abodes the snow began to fall again in blinding sheets. Darkness of the clouds filled in the blue sky above and once again it was as before. I reined Peton around in the direction of the frozen fall and put my heels to his side.

With the dull-edged sword I dug a hole down to the entrance of the tunnel and found that a hole had already been broken through the ice. I walked Peton into the tunnel and it felt good to once again be out of the pounding of the wind and snow. I tried my best to cover up the hole in the icefall with snow, but the hole would naturally be filled with snow in a couple of hours.

In the tunnel Peton and I walked with the excitement of returning home. At the top entrance I had to dig out into the open. Peton then made his way to the stone house with me trekking behind in his path. The house was buried but visible and a welcome sight. I decided to dig into the animal shed first, which was built off the back of the house, and bed Peton in a stall before I surprised anyone with my presence.

"All the stalls are empty," I said to Peton. All the beasts were gone including Neco's and the other white one. I put

165

Peton in one of the stalls, removed his saddle and rubbed him down. The pleasure and gratefulness of Peton was quite evident as he moved his head with every stroke of my hand. Every now and then he would utter a purring sound showing his approval of this much-deserved attention. I made sure he had plenty of mountain grass to eat, which I had cut and stored last fall. I filled an open clay pot with snow for drinking water when it melted.

After my chores in the animal shelter, I carried the remaining supplies along with my saddle and climbed back out into the weather and walked over the roof of the house. I dug my way down to the front entrance and knocked before I entered. The two rooms were empty of any life. I searched and called out like a wounded animal in the forest for his mate. Desiree and my son were gone. Neco, Theo, and Eviea were likewise missing. The thoughts that ran through my mind were overwhelming. Did soldiers from the valley below find them and take them to their camp, or more likely did Desiree decide to return to Castor? Then the last words of Vertunda resounded in my mind, 'Read the scroll later when you are alone at Farella.'

"My God in heaven, you knew they were gone. But where?" My cries comforted me not, and I fell into the straw bedding in the sleeping room and finally my sorrow turned to sleep. When I awoke it was night, but the storm was still raging outside. The house was freezing cold, and I built a fire in the fire pit. Then I went outside and cleared the snow off the roof, in order to keep it from caving in and from blocking the smoke hole. After I had completed this strenuous task I went back into the house that was now toasty warm. For the first time in days I was warm, and it lifted my lonely spirits. I took my elb robe off, and my eye caught the scroll with the red ribbon. I pulled it out and placed it on the stone table that I had built out of flat granite rocks piled one upon another and wedged to be level.

166

Round cut trunks of a medium size lowben tree served as chairs for the stone table.

"I must eat first, then read the final scroll," I said to myself as if I were talking to some invisible person. This was a habit developed from my lonely days as an elb herder and continued during my imprisonment in the pit of Petrapolis. I cooked wild pig meat that was preserved from last summer and drank berry juice.

After I had cleaned up my body and cleared off the table, I took a fish lamp and sat at the stone table, carefully unrolling the parchment. At the top I read the title, FARELLA.

"Holy One, guide my eyes and mind as I read this last scroll. Show me what I am to learn. And give me strength to endure what it says.'

Farella

The words of Elan, a member of the royal priesthood from the hidden and holy city of Rift, to whom the word of the Holy One came in the seventh year of the Petrapolis Order, which stands on the Wilderness of Death. The word of the Holy One came to me, saying, 'You shall hear and see what will come to pass in the age to come. This age will be the Kingdom Age for I will place a king on the throne of Rift. The king will be young, but filled with wisdom and strength from above. He will come from the land of Lepis and out of the Order of Petrapolis will he flee. He will be disciplined in the Holy Temple and from Farella will he vanquish the evil one. He will carry the Flaming Sword and it will be presented at the Gate of Virgins as a sign to the unbelievers.'

I, Elan, was carried ere these last days, and
shortly before the kingdom begins and stood with
a good pelot as he showed me the future king of
Ontelles. I watched as he slew a giant at the Gate
of Virgins with the Flaming Sword. Then I saw
him again cut the hand off of a mighty warrior in
the Warrior Council Chamber of Petrapolis. Then
lastly I saw him at Farella. The very same Farella
where Leatos, the pelot of darkness, fought with
Vertunda, written about in the writings entitled
BEGINNINGS. What I saw was the last battle
between Leatos and Vertunda. The king battled
with the champion of darkness, the mighty warrior with the missing hand. They both held flaming swords and fought bravely. The good pelot
removed me from the battle and I didn't see the
end. 'Write what you saw,' said the good pelot.
'This shall be a sign of the end of the last days,
shortly before the true kingdom begins and ends
and the Age of Truth prevails. These words will be
locked up until the last days when the city of Rift
will fall into the hands of the evil ones and then be
recaptured by the King's armies.

I, Elan, ten years after my first prophecy and
vision, was taken in the spirit and stood at the
edge of the Wilderness of Death. I saw a huge city
burning and the cries of women and children rose
with smoke. The good pelot as before stood by me
and spoke. 'The Order of Petrapolis will grow
and spread its power and influence into the
Wilderness of Lepis and Topan. Many years will
the wickedness grow and the pains of its selfish-
ness will touch many. But what you see is the end
of the city of wickedness when the King of

Ontelles arrives. He will free the people of Ontelles and he will instruct them in truth from the courtyard of my Temple and from the holy valley of Farella. But the power of the evil one will haunt the kingdom until the battle between Leatos and Vertunda. Then will the reign of Truth begin.'

I wrote down the words of the good pelot and what I saw, then handed the writings to the high priest of Rift, named Tepon. I was then called before the Holy Council of Elders and Priests and ordered to be beaten, because I claimed to have had a visit by a good pelot and witnessed the future. They said there could not be a King of Ontelles, for the Holy One was king. If the Holy One wanted a king he would surely make the high priest of Rift king. I was taken to the Gate of Virgins and tied to the wall. There I was whipped: one stroke by every priest and elder. Then my tongue was cut from my mouth so I wouldn't tell what I saw. But I secretly made a second copy since the first scroll was destroyed, and I added the remainder, in order to show the unbelief even by the ones who claim to
be the followers of God.

In the twelfth year of the Order of Petrapolis, and the twentieth year of the High Priest, Tepon, a decree was given by the Petrapolis Warrior Council to mark all babies with their name, village and date of birth. And it was at this time the word of the Holy One came to me again for a third time. He sent it through his messenger and highest pelot, Vertunda. I was herding elbs outside the city walls of Rift when he appeared and placed his finger on my lips. 'You now have your tongue restored, in order to bear witness of what I am about to tell you. Because of the evilness of the priests and elders of Rift, I will send the armies of Petrapolis to destroy and kill those that live therein. But for the sake of my Holy Word and of you, Elan, this will not take place until the last days. I will then send the armies of the king to take the city back and cleanse it. But the city of Rift will still be in danger as prophesied in the Holy Scrolls. There will be only one escape for Rift. If the inhabitants repent of their wrong and evil deeds, then I will save them. A prophet from Farella will come to Rift and prophesy before the true kingdom begins and ends. My servant of truth will also come from Farella to lead my people into the brightness of truth.'

Chapter Seventeen

"The Wilderness of Death? This must have been written back in the Ancient of Days. The Plain of Blood hasn't been referred to as the Wilderness of Death in my memory," I said to myself after I finished the scroll. Perhaps long ago it was, I thought. To read something as ancient as the dust, yet as fresh as a volsa rose was paralyzing to the mind. "The scroll is a prophecy about me," I cried aloud. "My God in heaven, I'm numb to all this. My mind, my spirit, my soul, and my strength are extended beyond their natural limits!" I pulled at my hair and fell to the floor and lay there with my eyes open and my mouth agape. How long I remained in this position I'm not sure. When I finally got up, my beard was several days old and I was famished. After I ate, I tried to reread the scroll, but I found it too difficult to even get close to the stone table where I had left it lay. I needed the presence of a living soul or I would fall to the floor again, and I was afraid if it happened I would never be able to survive.

"Peton! I shall visit my friend Peton." When I left the stone house and climbed over the snow-covered roof to the animal shelter I was given new strength. The sky was clear of clouds and the suns were high overhead. I found my white beast pounding his hooves into the dirt floor; his way of telling me he was hungry for mountain grass and attention from his master. I rubbed him with a stiff cloth while I talked to him for hours as he purred and threw his head up and down pretending he understood every word I said.

"Peton, what do you think? Have I lost my mind? Don't shake your head yes. I don't want to be king, but can I cancel what has been planned and foretold to happen? Don't shake your head yes to everything I say. I must be crazy to be discussing these things with a beast. But you are a loyal and faithful beast: don't get me wrong. I've just never seen nor heard of a beast that was as friendly with a human before. Yes, it is silly, but I am thankful. What about the soldiers? I forgot about the camp at the bottom of the tunnel. I will be back Peton."

I left the animal shed and made my way to the edge of the cirque and looked down to the valley below. There were thousands of campfires and the smoke was thick and almost hid the camp from my view. It looked like a legion, the one Joba spoke of in the temple. If I could reach Rift somehow I could tell Joba and we could corner them here at the end of the valley. But I knew it would take a miracle to pass through their camp to reach Rift.

I walked back to the stone house and everyday I returned, if the weather permitted, to watch the soldiers below. I was very lonely, the loneliest I had ever been. Six thousand men were within yelling range, yet I might as well have been on a different planet. My mind reminisced over and over about Desiree and the three most glorious days of my life that were spent here in Farella.

Before spring arrived I had made my decision, and I had discussed it over and over with Peton, who always answered yes. I was going to my home village and either take Desiree with me or die trying. All the power of being king did not mean anything without Desiree. She was my other half, and I wasn't complete without her.

When the first signs of spring did arrive, I began to grow

uneasy with what I had planned. I had hidden the scroll of FARELLA in a side pouch on my saddle and tried to forget about it. But it wasn't easy forcing it from my mind. It took two weeks before I was able to put the ribbon back on it, and it seemed strange to have had a fear over a piece of parchment; but the words within cut deeper than any sword.

On the first warm day of spring, green patches of grass began to show through the melting snow. I went to the animal shed and released Peton from his stall. I laughed as I watched him run around the lake as I walked to the edge of the cirque and looked down to the valley below. "The soldiers are gone," I whispered to myself. "They must have left in the night."

I ventured down the tunnel and explored the legion's abandoned camp. I found useful tools and equipment in their garbage dumps and it took several trips to carry most of my treasures up to Farella.

The next day around noon I heard a thundering crash in the valley where the soldiers had camped. I ran out of the house to the edge of the waterfall. Down in the valley lay huge pieces of ice from the frozen waterfall. Peton came running up to me hissing and snorting as he reared up and down, slamming his sharp hooves into the ground. I looked at the top edge of the icefall and saw his hoof marks. Peton had caused the huge icicle to fall, along with the help of the warm weather. I jumped on Peton's back and rode down the tunnel into the lower valley and what I saw scared me. The opening of the tunnel was visible to anyone. "Well Peton, let's just hope no one happens to come up the valley today. And let's pray that this warm weather keeps up and the melting snow will hide the tunnel entrance with a new fall." Peton hissed and shook his head yes.

The warm weather did continue and the waterfall grew and covered the tunnel entrance. Three days later I saddled Peton and with two weeks of supplies I left Farella and headed towards the Lepis Wilderness. The only weapon I carried was the nugget's sword, the one I had named Peton. I had tried to sharpen it but I found it wouldn't hold an edge. If I got into combat I would have to use it more as a club than a sword.

The next four days the weather remained pleasantly warm, and at the end of the fourth day I camped in the mountain pass where I had encountered the red giant. That evening I began to question my motives for going to my village, and I couldn't understand why Neco never returned to Farella with Eviea. The possible reason, I told myself, was that he couldn't return with the Petrapolis legion camping at the end of the valley. With that conclusion, I adjusted my saddle that I was leaning against, and I discovered something. "The FARELLA scroll," I said in surprise. I had forgotten that I placed it in my saddlebag. I opened the side pouch on my saddle and there was the red ribbon around the scroll staring at me. I quickly closed the flap on the pouch and got up from my fire. I tried walking in order to get my mind off the scroll. "What a curse it was to know the future and then only in part," I thought out loud. How did it do any good? I knew I had to have combat with Castor but Elan was taken away from the battle scene. "Who won?" I yelled up into the heavens. "My God, is that how I'm going to die? At the hands of the man whom I hate?"

I pulled my clenched fist down and in my anger I saw something. At first it looked like a stick, but at second glance I saw the sword I once owned. My very first sword, the one the giant had broken and tossed away when I was a nugget. I bent over and pulled on the handle and out of the slush came the shattered sword. I quickly saw that I had a better opinion of it when I was a nugget than I did now. The blade, besides being rusty, was just as dull as the sword under my elb robe. I carried it back to camp and tied it to my saddle next to the pouch that held the scroll.

The next day was chilly. A wind out of the west blew along the rolling wilderness of Lepis. The landscape was familiar, since I spent my boyhood days herding elbs here. Before sunset I saw in the distance the giant lowben tree that stood by itself and the village beyond. I had made good time with the strong wind at my back. There were still a couple of hours of light left, so I decided to enter the village before dark and find Desiree.

Strangely enough, as I trotted my beast towards the village, I felt no fear of losing my life. When I entered the main street I saw many of the men sitting outside their huts smoking long pipes and telling stories before twilight. This was a custom of my village as long as I could remember. There was one such story I remember that was told to me by the old elb skinner, named Zepatum. The story was about Kentu the nugget. Kentu had left one winter on his twentieth birthday but returned to his village six months later. The boy said he couldn't take it out in the mountains alone and he couldn't kill someone just for their head. The crying nugget was then tied up in the center of the village and all the women passed by and spat upon him. Then his own mother came last and threw mud in his face. His father took a sword and delivered a blow that cut the boy from the head down between the legs. The other men cut him at the waist and the four pieces were thrown to the four corners of the village. It was a gruesome story and I hadn't believed it was true until that morning at the walls of Petrapolis when I witnessed the slaughter of women and children for myself.

As I rode towards Desiree's hut, I looked at the old and young men outside their huts and felt no remorse for what I was doing. I reined Peton up at the hut next to my parents. Both my parents' and Castor's hut were free of any pipe-smoking men or curious boys. I was about to dismount and knock on the door when I heard someone yell from across the street.

"You are a dead man, Tobe!" and then there were three long blasts from a bull-delf horn. Within minutes all the men of the village came running with swords. I tried to pull Peton out into the street to make my escape, but it was too late as I found myself encircled.

"You aren't very smart, my son! And I heard you have corrupted the mind of your brother, Jeeba!" I turned towards the voice and saw the face of my father. He was old looking, and weather beaten with deep lines around his eyes. "State your business before we kill you."

"The old laws of Petrapolis are no more, and the city Rift has also fallen. I'm now the king of this planet and if anyone touches me he is a dead man along with this entire village. My business is with Desiree. I have come only to speak with her and see my son."

"You evil beast!" screamed a man from the other side of the human circle. I turned my head and quickly recognized the one-handed man, Castor. He wore an old beaten elb robe, and his black greasy hair was long to his shoulders. His eyes burned with hate and revenge. "You took her from me and now you come here asking for her?"

"She isn't here?" I asked not realizing what I had said. The villagers all began to laugh except Castor and my father. I began to feel sick. Where was Desiree?

"Get off your beast and fight your father like a man!" yelled the old elb skinner.

"No!" called out Castor as he stepped out into the empty ring with me. "He carries a powerful weapon, the one that cut my hand off. It's called the Flaming Sword and he can kill us all. Let the beast alone, for he is mine and I will fight him on another day when the conditions are more equal."

"I don't care what type of sword he has!" cried out my father and he began to run towards me with his sword outstretched in his hand. Castor rushed out and intercepted him before he reached me.

"Stop Father!" said Castor as he held my father. "I beg you not to do this. I will kill him for you on another day; I swear this with my life."

"I hate you, Tobe! I hate you!" screamed my father as white foam formed at the corners of his mouth. I nudged Peton with my knees and he moved cautiously out of the circle. I looked towards my parent's hut and in the doorway stood my mother with hands covering her face. When I reached the edge of the village, Peton began to canter, and he didn't stop until late that night.

I camped in the wilderness without a fire and slept very little. In the morning Peton and I headed towards the mountains in the direction of Farella. Four days later I was back at the hanging valley. All the way up the tunnel I shivered because of the drenching of ice-cold snow water. Most of the snow around the lake had melted and green grass along with mountain flowers was everywhere. All looked to be in order until I found two beasts tied in the animal shelter. I didn't recognize the beasts and pulled the dull sword out from under my wet elb robe. When I came out of the animal shelter, there stood Neco and Joba, both smiling and holding cups of cream juice.

"Welcome you old magician," said Joba with a laugh. "Back at Rift we were all waiting for our king and no one could find him. Then this nugget, named Peton or Taman, shows up and says you bolted to Farella, wherever that was."

"I had no choice," I said very seriously, not being loosened by the cream juice. "Neco, where is Desiree?"

"She is at Rift, where else?" he said in a jovial manner then taking a sip from his clay cup. With my left hand I knocked the cup from his hand and grabbed him by the throat.

"I told you to watch her and only escort her to the village if she wanted to go!" I yelled. Joba pulled me off Neco.

"Put that sword away before someone gets hurt," said

Joba. "Desiree is safe; she is all right."

"I'm sorry Zeb," Neco said. "After you left she went into a rage and demanded that I take her to you at the stone fortress. I didn't have much choice and I didn't want to leave Eviea here alone. When we all arrived at Stone Fortress, you had already vanished off to Rift."

"I'm the one who should be sorry," I apologized. "I'm wet, I'm tired and I almost got myself killed at my village looking for Desiree."

"You went back to the village looking for Desiree?" asked Joba as he found humor in this and began to laugh so hard he fell to the ground holding his sides. When I was overtaken by Joba's contagious laughter, Neco joined in. I told them how at the village they thought I had the Flaming Sword and they all backed off. Then Joba asked if I pulled out the dull sword and slew them all with laughter. It was all very funny and that evening we barbecued elb steaks and ate cooked bluebon roots and drank all the cream juice Neco and Joba had brought with them. After dinner we sat outside the house and just relaxed, as the clouds turned fire red from the dropping suns.

"Tell me about the battle for Rift. I'm sorry I didn't stay to find out."

Joba began to glow with pride and thought for a second before he began. "Well, we came to the conclusion you had gotten yourself captured or something worse, so we went ahead with our plans. We gave Neco the command of your group and everything went ahead with timetable precision. The weather stayed pretty good after you left, no big storms and the mountain climbing was probably the hardest part of the entire operation. We lost more men on the ropes than we did in the city. We found climbing the city walls unexpectedly easy."

"Yes, mounds of human bodies on all four sides of the walls," I cut in.

"We have burned the piles and marked the locations for our children's education in the future," said Neco.

I gave him a sad smile and Joba continued. "We hit the city all at once and caught everyone asleep. It was a horrible slaughter and the streets ran with blood. All was a total success except for the legion that we missed because it was out on patrol."

"Do you know where the legion is now?" I asked.

"No idea. We think they held up last winter in the wilderness somewhere or went back to the ruins of Petrapolis," answered Joba.

"They spent the winter in the valley below, right next to the waterfall."

"You're kidding?" blurted out Neco. "They didn't find Farella did they?"

"If they did, I wouldn't be here now. But I'm sure they saw the cirque, but didn't see a way up."

"By the way Zeb, where were you all those weeks after you left Stone Fortress?" asked Joba.

"I was right where you found me. Vertunda was with me and he had me read all the scrolls in the room. I didn't sleep day or night, and when I had any questions, Vertunda answered them for me. Did you close the room up like I asked, and is the city in order?"

"Of course. We are all obedient servants to the King of Ontelles," jested Joba. "And tomorrow we will leave and you can be united with Desiree and start acting like a king."

"That sounds fine, very fine," I said feeling and enjoying the smoothness of the cream juice.

I lay back on my saddle that I used as a rest, and Joba pulled out a black pouch and began to pack a pipe with the contents of the bag. Neco left and went inside the house, and I just stayed where I was and watched Joba's huge hands pack his pipe. He then put a sulfur stick to the pipe and began to puff causing a blue flame to form over the pipe leaves. Joba began to take deep drags of the smoke and didn't exhale until he held it as long as he could. I thought this strange even though I never enjoyed smoking. Then when I smelled the foul aroma of the smoke, my mind promptly flashed back to the Warrior Council Chamber, when Joba and I first visited Petrapolis. "What is that you are smoking?" I finally asked.

"Good stuff. Your brother introduced me to it. You probably remember the smell from the council chamber when we were in Petrapolis. Do you want to try it?" I shook my head, no, and thought no more of it. I left Joba and his pipe smoke and went to find sleep.

Chapter Eighteen

That night as I slept I had a dream that troubled me deeply and caused great grief. In the dream I saw Vertunda and he stood at the tunnel entrance of Farella. In his hand was the Flaming Sword and he told me not to leave Farella. He said I was to stay, as Neco and Joba were to return to Rift. I became angry and told him I wanted Desiree. He said she would join me when the time was right, but it was important that I stay. I awoke in a cold sweat and laid awake for about an hour before I finally got up. I found Joba asleep next to Neco so I went into the other room and lit the fish lamp on the stone table. Mixing some writing ink and with the feather pen of a tish bird, I began to write a song to Desiree on a piece of vellum. After the song was completed, I broke down just as I had the day my mind tore in Petrapolis, and I wept.

Song of Zebulum to His Lost Love

> The beauty of your smile - The shine of your eyes - The wisdom of your mind - The strength of your faith. These are the ingredients of your appeal. And to further this attractiveness is a fire deep inside that cries for truth to fuel you to peace.

The death of a touch, no matter how intimate, is only a memorial to the future rest that will come.

To enter into a heart isn't an easy task and once it is taken there is the tragedy that it can be spoiled by abandoned plunder because of the drunkenness of success. To guard against this evilness is the gamble of life; and there are many woes and troubles for those who suffer from the results of this great error.

The hot consuming mixture of ores becomes stronger than the original metal. When the waters of life cool the fire, it will hold and only a new consuming heat can break that bond.

A friend who is closer than a brother is a prize indeed, and through the toils of life, the bond will not break no matter what adversities. Time is no enemy if the bond is love, a love that is grounded with compassion and selflessness.

Now for the pain of truth and its agonizing victories. To seek God is to die to self, and follow a path that is foreign to this world. Many temporal pleasures must be abandoned for peace of conscience, which sustains us to continue when all seems dead and futile. Seek this purity and only then may you begin to walk in the truth no matter what color this life seems to tint it. For that innocent knowledge was first placed there by Him, who knew you before the beginning of time.

What the future holds is in His hands and to live the present, and its circumstances is the duty you now have. Live it according to His law that is written on your heart. Fear not the past, the present, nor the future. Painful is your life, yet only the overpowering love of God can sustain you. Allow this knowledge and living water to flow from you; then to your loved ones, and then to the world. Open these gates and healing will begin.

Forgive the thoughtlessness and wickedness around you and forget not those who love you and wait for your return when all will be prepared. Remember you are always being lifted up in prayer.

"I'm not going; you and Neco will have to go without me."

"You are crazy. Neco is saddling your beast, and you said you were going last night."

"I'm sorry, but there has been a change in plans."

"What's going on in here?" asked Neco peering in through the front door. I saw the three beasts through the open door saddled and ready to travel.

Joba pounded his fist on the stone table. "What's wrong Zeb? I don't know who you are any more!" screamed Joba. I said nothing but instead walked outside and opened the side pouch on my saddle and pulled the scroll out with the red ribbon tied around it.

"Neco, please take Peton back to his stall and unsaddle him."

I walked back into the dimly lit room of the house and placed the FARELLA scroll in front of Joba. "Read it. It is the last of the holy scrolls." With a disdainful look on Joba's face he slowly untied the ribbon and unrolled the parchment. "And as you read it, remember that it was written in the Ancient Days, when the Plain of Blood was called the

Wilderness of Death."

A sober look came over his features as he read the scroll. When he finished he looked through it once more then he quietly asked me one question. "All right, this is very impressive; but tell me, are you staying in order to fight Castor?"

"I don't know why I am to stay. I was just instructed to do so by a dream I had last night."

"I see, you had a dream. Well it says here in the scroll that you are going to instruct the people in truth from the courtyard of the temple and from the context of this, I take it this will happen before the big battle."

"And it also says I will instruct from the valley of Farella if I'm not mistaken, and if anyone wants to talk to me, this is where I will be until God tells me otherwise."

"You're impossible. Don't you realize Rift needs you? The people have no guidance or direction. In the stone fortress it was different, we had an objective: a goal to obtain. But now that Rift has been taken everyone just sits idly by, waiting for who knows what."

I walked over to a shelf and took the vellum I had written on in the night. It was rolled and sealed in wax. I handed it to Joba and said, "This is a private letter to Desiree. After she reads it I want it to become the common property of the people of Rift. The first instructions from the king are to have it read once every hour, day and night in the courtyard of the temple. Tell the people to memorize the words and then to do what it says. I want them to seek God and His purity. Tell them this, and tell the people this is what I would say if I were there."

"I'm sorry Zeb, but this is all very hard for me to understand. I'll do what you say. Is there anything else you want me to do?"

"Send out scouts to find that missing legion and as soon as it is located send a messenger to me. Always be prepared for a surprise attack from them, especially at night. And remember to let Desiree read the scroll first."

"I will my king. Watch yourself."

Neco called from outside that he was holding the beasts and all was ready. Joba and I embraced and kissed each other on the cheeks. Outside I embraced Neco and told him to watch Desiree and Tobe for me and to send them my love. I stood at the house as the two riders left and then I ran and watched from the top of the fall as they disappeared down the green valley.

That summer passed very slowly, and no one came to visit me from Rift. I was hoping Desiree would come, but as each day passed, so did my hopes. I spent most of my time hunting and preparing for a long winter. There were repairs on the roof and walls of Stone House to be made, harvesting of mountain grass and the collecting of wood below the timberline. I also spent time picking berries and digging for bluebon roots. When I wasn't making pottery, I fished in the lake, or made vellum to write on. At night I squeezed fish on a press I had constructed and collected the oil for the long winter nights. By the time summer was over and fall began I had enough provisions for a small army.

A few weeks into fall I became ill and was running a high fever. For two weeks I wasn't able to get up out of bed. Peton was neglected, but I knew he wouldn't hold it against me. I had a hard time feeding myself and at times I felt like I wasn't going to survive the sickness. When the first storm of winter hit, the fever broke and my strength began to slowly return.

Within the first month of winter my health was back to normal, except my mind began to slip into a state of deep depression: a depression that was dangerously approaching the same level of subversion I experienced in the pit at Petrapolis. I couldn't understand it either, for I knew that

Desiree was well and alive and that she loved me. But why the low state of mind? I finally came to the belief that it wasn't the absence of Desiree that depressed me, even though I was anticipating a long lonely winter without her. It had to be the FARELLA scroll. The last battle was to be fought at Farella and it was going to be between Castor and myself. Castor swore his life away to my father, if he didn't succeed in destroying me. I had no weapon except one dull sword and a broken rusty one. I was sentenced to stay in this mountainous valley of ancient legend to either die or live. "But the scroll did say I would have a flaming sword, except Leatos has the Sword of Truth and Vertunda has the Sword of Guile," I said to myself as I sat at the stone table drinking berry juice.

"And now I give it back to you."

I looked up and standing at the open door of the stone house stood Vertunda. The low flying clouds behind him enveloped him like giant wings. Light and shadows from the passing clouds blinked behind him. I saw Peton running in the snow by the frozen lake, throwing his head up and down. Vertunda held out his arms and in his hands was the black handled sword in its black sheath.

"It is time; Leatos waits and the evil pelots have all gathered. Now take the sword, it is all we have."

I got up from the stone table and walked towards Vertunda. I took the sword from his hands and as I touched the sheath I noticed a tear drop from Vertunda's right eye and I watched it run down his cheek. I wasn't able to ask him why he wept for he disappeared, leaving me the sword. I stood there in the open door and my eyes beheld a strange looking creature standing on the frozen waters of the lake. It looked like a man but I knew it was a pelot. He had long red hair that blew in the wind, along with a long red and black cape. Then this strange creature began to point at me and snickered a hideous and sickening laugh. Behind him and around the lake thousands upon thousands of ugly looking pelots appeared and they were also laughing in a high-pitched giggling. I stood and watched in awe. Peton sensed their evil presence and turned towards Stone House and galloped towards me.

"Worship me and you will not die," said the creature standing on the lake. "I have the Sword of Truth. Worship me and I will make you a god."

"Peton, do you see him? It is Leatos, the Dark Prince," I said as he now stood next to me at the door. The huge girth of ugly pelots vanished and only Leatos remained in sight.

"I serve only the Holy One, the God of Vertunda. The holy scrolls say no one is to worship anyone except the Creator. And you are not the Creator, but only one of His many creatures."

"Serve yourself and perish into dust," and he vanished. The clouds flew by as if nothing had happened. I exchanged the evil sword with the dull sword under my white elb robe.

"Wait here Peton," I ordered and went and got Peton's saddle. My faithful beast stood silent while I saddled him. I put my hand on the broken sword that was still tied to the pouch that held the FARELLA scroll.

"Zeb! Zeb, it's me, Desiree!"

I looked up over Peton's back and standing by the tunnel at the end of the lake where the ugly pelots had been only moments ago, was Desiree on top of a white beast. I waved and she kicked her beast into a run. I mounted Peton and raced towards her. Her long hair was flying in the wind and I could see her beautiful smile and the shine of her eyes, as we drew towards each other. All the fears and evil feelings that had come upon me when I saw Leatos vanished as Desiree jumped from her beast into my arms. We kissed and kissed on top of Peton as he hissed happily and threw his head up and down.

"You came; you finally came."

"Yes, but I'm not alone," and she pointed towards the tunnel. Neco and Eviea, came out holding Theo and Tobe. Behind them were Joba and Lydia leading several pack beasts. Then came an elderly man at the rear whom I didn't recognize, but as the group drew closer I recognized the man to be old Topaz, the high priest of Rift.

"Topaz, I though you were dead!" I cried out and the echo of his name mixed with the word, 'dead', as my voice bounced around the mountain peaks.

"I'm very much alive!" he laughed.

We all embraced and kissed in this great reunion of friends and family.

"What are all the pack beasts for?" I asked Joba.

Joba answered as he slapped me on the back, "We came to take you back to Rift, but if you refuse, we plan to spend the winter with you here at Farella."

"You bunch of crazy idiots. Everyone to the house, this calls for a celebration."

"I don't know Zeb," said Neco. "We think we were followed here."

"By whom?" I asked.

"Maybe soldiers from that missing legion," answered Joba.

"And you led them to Farella. And the ice, did you cut a hole in the icefall?"

"What did you want us to do? This is a dead-end valley. If it were the legionaries we couldn't make it back to Rift," answered Neco.

"All right, all the women and children to the house. Topaz, you go with them," I ordered. "Neco, go to the tunnel and defend it with your life if anyone tries to come up. Joba, come with me." The women and children began making their way to the house along with the string of pack animals.

"Be careful Zeb; I've waited a long time to see you!" cried out Desiree, holding Tobe up in the saddle with her.

"I've waited a long time for you too, my love."

Joba was the first to spot the soldiers, the advance guard of a legion. The guard consisted of twelve men riding beasts apparently following the fresh tracks in the snow.

"The legion is probably not far behind," I observed.

"We have to block or cave-in the tunnel somehow and do it quick."

"How do you propose we do that?"

"I have an idea, but first we have to deal with that advance guard. Go wait with Neco and I'll fetch Topaz to be our lookout."

Joba saluted with a clenched fist against his chest and ran through the snow-covered meadow onto the ice lake. I ran to Stone House and circled around to the animal shelter. I found Topaz trying to remove the loads off the pack beasts.

"Topaz, you were followed here by a dozen men. We believe they are an advance guard of the missing Petrapolis legion."

"What can I do, my king?" he asked very subserviently in his old deep voice. His manner filled me with a strange sorrow because of the other encounters I had had with him, when his unbelief and arrogance had caused such grief. But I knew he was an intelligent and scholarly man, capable of making wise and sound decisions.

"If we can make it through this day, I'm going to need your wise counsel. Men of great learning are rare indeed these days, but this is something we will change someday. What I need of you now is to stand at the edge of the cirque and be our eyes, while Joba, Neco and myself do something about that advance guard."

"Do you want me to leave the animals the way they are and go now?"

"Yes, and if you spot any more soldiers besides the advance guard, wave your arms and yell."

Topaz bowed twice and started running in the almost comical way that old men run. I walked around to the front of Stone House leading Peton and I saw that Neco and Joba were waiting for me at the entrance of the tunnel. When I opened the door to the house the cold air rushed in chilling the women and children. They were waiting for word of what to do. Desiree was trying to hide her nervousness by picking up wood chips, which had been carelessly thrown on the floor next to the fire pit.

"There are a dozen men following your tracks up the valley and they will probably try to come up the tunnel. I sent Topaz to be our lookout and I want you to take the children to the animal shelter and hide them in the stalls. Stay there and be quiet until one of us tells you to come out." Panic and fear began to spread over the women's faces. As I stood there watching this frightening display of terror, I hated being the bearer of such disturbing news.

"They are coming Zeb!" yelled Joba. I left the house and mounted Peton. Turning him toward the tunnel, I looked over my shoulder and winked at Desiree, hoping that this small gesture would somehow ease her fears. She forced a smile and tilted her head to the side like always, reminding me of the day I left her standing alone by the lowben tree on my twentieth birthday.

At the tunnel both Joba and Neco had their swords drawn. "They are coming up the tunnel," pointed Joba.

I looked down the dark shaft and saw that they were about half way up, all of them on foot. "Are you two ready?" I asked, looking both in the face with a false smile. They both nodded zealously. "Peton and I will charge through them, then you two will follow on foot and work together as a team. Don't let any of them get past you or we're all dead."

Both men saluted as I removed my elb robe and tossed it on the snow. I then pulled Peton's head towards the tunnel with my reins and took the broken rusty sword into my hand instead of the long Sword of Guile, which would be too long to use in the cramped quarters of the tunnel. I looked over my shoulder at my general and his aide before I charged, and I thought of how innocent they both looked before this desperate fight for survival. My mind was void of the thought that possibly a myriad of ugly pelots were watching at this very moment. My heels drove deep into Peton's sides and he snorted a vicious sound, showing his razor sharp teeth, which flashed in the sunlight, before he began his onslaught down the tunnel. We met the wall of human flesh about half way up the tunnel and they weren't prepared for a charging beast. Peton plowed into the bunched-up group smashing most of them to the floor and rock walls. Yells and screams of death deafened my ears as Peton and I passed over the fresh carnage. I looked over my shoulder and Neco and Joba had the element of surprise on their side as they chopped and thrusted their swords into the disordered mass of men who were trying to gather themselves. There wasn't any room in the tunnel to turn Peton around, so I decided to continue out the tunnel and challenge anyone who was still in the valley.

I found only two men holding all the warrior's beasts, unaware of what was happening to their comrades in the tunnel. Both dropped the reins of their beasts when they saw me and drew their swords. I charged towards the man who had his sword cleared of its scabbard first and drove Peton into him before he could use it. Peton took the warrior's helmeted head into his large mouth and crushed it in his vise-like jaws. I quickly threw my broken sword like a throwing knife at the other soldier and the jagged end cleared his metal breastplate above his collarbone and sank into the white fleshy part of his neck. Bright red blood gushed out of his mouth and neck in a sickening choking fit of death.

I waited until he stopped moving and salvaged the broken sword. I then pulled Peton off the other ravaged soldier and reined him back towards the tunnel. Smells of blood, urine and other foul odors filled the tunnel as I waited a moment to allow my eyes to adjust to the darkness. Joba and Neco had finished with the ten who had carelessly ventured up the tunnel.

"Join me down here and we will collect these beasts," I called up to my two men.

"What about these bodies?" asked Joba.

"Leave them."

Outside on the blood-covered snow, the dozen beasts were all like a pack of wild animals, ripping and tearing at the flesh of the two fallen soldiers. After we pulled them away, we led them up the tunnel and stripped off their saddles. I told Neco to hold all the beasts by their reins and instructed Joba to bring me one beast at a time to the tunnel entrance.

"What are you going to do Zeb?" asked Joba as he brought me the first beast. I didn't answer but instead took Joba's bloody sword from his hand. Joba's eyes opened wide as he watched with horror as I shoved the sword up to the hilt into the beast, just behind the shoulder. The beast dropped instantly like a rock, and I pulled the sword out as the shaggy creature rolled down the tunnel stopping on the pile of human bodies.

"Get another...we don't have much time. The next dropped like the first, and after all twelve beasts had been killed and rolled down the tunnel, I ordered Joba and Neco to begin plugging up the holes with the saddles and snow.

"This won't stop them Zeb," expressed Joba with his dark features showing his disapproval of this unnecessary slaughter. I turned and left the two men to do what I had ordered. I hated being in the position of authority, but someone had to be the leader and they all recognized me as their king. It was a lonely and cold feeling at times.

"What do you see, Topaz?" I called out from Peton's back, halfway between the lake and Stone House.

"They are coming... the entire legion. We may have only an hour before they get here."

"Keep watching!"

When I entered the animal shelter the women had all the pack beasts unloaded and tied up in the stalls.

"Lydia and Eviea, I want you both to go to the tunnel entrance and help your husbands. Tell them to keep packing the tunnel with snow." I looked towards Desiree and the two toddlers standing around her legs. I recognized my son at once and he looked at me and said, "Ba, Ba." Desiree laughed and then asked what she was to do.

"You might as well take the boys into the house and watch them there." As I looked at my son I said, "He looks like his father, doesn't he?"

"He has his mother's eyes, everyone says."

"Did you get my letter?"

"Yes, and so did everyone else. It is hard sharing a woman's husband with everyone."

"You consider me your husband I take it?"

"You have always been my husband."

I took her into my arms and our mouths didn't part for a long time. When I stepped out of the shed the white puffy clouds were still indifferently drifting above the cragged peaks.

"What's going to happen?" asked Desiree as I mounted Peton.

"We just try and stay alive. I love you." I didn't hear her reply but read her lips as she responded the same to me.

I kneed Peton and when I reached Topaz at the edge of the fall, I could see the black mass of soldiers moving wagons and beasts through the snow.

"That was quite a battle down below," Topaz said as he pointed to the blood-stained snow.

"If there was some way to hide the blood we might be safe. If you see any more advance guards approaching ahead of the legion, be sure to alert us. I'll be at the tunnel."

He bowed again in submission and I trotted Peton across the frozen lake to the two men and two women who were frantically working at plugging the tunnel. I mentioned that Topaz had spotted the legion and we had maybe an hour. Joba had a dark look in his eye and walked out onto the ice to have a private talk with me. I dismounted and followed him. About twenty bodies out onto the ice he turned and pointed his finger at me. "Dead bodies and snow won't stop a legion from coming up this tunnel."

"General, I'll give you my plan. This tunnel used to be the drainage system for this lake, before there was a waterfall. Now if we can make a ditch between the lake and the tunnel, and make it lower than where Topaz is now, then the lake will drain down the tunnel."

"But the lake is frozen...have you forgotten? This isn't summer," he said sarcastically and with bitter anger.

"I have two barrels of fish oil in the house that we can spread on top of the ice and then flame the lake. That should melt the ice and hopefully it will drain into the tunnel."

"All right, say this works, in spite of the fact that I have my doubts. How is that going to stop the warriors?"

"The water will either freeze and make a solid ice plug, or it will flood anyone trying to come up. But if you have a better plan let's hear it," I said very cuttingly.

"Nothing at this point, so let's start digging."

"Good," I said as I went over and began to dig into the frozen ground with my broken sword.

Chapter Nineteen

The two women and the three men dug and dug. All we had were swords as tools and the frozen ground gave up only a handful of soil at each thrust. While the men used swords, the women clawed at the soil with their hands. Lydia's and Eviea's hands were covered with blood.

My mind became deliriously lost in my toil until my eyes saw the beautiful white elb robe crumpled on the snow where I had thrown it earlier. Sweat poured from my brow, my arms were muddy and my mind raced with thoughts of the past and my white elb robe. The fur robe that took years to breed and select the perfect elbs. Then there was the red giant that had taken it and stained it with his drool. Then Topo had tricked me into leaving it with him. After I took it back, the magnificent robe reeked of foul pipe smoke from the warrior council meetings. Since then I had stained it myself with animal blood, grime and dirt from the mountains and wilderness. Yet as I looked at it on the snow, the robe still looked beautiful and majestic: the true robe of a king.

I focused my attention to the sky with its white puffy clouds still floating leisurely without a care. There were patches of light and shadows over the entire scenery of Farella. The suns were together and high above our heads. So much had already transpired since this day began. First, the spirit world had appeared to me, secondly, warriors had been killed and innocent creatures of burden had been slaughtered; slain with my own hands. I hesitated in my thoughts to search for Peton. I saw him hunting for grass under the thin layer of snow. He was unaware of my gaze upon him and my lips curled upward in a grateful smile as I stared at him. I could see his bulging muscles under his long shaggy hair, and those sharp teeth gently nibbling at the blades of grass he had uncovered.

I chopped at the solid ground again and again. When I looked up I saw Desiree walking towards us carrying a large basket and a huge jug. "My love to the rescue," I said to myself. Food and drink were a lovely sight indeed. She wore no hat and her long blond hair flowed gracefully over her shoulders. She smiled when she saw me staring at her. When she reached our shallow trench we all collapsed in exhausted fatigue. She passed out bread and dried meat to each of us and poured berry juice in clay cups.

"Girls, look at those hands! This is horrible. Oh Zeb, why are you forcing Eviea and Lydia to become common slaves?" rebuked Desiree with her charming eyes ablaze with innocent concern.

"I don't think it is going to work," I replied looking at the sweaty and exhausted men. Desiree meanwhile pulled at my sleeve to regain my attention.

"This is outrageous. These women aren't men."

"Listen, I told you to watch the children...now where are they?" I flared up at her in my anger.

"Sleeping! And if you don't appreciate the food I brought you, you can hand it over and I'll take it back to where I found it."

"We won't be able to melt the lake. It's a stupid dream," continued Joba discounting Desiree. "The fish oil won't burn long enough and even if it did it would only melt the top of the ice which would only leave a thin layer of water."

"He's right Zeb," said Neco. "If that is what you're planning, it won't work."

I began to understand that maybe Joba was right. I didn't reply, but just sat there and watched Desiree walk away towards the lake. She had taken a piece of cloth and dipped it into the edge of the lake where there was some water.

"The lake isn't frozen solid!" I yelled. "Look where Dez is! There is still an entire lake under the ice. We only have to dig the ditch deeper below the ice and it will drain.

"Yes, you're right," complimented Joba.

Desiree wasn't enlightened with our discovery and was obviously hurt by my harsh retort. I turned my palms up to her as she walked back from the lake and gave her a little boy smile that always melted her anger.

"Well King Zeb, what about these girls' hands?" She asked coyly after she cleaned Eviea's and Lydia's hands with the wet cloth.

"Yes, you better take them to the house," I said and Desiree lifted Lydia and Eviea to their feet. "And Dez, see Topaz and ask him how much longer we have."

"Yes, my master," she said with a cute smile, but then changed to a mean stare to let me know she was still angry.

"All right men, let's get back to work."

Time began to melt away as we dug and dug. When Desiree returned with news from Topaz, the sky had turned angry black and the huge boiling clouds were massing together as they turned over and over.

"Topaz says the soldiers are below the fall. He said they have found the tunnel."

"God in heaven we are too late!" bawled Joba.

"No, the water is beginning to run," I said as I pointed to the ditch. A small trickle was rushing its way down the trench towards the tunnel.

"Hurry, let's make it deeper and it will run faster," yelled Neco.

"Dez, tell Eviea to hide the children in the stalls, then you and Lydia come back here."

She turned and began to run. I joined my comrades and we dug harder and deeper. The ground was softening as we got beyond the frost line and the water began to flow towards us. All three of us were covered in mud when the two women returned.

"Zeb! Zeb! Look!" screamed Desiree as she pointed behind me. I looked over my shoulder and there stood a Petrapolis warrior.

"They made it through!" yelled Joba as he ran to challenge the invader. Neco was running behind him. I heard the clash of steel against steel as I ran to the lake to see why the water wasn't flowing any faster than it was. The black angry clouds were now passing at our heads and it would only be minutes before we would all be covered in dense fog. Desire was at my side when I reached the lake. The ice had broken and a huge piece was damming the water. I turned to Desiree and handed her the broken sword. "Start chopping the ice. I'm going to get a barrel of fish oil." She took the sword and began to chop with a lack of coordination. I whistled for Peton and he came running. I rode him to the house. Inside I grabbed a handful of sulfur sticks and put them in a waist pouch that hung from my belt. My elb boots were black with mud and I noticed that I had tracked up Stone House, which had been carefully cleaned by Desiree and the women. There was a clean smell of soap everywhere, and a warm feeling filled my heart as I thought of the little joys women give without realizing it. Standing in the spotless room I almost forgot why I was there. "Oh yes, the fish oil," I said remembering.

The barrel was huge and almost too heavy to roll. It had taken me a week to build each wooden barrel and the rope bands that held them together. Once outside I tied a rope around the middle of the barrel and the other end to Peton's saddle. He then slowly dragged the flammable fluid over the snow while I led him towards the tunnel. To my right I could barely see Topaz covered in moving clouds at the top of the icefall. He waved to me to come look at something, but I was too busy to stop what I was doing. At the tunnel, Neco and Joba were still fighting those that had broken through the wall of snow and flesh. Eviea and Desiree were eagerly waiting for me at the edge of the lake. Desiree had failed to break up the ice with my sword and was looking sadly at me with the rusty sword dangling from her hands. Her elb robe had been discarded on the snow and her slim and supple figure enticed a deep passion within me for her, even at this time of grave danger.

"Don't you think your mind should be somewhere else?" she said, almost comically noticing my gaze.

"Help me with this oil," I barked, shifting back into my king role but with a smile.

Lydia and Desiree helped me drag the barrel to the ice and I smashed it open with the Sword of Guile, which didn't flame when I unsheathed it for the first time since Vertunda had given it to me. Black, stinking oil spilled everywhere on the ice. I told the women to get back and I sloshed it around with my muddy feet. When the ice was covered in oil I struck a sulfur stick on my sword and tossed it towards the oil. With a WHOOP the oil ignited in a blazing red and yellow flash. I had seen this sight only once before. It was when I was a small boy in my village and a spark flew from the furnace at the village foundry and landed on some spilled oil from a fish lamp. Veatus, the son of the founder, had purposely knocked it over. Veatus was the nugget I had encountered in the mountains and whom I killed after he chased me down with the beast I hadn't been able to hamstring. He always detested me because of Desiree, and when I was in his father's shop that day of the explosion, he had intentionally tried to throw the oil on me. When the spark hit the oil on the floor it made a loud boom and almost burned down our entire village. I never told anyone what really happened even though Veatus was younger and not someone I feared. Veatus was grateful for my silence even though he still disliked me even to his death.

"Is it going to work?" called out Desiree as the blazing flames leaped up into the smothering fog, crating an eerie sight. It was now late afternoon but the dense clouds turned the sun's light into a gray darkness.

"We will have to wait until the oil has finished burning to see if we can break up the ice."

"Zeb, I don't think they can hold much longer," said Lydia pointing to the tunnel. I left the burning lake and ran next to the ditch that was about a body wide and a body deep. At the mouth of the tunnel I saw bodies lying everywhere. The ground was muddy from blood and lake water. The tunnel was sheathed in darkness and every few seconds a warrior came running out of the shadows towards Joba and Neco. Neco was holding his side and I noticed his hand drenched in blood.

Joba saw me and pointed to Neco's side, then prepared for the next warrior to exit out of the black throat of the passageway. I helped Neco reach Lydia who began to apply pressure to the wound with a cloth.

"Zeb, look the ice is breaking up!" shouted Desiree. I looked towards the fog-covered lake that was aglow by the fire.

"Joba! Get away from the tunnel!" I turned and yelled as the ice dam gave way. Joba barely jumped away in time to save himself from a huge wall of icy water that came rushing through the wide trench and into the mouth of the tunnel. There were shouts of drowning men who had been lurking in the darkened shadows of the inclined passageway. Huge chunks of burning ice sailed on top of the moving water and disappeared down the dark throat.

"Zeb! Come quickly...they are climbing the ice!" cried a deep voice. I turned and saw Topaz ringing wet from the clouds. "A hundred are climbing up the frozen waterfall. I came to warn you!"

I turned back and yelled to my general. "Joba, there isn't going to be anyone coming through the tunnel for a while...I'll need your help!"

"Where do you need me?" he asked.

"Run to the fall and keep anyone from reaching Farella and I'll meet you there shortly." I turned to Desiree who was helping Eviea bandage Neco's wound. "Dez, I smelled soap in the house, is there any soap left over?"

"Well yes, Eviea and I made Joba and Neco pack one entire beast with soap. I surely wasn't going to spend an entire winter in that filthy house."

I whistled for Peton and he came running out of the gray fog. I pulled Desiree up in the saddle behind me and we passed Joba and Topaz on our way to Stone House. After she dismounted I asked Desiree where the soap was and she said it was in the animal shelter. I told her to load the glutinous substance on a beast and bring it to the waterfall. I went into the house and rolled the last barrel of fish oil out onto the snow. By the time I had the barrel tied behind Peton, Desiree was leading a beast around the house loaded down with about a dozen soap jugs slung over a beast pack-rack.

"Let's get this stuff to the fall before any warriors get to the top," I said.

When we arrived at the U-shaped edge of Farella I saw that we were too late. Half a dozen warriors had already made it to the top and were fighting with Joba and Topaz. Several were dead on the ground, killed by Joba, but he was now surrounded and in grave danger. Topaz likewise was trying to fight two of the warriors. He held my broken sword, which he must have recovered from where Desiree had left it. One of the men circled around Topaz and before I could call out to warn him, the soldier placed his sword into the lower part of his back. I saw Topaz drop my sword in pain and the warrior in front impaled him in the stomach. I quickly cut the barrel loose from Peton and ordered my loyal beast to attack the two men who stabbed Topaz. Peton showed his long white teeth and lunged forward. Meanwhile I went to Joba's aid. The four men fighting with Joba had almost overwhelmed him. I noticed blood flowing down his leg and left arm. I slew the first warrior in the back before he knew I was behind him. The second man lost his head after I ducked from his sword, then swung mine when he tried to recover his balance.

"That a way, Zeb!" cried out Joba in berserk excitement. He then lunged forward and mortally cut one of the two remaining men but was stabbed in the side by the other when he was recovering his sword out of the dying warrior. I cut Joba's assailant down his middle with the flameless Sword of Guile, almost splitting him in half.

"More come!" gasped Joba as he fell to the slushy snow that was now spotted pinkish red with blood.

I looked towards the icy fall and two more men were pulling themselves up with ice picks. I ran to stop their ascent and saw Peton out of the corner of my eye, tearing the limbs off the two mutilated warriors he had attacked. He was throwing his head from side to side with such force it gave me a headache to watch. Desiree reached the edge of the cliff before I did and smashed the soap jug over one of the un-helmeted invaders. He gave out a scream as his soap covered head disappeared over the edge of Farella. The other man was quickly eliminated over the edge with a split head from my sword.

"Let's get the oil up here," I ordered Desiree. She had fear on her face as she looked at me. I tried to smile but it did no good. I ran to the oil barrel and began to roll it to the icefall. Desiree was at my side helping. Another warrior was breaching the top. I left the barrel and put the top of my boot into his face. He let out a scream and I momentarily watched him fall down to the thousands of soldiers below.

"What now?" asked Desiree.

"Get the soap." She turned and ran through the moving fog and disappeared. Meanwhile I broke open the lid of the barrel and dumped about half the oil down the frozen waterfall. There were screams and curses from the soldiers who were climbing the ice as the stinking oil splashed on them.

"What now?" she asked again standing behind me, drenched by the clouds. I pointed to the soap jugs and told her to start dumping the sticky liquid down the ice. She grabbed two jugs while I kicked an ice pick, which caused its owner to drop to the valley below.

Desiree and I emptied four jugs of soap, covering the giant icicle. I ordered her to step back as I struck a sulfur stick and tossed it on the oily ice. The flame blew out before it touched the ice. I lit a second stick and as I cupped the flame with my hands I bent down and laid it on the oil. It ignited and the flame threw me back with a whoosh sound and the explosion continued down the ice like liquid fire. Screams of death reassured me that my plan had worked. I turned to hug Desiree, but she wasn't behind me.

"Dez! Where are you? Are you all right?" I called into the dense fog with my hands to my mouth.

"I'm over here with Topaz!" she answered. I ran to the spot where Peton was still feasting on the unrecognizable warriors and Desiree was kneeling over the old man cradling his head in her hands. I could see that he was almost finished.

"Dez, find Joba and see if you can help him."

"Yes," she said with a sad look on her face. She waited for me to take Topaz's head from her hands before she left.

"How bad is it?" asked Topaz in a voice that was now very frail.

"You're bleeding pretty bad. To be truthful, I'd say this is it."

"It can't be. I had a dream while Rift was in control of

my brother and the warriors. In the dream the Holy One told me I wouldn't die until I read the scroll of FARELLA once more. After Joba and his men recaptured Rift I went to the temple to look at the scrolls. Joba told me no one was to enter the temple or the scroll room, according to your orders. Two nights passed and I decided to enter the temple by a secret passage. Once inside the hidden scroll room I found the FARELLA scroll missing. I took this as a good sign, and I believe the Holy One gave me the dream," and Topaz began to cough horribly, spitting up blood.

"You rest easy old man. I'll be right back," and I gently laid his head on the snow. I walked over to Peton who was still eating and opened the side pouch. My hand felt the scroll and I pulled it out. When I returned to Topaz, Desiree and Joba were there. Desiree eyed me with a funny look on her face since I had left Topaz alone. I asked her how Joba was and Joba himself answered, "I'm going to live." He had the shirt of a dead warrior tied around his wound.

"What's wrong Dez?" I finally asked.

"Why did you leave Topaz alone?"

"Here, read this to him before all light is gone," I said in a kind voice as I handed her the scroll and then placed the leather saddle pouch under his head as a pillow.

Topaz's eyes opened wide and tears began to flow when he saw the scroll. I felt horrible until I saw the smile on his face as Desiree unrolled the scroll and read the title, "FARELLA".

"Joba, I want you to listen to this," and I left the three and went and found the beast with the soap jugs. I led him to the burning waterfall of ice and began to unload the seven remaining jugs. Then I poured the rest of the fish oil into each jug letting the contents mix. After I had completed this chore I heard a snort behind me. I turned and there stood my white shaggy beast with his snout covered in blood.

"You crazy beast. Come and help me break the ice like

you did last spring." Peton lifted his huge head up and down. Then he trotted to the icefall and began to rear up dropping his powerful hooves onto the ice. Large chips began to fly and I helped with the aid of the black handled sword. It wasn't long before the giant burning icicle broke loose and fell, crashing down on hundreds and possibly thousands of the soldiers gathered below. I could barely see through the clouds as I crouched down and watched the flaming ice break and scatter over the valley, setting many of the trees on fire.

"The ice is damming up the lake," came a voice out of the clouds. I took my eyes off the valley below and Neco and Lydia came walking towards me. Neco's side was covered in blood and Lydia was holding my white elb robe.

"Here Zeb, you left this at the tunnel," she said. I didn't say a word but just remained in my crouched position. Lydia walked over and draped the kingly robe over my wet shoulders. Her long blond hair was hanging limp and wet from the moisture-laden clouds.

"Your father is over there Lydia, and I'm afraid he is in pretty bad shape."

"Oh God. Why...it can't be. He told me he wasn't going to die until he read the FARELLA scroll one more time."

"Well, the FARELLA scroll is being read to him right now by Dez."

Lydia left my side and ran into the clouds calling out for her father. I looked up at Neco and he had a very serious expression.

"You've turned out to be quite a warrior, Neco. To be honest with you I had my doubts when you brought me that old gray elb robe at the Gate of Virgins." Neco grinned with embarrassment and the serious expression left as he dropped his head like a little boy just praised by his father. "Now tell me...how long before the passageway will be opened to the warriors?"

"Well, the water flushed all the beasts and snow down the tunnel and it's still running fairly well, but I'd say it will be clear by morning. We could dig the trench deeper and try to burn the ice again."

"You see all those soap jugs over there? They are all filled with fish oil and soap. I'll help you load them on the pack beast and I want you to take them back to the tunnel." I handed him the pouch of sulfur sticks, keeping one stick in my hand. With the one sulfur stick I walked over to the jugs and separated one. I lit the stick on the side of the clay jug and dropped it inside. The oil mixed with the soap kept the oil from exploding but the viscous substance lit like a large fish lamp wick. I then tossed the jug over the edge of Farella and we both watched the jug tumble in the air, hit and explode sending burning soap everywhere. Men below began running with flames leaping off their clothes and elb robes.

"Now I know why you are the king," complimented Neco.

"You had your doubts I see," I said jokingly. "Now let's load up these six remaining jugs and check your father-in-law.

Chapter Twenty

An hour before sunset a knife-edge wind began to blow the heavy snow-laden clouds over the frozen surface of Farella. The temperature began to drop dramatically and all the sweat on Neco's face turned to hoarfrost. When Neco and I found the group huddled around Topaz I could see that he was moments from death. Desiree was just finishing the reading of FARELLA as I knelt beside the dying priest of Rift.

"A prophet from Farella will come to Rift and prophesy before the true kingdom begins and ends. My servant of truth will also come from Farella to lead my people into the brightness of truth." Desiree rolled the scroll back up and her tear filled eyes looked up to me. I lowered my eyes in order not to betray my feelings about the scroll. I had only read it once and at that time it devastated me. Hearing the end of the scroll again was sending ripples of fear and panic through my inner being. I eyed Topaz who was watching me and he looked as if he were reading my mind.

"You, my son, are the prophet of Farella," said Topaz in his natural deep voice. "You are also the true king of Ontelles, but because of my unbelief I lost my daughter. You who came from the land of Lepis and out of the Order of Petrapolis, you shall today vanquish the evil one. Today is the last battle between Leatos and Vertunda. And you my king, shall battle the champion of darkness, the mighty warrior with the missing hand." Topaz closed his eyes after he spoke and gave up his spirit. Lydia fell over his warm body and began to weep. I reached over and touched Desiree's hand. She still had tears in her eyes, both awed and frightened by the unnatural and prophetic words that passed over Topaz's lips.

"Castor has a missing hand, it is Castor you are to battle?" she asked almost in a whisper.

"Yes, unfaithful wife, he is to fight me!" came a voice out of the howling wind. Everyone turned towards the voice not sure if we heard it or not, and there stood two men wearing black elb robes. I recognized the one who had spoken as Castor and the other was the false king, Topo. Behind them the yellowish glow from the burning lake silhouetted their dark and awesome figures.

"How did you two get up here?" barked Joba who lifted his sword off the snow and pointed it towards Topo.

"My lord, the Dark Prince showed us a secret way up," answered Topo. "I told you Zeb, that in exchange for your sword, the Dark Prince gave me special powers. For instance, I knew you were coming that night."

"Alright, what do you want?" I called out as I stood next to Desiree.

"The sword you carry. We have come for the Sword of Guile. As soon as we pull it from your dead hands my Lord Leatos wins."

"It isn't going to be that easy," I said very calmly and under control. I opened my white robe and pulled the black, cold steel from its black sheath. "As much as I hate this sword I'm not turning it over to you."

"Have it your own way, foolish one," and Topo opened his black robe and handed Castor the sword I recognized at once: the Sword of Truth. I saw the beautifully jeweled handle and golden scabbard. "He stole your wife, Castor, and now he defies the lord of Ontelles. Kill him and take his sword. You swore it to your father."

Castor dropped his black robe to the snow and unsheathed the beautiful sword as Topo held the golden scabbard. The blade didn't flame and small flakes of snow began to fall and melt on the cold steel blade. I likewise removed my white robe and handed it to Desiree who stood up and kissed my cold cheek.

"I love you Zeb. I always did and always will," she said as the tears in her eyes began to flood down her red cheeks. I was embarrassed in the company of everyone to return my affections to the one woman I loved.

"Watch my robe and raise our son in truth," was all I said.

"To the death!" yelled Topo, as he stepped back to give his champion room. I stepped towards him leaving Topaz's cold and lifeless body behind me.

"Now I will do to you what I should have done years ago in the council chamber at Petrapolis," breathed Castor in thick clouds of breath. The snow began to fall faster and heavier when Castor made his first lunge. Sparks and flames flew as I blocked his attack. He swung again and again, I was barely able to out-maneuver him. Flames leaped off our blades at each contact. He was very good with a sword even though he only had one hand. I began to feel my fatigue and lack of food. The digging of the ditch and all the fighting had taken its toll on my energy and strength. I found myself panting like a wind-blown beast as I tried to protect myself from Castor's attacks. Screams and yells were coming from my friends but the thick clouds of snow made it almost impossible to see them.

"Use what we taught ourselves in the Vth Legion!" called out Joba. "Come on you can do it. Try the drop kick! The drop kick!"

The panic that was holding me left as I listened to Joba. I blocked the next blow then dropped my sword, kicking the hilt with my right boot, inches before it hit the ground, sending the butt of the handle into Castor's face. He gave out a scream of pain and bright red blood began to flow from over his left eye. He stepped back and tripped falling backwards, dropping the Sword of Truth. I quickly grabbed the Sword of Truth from the snow and as soon as my hands touched the handle, the blade turned to flames. Realizing his danger, Castor snatched up the Sword of Guile and its blade, to my surprise, also lit up with flames.

"Creator in the highest, what is going on here?" came the voice of Neco.

"This is just like the scroll said!" yelled Joba.

"Be careful Castor!" screamed Topo. "The Sword of Truth is stronger than the Sword of Guile."

His words gave me the needed mental edge. I stalked around Castor now putting him on the defensive.

"You son of an ash lizard, I swear I'm going to kill you," breathed Castor. He prepared for his final attack as he wiped blood from his brow with his handless arm.

"Watch his shoulder and sword!" yelled Joba. "Fear not, you have the Sword of Truth." I waved my sword at Castor forcing him back. The weather conditions became severe and it was almost impossible to see each other except for the light emitting from the two swords.

"What is that?" I said under my breath as I noticed two men standing behind Castor. One was wearing a very thin green tunic and the other an old gray elb robe. "Elan, is that you?" I asked as I unwarily lowered my guard. The two disappeared in the clouds and Castor capitalized on my broken concentration. He thrust forward with his sword, aiming for my chest. I quickly gathered myself in time to step aside and swung my sword across his, hoping to block his thrust. I felt a burning sensation along my right side next to my ribs. I let out a groan of pain as Castor continued his charge and lowered his shoulder into my chest. I was knocked off my feet and landed on my back. With my sword still in my hand, Castor stepped back to gather himself. In his hand I noticed his sword was only half as long as before. I wondered at this until I saw the other half of his blade laying flameless in the snow. The Sword of Truth had severed it and the black steel stood out against the white snow. Now I understood what happened. My sword cut his instead of blocking it away. That's why Castor was able to cut me in his charge. I looked at my right side and I counted three charred ribs and cauterized skin still steaming.

"I have you now!" yelled Castor while he wiped away more blood.

"Zeb, are you all right?" called out Desiree somewhere behind me.

I didn't have time to answer as Castor was attacking again while I was still on the ground. I tried to stand but the pain was horrible and then I felt a thump on the back of my head. Topo was holding the golden sheath with both of his hands. I wasn't able to stop Castor's attack, but I rolled away. When I finally got to my feet I felt my face and realized Castor had cut me with a long burning slash under my right eye. Blood was oozing from the back of my head where Topo had hit me, and my other wounds were agonizing. My mind began to blank and blackness was beginning to cloud my eyes. Castor saw me sway and charged again with his shortened flaming sword and all I remember was lifting my sword with both hands and pointing the tip towards his stomach. He ran into it impaling himself as flames and steam hissed from his burning bowels. Castor let out an animal scream and dropped his sword and backed away as I collapsed to the ground, leaving my sword in Castor's abdomen. As soon as I released the jeweled hilt the flames ceased and Castor disappeared into the darkness. I heard a scream that was very distant and it echoed across the valley. Blackness took me into her arms as I collapsed onto the snow-covered ground of Farella.

When I opened my eyes, I found myself lying in Stone House. Joba and Neco were asleep next to me. I tried to sit up but the pain in my head and side were too overpowering.

"Zeb, lie still," said Eviea as she stood at the doorway. "Desiree, your husband is awake," and I watched as my beautiful wife entered the sleeping room. She wore white pants and a shirt made from the skins of a white bull delf. Her hair was long and clean and the smile on her face gleamed like the suns of Ontelles.

"The others are still asleep," whispered Eviea to Desiree as they both stood at the doorway. I also saw Lydia standing behind the two women and I heard the playing noises of the two toddlers in the other room.

"Who is watching the tunnel?" I asked very weakly.

"The tunnel caved in," answered Eviea very softly. In the night the warriors tried to rush the tunnel again and Neco dropped two jug bombs down the passageway. The explosion caved the tunnel in. No one can get to us now. Besides the snow hasn't stopped and it has been two days since it started."

"I'm hungry and I have to relieve myself, so please help me up." I said as quietly as possible. All three of the ladies pulled me up to my feet and helped me into the other room. Desiree put on my elb boots for me while Lydia placed my elb robe on over the white bandages that encircled my chest. I felt my head and face, finding more bandages.

"What would you like to eat?" asked Eviea standing next to the pit fire.

"Three elb steaks and a dozen tish eggs." I said smiling. "But first I have to go outside." Desiree kissed my mouth and forehead before I left the warmness of our stone abode. The snow was still falling just like Eviea had said and I trudged through the knee deep powdery stuff until I circled around to the animal shelter. Next to the shed I relieved myself in a small stone void house built after finishing Stone House. I then went into the stable and found it pleasantly warm from the beasts' body temperatures.

"Well Peton, no one has cleaned the blood from your snout and now it has discolored you. Maybe it makes you look like a warrior's beast." Peton gave a snort and threw his head back. I rubbed his neck until my eyes saw the shed door open and in stepped a visitor: it was Vertunda.

"Vertunda, it is good to see you," I said as I would to a good friend I hadn't seen in years. "How did the spiritual battle go?"

"You were victorious over the champion of darkness, but Leatos now possesses both swords."

"What? How could that be?"

"After you put the Sword of Truth into Castor, he fell over the edge of Farella. Topo recovered the broken Sword of Guile and escaped to pull the Sword of Truth from Castor. He is now marching towards Rift with the remaining troops to present himself as the king by right of the Flaming Sword."

"I don't understand?"

"Yes you do," said Vertunda very sternly. "Topaz prophesied before he died. You are the prophet that is from Farella who will go to Rift and prophesy before the true kingdom begins and ends."

I gave out a loud groan and hit my forehead on a wooden beam that I was standing next to. Blood began to drip from the wound under my right eye that was reopened with my gesture. "I really don't understand!" I cried out. "The pain hurts from the battle." I then turned thinking he was going to heal my wounds like before.

"No, not this time. The battle was lost. The Holy One has ordered all the good pelots back to His throne. We will not return unless the people of Rift repent and that is up to you."

"I don't believe this. How did you lose against Leatos?"

"He has the swords, but he hasn't destroyed the scrolls. Remember that, and if the people repent they will need the wisdom and truth from the scrolls to guide and prepare them for the servant of truth who will also come from Farella."

"Who is the servant of truth?" I begged to know before he left.

"The child born under the star," and Vertunda began to melt away. "Be brave and courageous, and although the pelots are gone you shall receive the Spirit of the Holy One," and as he was vanishing he pointed at me and smiled. The door of the shed blew open and a wind from outside blasted. I hugged the wooden beam until the wind ceased, awed by my visit and Vertunda's words.

"Zeb, are you all right?" I was looking at the door and then Desiree appeared. Her hair was cascading over her shoulders, and her head was cocked to the side. "We wondered where you were. Are you all right?" she asked as she walked towards me and took my hands into hers. She closed her eyes and with her head back she stood on her tiptoes and gently kissed my wounded cheek.

"I am all right," I said in a whisper after her kiss. "I was just talking to Vertunda."

"Vertunda, who is that?" she said with a quizzical look on her face. "The Vertunda in the scroll? Is he the one who made the foot prints in the snow outside the door?"

"Foot prints?" and I went to the door and there were huge prints in the snow. I turned to Desiree. "That's right, I never told you about Vertunda, have I?" She shook her head with a smile and I began to tell her the amazing story beginning with my first encounter with him in the forest after the red giant had broken my sword. We sat in the stable and I told her all the events of my life from the day I left as a nugget up till the present. Eviea came in with a tray as I was talking and left Desiree and myself alone with the elb steaks and eggs. We ate, talked and laughed.

Chapter Twenty-one

The winter of my twenty-sixth year was one of my most joyful and memorable. Stone House was stocked with plenty of food and wood. The house was filled with close friends and the pleasure the two boys gave us all was a joy beyond words. We all watched as they tried to master walking and talking. There were many laughs, which made a perfect environment to heal from battle wounds. The three women got along perfectly with each other and kept Stone House immaculately clean. There were a few complaints about the soap being used up or ruined, but it was all in jest. When things got boring, which they did at times, I would visit Peton and rub him down. Desiree began following me to the animal shelter on these visits and we discovered that the stalls provided a private place to be alone. Desiree and I grew very close, as she wanted to know all about the scrolls I had read when I was with Vertunda in the temple. She grew in wisdom, even beyond Lydia and Eviea who both had been instructed at Rift when they were girls. To Eviea and Lydia, the scrolls were common stories they had been brought up with. They took the privilege of knowing these truths for granted, whereas Desiree, who like myself was raised in an environment totally separated from the truth. The same was true concerning Neco and Joba. Joba, not being raised with knowledge of the scrolls, loved to hear me speak about them. Neco did not appear to show much interest.

When spring finally arrived, all the men were healed and Neco and Joba were ready to leave for Rift. I hadn't mentioned my visit from Vertunda in the animal shelter to any of the others, except Desiree. They had no idea that Topo had survived the storm and marched to Rift with the remaining Petrapolis warriors. There was no telling what was going on in Rift since the good pelots had gone away and Ontelles was under the total control of Leatos and his pelots. I often wondered if I would ever see Vertunda again.

As soon as the snow began to melt and the water began to cascade over the edge of Farella, the men recovered the frozen body of Topaz. We built a large stone altar and gave him a proper funeral. Lydia wept and the other women comforted her during the cremation.

The next day I ordered Joba and Neco to begin looking for the secret passage that Castor and Topo had used to find Farella. I stayed at Stone House and made repairs on the roof and outside. That afternoon Desiree and Lydia went to the lake with the children to wash clothes. Eviea stayed behind with me. No one saw this as odd, including myself. While I was working I went into the house to get a bucket. Eviea was sitting at the stone table with her eyes downcast and hands folded. Next to her hands was a pipe that I recognized as the pipe Joba had smoked from the night before I had written my letter to Desiree a year earlier. The room reeked with a foul odor. I perceived this as very strange, since Joba hadn't smoked from his pipe all winter, and I wondered how Eviea found it and decided to smoke from it.

"Eviea, what are you doing? Women don't smoke and especially not that stuff," I said, moving towards her.

"Everyone smokes this STUFF at Rift. Your brother, Dee, made it an edict, even though very few objected."

"What are you talking about? What does that stuff do to

your mind?"

"It makes everything beautiful; euphoric. Everything floats and colors are so much brighter," slurred Eviea.

"You are drugged. Why do you smoke this?" I asked picking up the pipe in my hand.

"I love you Zeb, do you know that?" she said looking into my eyes to see my expression. "Do you love me?"

My mind flashed back to that fall day when I left Farella to ride to Rift. Eviea was washing clothes where the other women were today, and I had asked her the same question. I looked at her dark eyes, the attractive face, and her long black hair that was silky and shiny as oil.

"I love Desiree and you love Neco," I said very quietly hoping no one was standing at the door.

"Yes, maybe you are right, maybe we are just fond of each other like you said long ago. But I fell for you the day you saved my baby and me. Do you know who my son is?" she asked, trying to change this embarrassing conversation.

"Yes I do," I said as I sat down and placed my hands on top of hers in order to comfort her. Her downcast eyes opened wide and looked into mine.

"Who is he?"

"The servant of truth who is to come from Farella...the one mentioned in the last sentence of the FARELLA scroll."

After I made this proclamation, Eviea smiled, "Thank you Zeb, and in a close friendship way....I do love you."

At that very moment, as Eviea finished her sentence, I heard someone say, "Oh my I don't believe this!" and then the door slammed. I jumped up and ran outside and saw Desiree running towards the lake. When I caught up with her, halfway between the lake and the house, she turned on me and tried to hit me. I held her hands and she screamed and called me a deceiver and a liar. "I hate you and I hate Eviea!"

"No Desiree, please it isn't what you think," cried Eviea who had followed us out the door. "Zeb doesn't love me, he loves you...he told me so."

"I read your lips, you said, "I love you."

"She said in a close friendship way I love you," I explained. "I love you Dez, you know that." Desiree fell to her knees sobbing.

"This is the second time I've been jealous because of you, Eviea," cried Desiree. "I'm sorry." Eviea knelt down with her and the two women hugged in their tears. I stood there feeling stupid, and I desperately wanted to leave and find Peton, but Desiree would certainly be upset with me if she found me talking to my beast and not her.

As the two women huddled, I saw Neco and Joba standing down at the lake with Lydia and the children. They hadn't seen us and the three of them were laughing as the boys were playing together at the water's edge. Lydia was bulging at the stomach being heavy with child.

"Dez, I will be right back, I want to see if Neco and Joba found the secret passage." I didn't think she heard me but I left anyway. At the lake Joba said they found it.

"It's a snake path that is only big enough for humans, and it's probably too narrow and steep for the women," Joba said. I told them to sharpen their swords and prepare to leave in the morning.

"Joba, I would like to speak with you privately if I could." I said as the two men began to head towards Stone House.

"What is it?" he asked as Neco continued on.

"Walk with me to the waterfall." We walked in silence before I stopped and began to speak. "I found Eviea smoking your pipe a little while ago. First, I want to know how she got it."

Joba stood there and looked frightened even though he never moved his eyes from mine. "She asked me if she could smoke some pelot leaves while I was away today. I said, 'sure'. Why do you ask?"

"Pelot leaves, what's that?"

"A plant that grows only on the Plain of Blood. It's a stimulant if smoked. That's why Petrapolis was built out in the middle of nowhere. That's where the plant is most abundant."

"Then it is evil. Why do you smoke it?" I demanded.

"I haven't smoked any since I've left Rift."

"Yes, and that is another thing. Eviea said my brother made an edict, which makes it compulsory for everyone to smoke pelot leaves."

"No, no. She is wrong there. That's crazy."

"You wouldn't lie to me, would you?"

Joba's brow was covered in beads of sweat and I wondered if I should believe his last answer or not. I looked away from him and stared blankly out into space and asked the Holy One if Joba was telling me the truth. In my mind I heard the words, 'Test him with the sword, test him with the sword.' I looked down to the ground confused at what I heard in my mind when my eyes saw the severed section of the Sword of Guile. I looked around and realized this was the spot where Castor and I had fought. "Joba, pick up that blade." I ordered as I pointed to the black steel, which was laying in the grass, with tiny little mountain flowers growing up around it. Joba smiled with an amused little laugh when he saw what I was looking at. He seemed almost too eager to obey my order and bent at the waist to pick it up. When his fingers touched the tip, the blade turned into burning flames. Joba let out a scream of pain, and I saw that his left hand was badly burned.

"You tricked me!" he said holding his injured hand close to his chest.

"No, you tricked yourself by lying to me and the Creator," I answered as I bent down and reached for the broken blade. When the sword didn't flame as I picked it up, Joba dropped his head.

"I'm sorry my king, I did lie. Your brother Dee did make

it an edict. Everyone has to smoke pelot leaves at the morning, noon, and evening hours. It is the law of Rift."

"Why would he do such a thing?" I angrily asked.

"He said it would keep the people under control and they would love him and not you. You see, Zeb, you were the king but you were nowhere to be found. We thought... I mean he thought... all right we thought you had lost your mind. Then when you didn't return with Neco and myself last year that was the end of it. I tried to get you to smoke the leaves that night before we left but you refused. Had you started smoking the stuff you would be hooked today and in the control of us. But understand this, I was with Dee, but I've changed. That's why Topaz, Neco, the women and myself left Rift. We were evil, and the edict was wrong and we came to be with our king. Everything was great all winter but now that spring is here we all realized we would be leaving for Rift, and Neco and I decided to get you hooked on pelot leaves so you wouldn't be angry at Dee and kill him when you found out."

"And Eviea was chosen to entrap me?" Joba nodded his lowered head. "Why not Desiree?"

"She had nothing to do with it. She was one of the guiltless ones at Rift who refused to smoke the leaves. Believe me it was mostly for her safety that we left Rift to find you."

"What about the letter I asked to be read day and night at the temple?"

"It was read but everyone laughed at it. Topaz was the reader and after the first week only Desiree listened to each reading and she was the only one who memorized the words."

"This truly is a wicked world we live in." And in a burning rage I tossed the broken sword with all my might into the air and it fell into the center of the lake, making a loud splash that sent ripples out to the shoreline.

After our evening meal and the children were put to bed

I asked everyone to assemble outside Stone House. When we were all gathered, I stood alone before the people who were my closest friends. Desiree, my love, sat at the far left and the suns that were about to set behind the peaks of Farella cast a pinkish glow on her face. Next to her sat Eviea. This I was happy to see considering the earlier events of the day. With Eviea sat her husband, young and handsome with fuzz of a beard beginning to appear on his chin. Next in line leaning against the stone house was my general, dark and fearsome on the outside, but on the inside kind and compassionate. With him was Lydia, sweet and innocent in appearance. Her arm was hooked inside Joba's and they both kissed each other before I began my address.

"I have asked you to step outside because I have some burdens that hang heavy on my heart. I stand here before you first as your friend, and with more difficulty I stand here by holy providence as your king. To be truthful I don't feel very kingly, for I really don't seem to have a kingdom except you here at Farella. I have ordered everyone around at times, and if anyone has been offended, I apologize and I do plan on being kinder in this regard." Everyone began to shake their heads to say I was wrong and not to worry but I knew their hearts and they were only being kind to me. I held up my hand to stop this and go on.

"I have been informed that Rift, the city of mystery for centuries and bastion of truth, has fallen into the hands of the evil ones and is the new throne of the Prince of Darkness."

Joba and Neco looked at each other as the women gasped. I raised my hands to keep anyone from questioning me until I had finished my address.

"Before Topaz died he said I was a prophet. I doubted him at the time, but today I believe it to be so. Topaz's brother, Topo, is now sitting at Rift with the remaining warriors from the Petrapolis legion. He has presented himself as king by right of the Flaming Sword. He possesses both the sword of Truth and what remains of the Sword of Guile. These things were shared with me by the great pelot, Vertunda, shortly before he and the legions of good pelots departed from this planet and returned to the throne and temple of God in heaven."

Once again I had to raise my hands to quiet my friends and to refuse any questions.

"Please allow me to finish. Yes, Rift has become a Petrapolis, yet it was heading in that direction before you fled from there last fall. We are only three men who can wield a sword, and three women, one quite pregnant, along with two toddling children. Not much of an army to break the evil back of Topo and his army. Nor do we have the spiritual help of the good pelots any longer; help that we took for granted. My friends, now comes the moment of decision. What do we do? I see only two options. One: stay here at Farella and live out our lives; impart the truth to our children, hoping one may someday carry on and lead the people of this planet to truth. Second: go to Rift, and try and lead the people into repentance. This is our only hope for the return of the good pelots and the salvation for the truth preserved in the holy scrolls. Now the basic question is this: do we save ourselves, or do we forfeit ourselves for the sake of others. I will tell you what I've decided, and I'm not ordering this upon you. You all may do what you wish. In the morning I will only ask Joba to come with me to Rift. Neco, I would want you to stay here with the women and children."

"My king, please let me come along," blurted out Neco.

"The work here is of more importance Neco. You will not be idle. There is wood to collect, much hunting and fishing to be done. Farella will need to be prepared for another long winter. Now if Joba and I are successful, with God's help, we will send for you all to join us at Rift...that is, if anyone wants to come. If we fail, we will return to live a life of peace and isolation here in this beautiful cirque. If we die, you all will join us in the next world, the one we are going to be in forever. Remember, what we do here will resonate into eternity. Be strong in the grace that the creator has given you all." I grinned, signaling the finish of my speech and walked over to Desiree. I put my hand on top of her head and asked her to walk with me. We walked arm in arm to the lake that was reflecting Lepis and Venu which both appeared as full orbs in the night sky. Thousands of stars twinkled and at one point there was a shower of falling stars. Hundreds of arching lights lit up the sky. I lay on my back in the short grass next to my childhood love.

"I love you, Desiree," I said looking over at her. She turned her gaze upon me, and didn't answer but looked long into my eyes with a wonderful smile on her face. "What do you see?" I finally asked.

"I see myself," she answered.

"Do you love me?" I asked very softly.

"Yes, I love you very much."

"Do you love me because I'm a king or because I'm a prophet?"

"I loved you when you were nothing but an elb herder, or have you forgotten?"

We embraced and kissed under the stars and it was late before we got back to Stone House.

In the morning Eviea and Lydia prepared a huge breakfast. Tish eggs, hog meat and berry rolls. We all ate heartily and even sang old village songs while the women cleared up the dishes and the children entertained. While all this festivity was going on I slipped out to say good-bye to my beast. I found him in his stall waiting to be released so he could frolic out in the meadow.

"Peton my good and loyal friend. I will be gone for a

while, and during that time I want you to protect the ladies and children if any intruders happen to venture up here." My beast nudged me with his snout that was still a little discolored and purred as I stroked his neck.

"You know, a woman could become jealous over that beast," said Desiree who was standing at the shelter with her hip to one side.

"This old boy has saved my life several times and he isn't just an old indifferent beast. He loves me just like you do, so you two ought to get along well." We both laughed, and after I released Peton from his stall to run in the meadow, Desiree and I fell into one of the empty stalls embracing and laughing. As she lay in my arms, I could smell her sweet breath and her clean hair. "You know something, we have never properly been married."

"What do you suggest?" she asked in a whisper.

"A marriage ceremony before Joba and I leave."

"That's a grand idea, and you know Neco and Eviea have never had an official ceremony either."

When Desiree and I broke the good news about our marriage ceremony everyone called for a celebration. Joba immediately asked if this was going to postpone our trip to Rift. Desiree answered quickly, "I'm not going to get married and then let my husband walk off after the ceremony for who knows how long."

That evening Neco, Eviea, Desiree and I, stood at the edge of Farella as Joba, in his official role as general of the king's army, performed a ceremony that Desiree and I spent the whole day composing. We made vows to never leave each other and asked the God of heaven to help us uphold our promises. Afterwards, I read a song I had written and Desiree recited SONG OF ZEBULUM TO HIS LOST LOVE by heart. She did it so well that everyone became misty eyed and had lumps in their throats. That night there was much cream juice, singing and dancing. Neco and Eviea spent the night in Stone House while Desiree and I slept in the animal shelter. It was a night to remember as Desiree and I held each other in a stall full of newly cut mountain grass. We told each other, 'I love you' a thousand times during the night. When day finally came, Lydia had cooked a huge breakfast much like the day before.

"When do we leave?" asked Joba while everyone sat at the stone table eating.

"I suppose we could delay another week," I said as I winked at Desiree. She smiled back and touched my knee with her hand under the table.

The next seven days went by quickly. Desiree rarely left my side. She even fished with me and helped repair some stonework on the house. On the night before Joba and I planned to leave, she wept in her sleep and begged me not to leave her. I felt badly to be leaving, but in the morning Joba and I packed two small bags full of food and rolled up our elb robes.

"Zeb," said Desiree while I was rolling my elb robe. "Put this in your robe and return it when you get to Rift." In her hand was the scroll with the red ribbon tied around it. She had a sad face and her eyes were puffy from weeping most of the night.

"Everything is going to be all right," I said trying to comfort her as my hand touched her cheek.

"I just wish I felt that was true. I don't understand it, Zeb, but I have a bad feeling."

"Pray for me and the Holy One's spirit will take care of me." She kissed my mouth with moist lips and her slim body quivered in my arms. "I will," she whispered.

Before late morning Joba and I were ready to leave. I placed the nugget Taman's dull sword, which wouldn't hold an edge, in the black scabbard that once held the Sword of Guile. We said our farewells and left by foot for the secret passage out of Farella. While Joba led the way I was amazed how Topo and Castor were able to pass on this thin and dangerous trail that day of the thick clouds and darkness. At some points we were practically hanging from sheer death by our fingernails. When we reached the valley below, the traveling became much easier. We walked long days and made it to the Gate of Virgins in seven days. At the crack in the wall there were four Petrapolis warriors standing guard.

"Name yourselves," commanded a warrior with a sixth class helmet. "Surely you're not nuggets, but you don't look like warriors either." I saw a black bound book on a table much like the scene outside the gate at Petrapolis. "Do you have tattoos on your necks?" questioned the soldier eyeing us and disturbed over our silence. "Answer or you will not gain entrance into the capital of Ontelles."

"Very well, we will pass on," I answered.

"Hold it. You both carry swords. Have you ever used them?"

"Who is the king or is there a warrior council like there used to be at Petrapolis?" I asked, revealing enough information to satisfy the soldier and who might possibly give us some answers.

"So you know about Petrapolis. I don't recognize you, are you Petrapolis warriors?"

"We are elb herders looking for some lost elbs. You four wouldn't be elb thieves would you?" Joba said gruffly. I gave Joba a stern look, noticing the irritation he had caused the soldiers. Hands went to swords and we all stood at a critical moment before a possible life and death struggle.

"The tongue is small but causes great harm," I coldly said to Joba relieving the tension that was standing at the surface of the four men's faces. Joba slowly moved his hand from his sword's hilt, as did the others.

"We will leave you protectors of the capital if we may," I said with pretended servility.

"Pass," ordered the soldier. Joba and I walked south

around the rocky, vertical wall that surrounded the meadow of Rift. When we came to the famous chimney running up the side of the rock faced mountain I began to feel ill. My hands were trembling and great drops of sweat fell from my brow.

"Joba, climb the chimney and see if there is a rope at the top." I said as I dropped my bag of food and slid down with my back against a tree. There I stayed until Joba returned.

"You don't look well," commented Joba as he came towards me. His face was reddened from his climb and descent of the rock wall.

"I don't know what's wrong...did you find the rope?"

"It's up there and you were right, the city is in the hands of the Petrapolis warriors. They are all over the walls."

"Listen, it's going to be dark in a few hours. Why don't we make camp here and enter the city after sunset."

"Sounds like a good plan to me," responded Joba as he began to hunt through his food bag.

That afternoon my illness became worse. I began to shake with chills and burn from fever. Joba was busy building a fire and cooking while I was barely able to untie my elb robe and roll up in it to try to sleep. When I awoke it was night and Joba was waiting with some overcooked meat and roots for me to eat.

"How long has it been dark?" I asked.

"Four or five hours. I have been waiting for you to come out of your nap."

I tried to sit up but I was too weak. I began to fear that I had the same sickness that had me bedridden for two weeks last fall. Joba placed a callused hand on my forehead and declared that I was running a beast of a fever. "My...my, Zeb, are you going to be able to make it?"

"I don't think so. Maybe you should leave me here and go spy out the city yourself. Learn who's in control and what role Dee has in the new order. Make sure no one finds you out and come back before morning light."

"Do you want anything before I leave?" asked Joba with a fearful look on his face.

"Leave me some water and then be on your way."

During the night I tossed and turned on the forest floor hoping for morning. I couldn't find sleep and my fever was causing horrible nightmares when I did rest. I had dreams of Castor cutting me into little pieces with a flaming sword and Topo eating the cooked bits at a huge banquet with warriors and unclad women. I woke several times calling out Desiree's name begging her to cool the fire that was burning me. Finally a hand woke me from my dreams and in a blur I saw Joba.

"Zeb, it is only a dream. Wake up, it's only a dream."

"Joba, what did you find?" I asked after bringing myself back to reality.

"The city lies in gross wickedness. Women give themselves to men for a wink and the temple has become the market place of human flesh. Murder, slander, vileness have become the code of the city. The streets are red with blood and men even turn to men, and women to women for vile favors. Zeb, if you weren't so sick, I would take you back to Farella and we would forget this evil night."

"My brother and Topo...what did you find?" I asked in a weak and trembling voice.

"Topo is the king and Dee is his general. I saw neither of them, but that is what others told me when I inquired. Maybe I could try to get near Topo and assassinate him."

"No! He has to repent like the rest. That is the only way...the only way." This was all I remembered in the forest after Joba returned from the city. When I awoke from many hours of sleep, I found myself in the infirmary at Rift. Joba was in the room with me. I asked him where I was and he shared with me what had happened. He had tried to cool me with water compresses after I went into unconsciousness.

My fever continued so he decided to tie the rope around my unconscious body and climb to the top. Once up at the summit he slowly hauled me up and then lowered me over to the other side. He then carried me into the city. Once in Rift we became just two more people; a friend carrying what looked like an over indulgent mate. I was cared for and packed in snow until my fever broke. When I finally opened my eyes, Joba told me a week had passed since I fell under the effects of the illness.

"Joba, are we in Rift?" I asked still unable to sit up or barely able to speak.

"Yes, and praise the Holy One for bringing you back."

"I'm not to die. The people are to repent. That's why I'm at Rift."

"No, No. This city is worse than Petrapolis ever was. The people are all drugged on pelot leaves and they won't repent. As soon as you are able to travel we are getting out of here."

I couldn't argue with my friend so I just closed my eyes and tried to relax. Another week passed before I was able to feed myself and sit up. I was still weak from not eating, and I had lost a great deal of weight. Joba never left my side and I saw no one else come into the infirmary room during my illness. A third week passed before I was finally able to walk. It was at this time that I decided to leave and visit the temple.

"No one knows that we are here...is that correct?" I asked my general as I sat up from my cot in the white-washed room.

"Not that I know of."

"Good. Now if you will please hand me my pants and shirt." Joba did as I asked, but he had a somber look and dragged his feet as he crossed the room. "Why are you so gloomy?" I asked.

"Here are your pants and shirt," Joba said handing me

my leather clothing but trying to evade my question. Realizing he couldn't, he asked, "You are leaving this room to go to the temple aren't you?"

"Of course, did you think I was going to leave and hide the rest of my life at Farella?"

"Then we will die today," stated Joba slapping the palm of his hand hard against the handle of his sword.

"I don't plan on dying today and neither should you. However, if you save yourself, you lose yourself. If you lose yourself for the truth, you will save yourself. That is in the scrolls."

"You said all the good pelots have left Ontelles. This city is in the control of evil men. Spiritually it is in the hands of Leatos. Now tell me why my thinking has gone awry? We will surely die if we declare who we are."

"Where is my elb robe?" I asked not seeing it in the room and trying not to respond to his emotional lecture.

"Didn't you hear me?" Joba yelled in a hushed voice.

"I heard you, now where is my robe?"

"How do you think we paid for this room for three weeks… with a handful of bluebon roots?"

"You sold my elb robe?"

"Yes, yes. I sold it. The robe was once elegant but it's old and stained now. Besides, it is a small price to pay when you have your life in return."

"Who did you sell it to?"

"Some man that works here at the infirmary."

"All right, let's find him," I commanded. I stood and looped the strap of my sword over my shoulder. On a table against a wall laid the scroll with the red ribbon. I took it in my hand and asked Joba to open the door. We walked out together and found the long hallway of marble deserted. We walked down the corridor until two men in front of us stepped out of a room laughing. One of the men saw me and stopped in his steps.

"That's the one," cried Joba, pointing to the person standing like a stone statue.

"My king," said the surprised man, then he bowed at the waist.

"What's going on here?" the second man said as his friend bowed.

"What is your name?" I asked looking at the man who had bowed.

"You named me Peton. Remember I was Taman the nugget," he answered.

"Yes, now I remember. My friend here says you bought a white elb robe from him," I said glancing over to Joba.

"Yes, this is true."

"Do you still have the robe?" I inquired trying to smile and be polite.

"Yes, I will get it. Please wait," and he turned and ran out of the building.

The other man stood awkwardly eyeing both Joba and myself. "Listen, I have work to do if you both will excuse me," the man said stumbling over his words. He turned and walked out of the building in a fast step.

After he had exited Joba turned to me in rage. "Very good, now we are known. The element of surprise is gone."

"Fear not my commander, all things are set and ordained to happen. Believe and you shall see."

Joba shrugged his shoulders, and coming down the hall with my elb robe in hand was the nugget warrior, Peton.

"Had I known it was yours I would not have taken it for any price," he said as he held it out to me.

"Thank you my servant," I said. I then passed the rolled up robe over to Joba to hold as I removed the dull sword and the black scabbard. "This is now being returned to its original owner."

"I can't take it back," Peton refused.

"Take it and I will also pay you back later what you gave

my friend for the robe. Now follow me to the temple." My command was given with power and authority. Peton grasped the scabbard and shouldered the scabbard strap. I took my elb robe back and with the scroll in hand I led the way out into the morning light. The sky was brassy blue with no clouds in view. People milled in the streets, much like I had remembered Rift in the past. Joba and Peton walked behind me until we entered the temple compound. The open courtyard was vacant of life. There were signs of great festivity and debauched behavior that must have occurred in the night. Women and men's clothing were scattered all around where apparently the entire compound had become a sea of naked people. Broken jugs and smoking pipes were scattered amongst the clothing. As we passed the giant altar I saw the most horrifying sight of all. A young naked woman lying flat on her back with a huge gaping hole cut in her chest. Blood was thick and black down the white marble sides of the altar where the girl had bled to death. Her long blonde hair hid her face.

"Human sacrifice?" I asked Peton who now walked at my left.

He nodded, "One at midnight by order of King Topo. It's a new way of dealing with women who reach their thirtieth birthday and are unwed. It's more entertaining than the old way whatever the old way was."

We mounted the temple stairs in silence and at the huge open doors I asked the two men to stand guard as I ventured into the high vaulted room. The temple reeked with the foul smell of pelot leaves and when I reached the broken altar, at the front of the temple, I saw a pile of leaves still burning. Torn clothing and smears of blood were everywhere. Resting by itself on the table where I had once found loaves of bread, lay the red and bloody heart of the girl I saw outside. I turned my eyes away blocking the sight from my mind. I got to my knees next to the hidden entrance to the scroll room. With my fingers barely in the crack in the stones I tried to lift, in order to trigger the mechanism controlling the pulleys that opened the stone door. I couldn't budge it.

"They are coming Zeb!" yelled Joba as his voice echoed in the huge room. I picked up the FARELLA scroll and robe and tried to run to the open door. I was still somewhat weak or just out of shape. Joba and Peton had their swords out and ready. Over their shoulders I watched an angry looking mob of men and women pouring into the compound. Leading the mass were three men. The one I had met in the infirmary, Topo, and my brother Dee.

"Listen my two friends," I said to Joba and Peton. "Go and mingle in the crowd. If they kill me, I want you Joba to leave and remain at Farella and forget this day and this city."

"I will stay and die with you my king," answered Joba.

"You're brave and noble, but do as I say and anger me not," I barked.

Joba looked at Peton, the warrior, and with his eyes he confirmed my request. The two men left me with their swords placed back in their scabbards. On the top of the steps I stood alone. The compound was filling quickly. I unrolled my elb robe and put it on even though the day was warm and sunny. I watched Joba melt into the crowd of men and women unnoticed. Peton was not as fortunate. His friend from the infirmary pointed him out to Topo. Two Petrapolis warriors grabbed and disarmed him before he was able to get his sword out of his scabbard. He was then dragged to the feet of Topo who withdrew the broken Sword of Guile from a new sheath, and with a flick of his wrist the short flaming blade lopped off Peton's right hand, the one that held the sword. His body shook with muscle spasms in the warrior's grasp as his severed hand fell onto the marbled pavement stones.

"Now it's your turn, deceiver!" screamed Topo, whose

features were distorted by his hate and anger towards me.

I raised my right hand in order to quiet the crowd, thinking it too might be cut off if not my head in a few moments. Miraculously they halted at the base of the temple steps and I knew if I was going to speak, now was the time. I quickly glanced at the scroll in my hand and my spirit called out for the Holy One to fill my mouth with words.

"People of Ontelles, citizens of Rift, hear me before you judge me," I called out in a loud and penetrating voice. The angry mob quieted for what seemed to be for only the sake of curiosity and entertainment. "Many of you from Rift remember me as the one who held the Flaming Sword of Truth and slew the red-bearded giant at the Gate of Virgins six winters ago. During the funeral of Lindas, the high priest, brother to the man who you now call your king, repented to the Holy One and begged him to send the king back. Today I have come and I have come to stay and rule with truth... but only if you repent from your wickedness. Your wrong actions must be changed into right actions. You people of Rift who have now mixed with those from the outside have fallen from the foundation of the written truth. You seek self-interest rather than self-sacrifice to follow the Holy One. Pleasure and greed have supplanted the truth which you were taught as little ones." I paused a moment to allow my words to sink into their minds.

"Those of you who are from the wilderness and the fallen Petrapolis, you have embraced the laws of Ontelles unaware, but your hearts condemned each one of you when you were children and your parents demanded that you never question the ways of Ontelles. Now tell me, is it right to dismember a man and chop off his hand without emotion, just as Topo did before our very eyes? This is nothing but cold and heartless barbarity. And the woman on the altar, what was her crime? She had a birthday and no man married her? Is that reason to kill someone? You evil and wicked generation! Tell me what prevents the loving god of this world from striking it with either fire or water? Look at the suns in the sky. They could explode in a second and it would be over, but does this thought frighten you? Lord have mercy upon you if you all would only change your minds and turn from your wicked ways."

My eyes surveyed the solemn crowd and I looked deeply into the people's eyes. Many turned their faces or looked down. "I sent a scroll to be read one year ago and I was told that you laughed and mocked at this. Tell me, if a man who hired someone to watch his elbs and when he returned he found that the hired man had allowed wild hogs to eat the elbs what would the owner do?"

"Kill the son of a beast!" yelled a man in the crowd causing great roars of laughter.

"You speak rightly," I said and the crowd quieted again. "And yet the true king has arrived from the Holy One to call forth His judgment."

The people began to murmur among themselves and Topo and Dee looked at one another, realizing I had to be silenced and silenced quickly.

"I'm the king of Ontelles by right of the Flaming Sword!" screamed Topo as his hand went to the hilt of the Sword of Guile. My eyes noticed the Sword of Truth also hanging at his side but he dared not touch the beautifully jeweled handle. The broken blade of the Sword of Guile leaped with flames as he withdrew it and the people stepped back in fear as he held the flaming sword above his head. While this was happening I searched the crowd with my eyes for Joba and I found him squeezing towards Topo. There was death and murder written in every line of his face. He was going to assassinate Topo if he could get to him. What was I to do or say that could prevent this? I held up the scroll with the red ribbon in my hand and called out in a loud voice.

"Hear me everyone. In my hand is a sword sharper and

more powerful than the one in Topo's hand."

The crowd began to explode in laughter and Topo sheathed his weapon in order to watch me prove what I had just proclaimed. "Prove it or I will cut you in half!" yelled Topo in a sickening scream.

I untied the red ribbon and unrolled the parchment. "This is the last of the Holy Scrolls, written centuries ago by the prophet Elan. The scroll reads concerning the kingdom age." My eyes went to the parchment and I read. "'I will place a king on the throne of Rift. The king will be young, but filled with wisdom and strength from above. He will come from the land of Lepis and out of the Order of Petrapolis will he flee.'"

After I read my eyes left the scroll and fell upon my brother Dee, who still stood next to Topo. I pointed down to him and addressed him. "My brother... tell the people what wilderness my village is located in. Tell them!"

Dee stood silent as the people waited for his answer.

"The Lepis Wilderness!" I answered for him. "Also I was a soldier from Petrapolis but I fled from that wicked order. Now tell me Topo, what city are you from?" I now pointed at Topo and his closed and pinched lips never moved. "I will answer this also. Topo, the brother of Topaz, the high priest of Rift is from this very city, not the Lepis Wilderness and he is still in the Petrapolis Order." I hesitated as I scanned the crowd then asked, "Tell me who is your king according to prophecy?"

The crowd was silent, not a soul moved or spoke. My eyes went back to the scroll. "'I, Elan, was carried to the last days, shortly before the kingdom began, and stood with a good pelot as he showed me the future king of Ontelles. I watched as he slew a giant at the Gate of Virgins with the Flaming Sword.'" I lifted my eyes to the people, "Six years ago this occurred. This prophecy in my hand also speaks of the evil that will come upon Rift and the king's armies who recaptured it. I ask those who served under my kingship from Stone Fortress, who has deceived you so quickly that you should fall into the grips of an ash lizard such as Topo?"

The crowd let out a loud murmur but this time it was directed not towards me but Topo. I lifted my hand to quiet the thronging crowd in order to read on in the scroll that I had only read once before, and at that time I had been totally devastated by its words.

"'I will then send the armies of the king to take the city back and cleanse it. But'... and I repeat, 'BUT ...the city of Rift will still be in danger as prophesied in the Holy Scrolls. There will be only one escape for Rift.'" I looked up from the scroll and eyed the crowd as I continued from memory. "'If the inhabitants repent of their wrong and evil deeds, then I will save them!'"

I saw several of the women pull at their hair and fall to the ground weeping. My eyes looked back to the scroll and I read the ending: the same as Desiree read to Topaz before he died. "'A prophet from Farella will come to Rift and prophesy before the true kingdom begins and ends.' And today this prophecy has been fulfilled."

I stood silent, rolled the scroll up, and tied the red ribbon around the tube. More women fell to the ground in tears. Others in the crowd, including men, cried out, "He is the true king!"; "No, he is the prophet!"; "We must repent or God will destroy us!" Many more began to wail and beat on their chests and confess that they had acted wickedly and begged the powers in heaven to forgive them. I looked towards Topo and I noticed Joba was behind him waiting to kill him. I stood silent and Dee ran up the stairs towards me and stopped halfway up, withdrew his sword and turned the blade towards his stomach in order to fall on it. I ran towards him and knocked the sword out of his hands before he fell. His face was streaked with tears and he dropped to his knees weeping like a baby. I looked over at Topo again and he began to run towards me before Joba was able to plunge his sword into his back. I moved away from Dee and Topo as he stopped on the step next to me raising his fiery sword above his head.

"Why don't you kill me?" I asked very calmly.

"I can't move my arms," replied Topo in a frightened voice. Then before my eyes I saw something assuming form. A man appeared standing next to Topo holding back his arms.

"Praise God!" I shouted as I recognized Vertunda. "Praise God!" I looked at all the people in the compound and standing with them and on the walls and roofs of the buildings were thousands and thousands of pelots dressed in white, green and powder blue tunics. I cried for joy as the city wept in its sorrow.

Topo finally dropped his sword and Vertunda released him only after he had removed the Sword of Truth from Topo's waist. Topo turned and ran out of the compound along with a number of Petrapolis warriors who hadn't repented. Joba later reported that Topo had left the city with close to a thousand warriors and headed west in the direction of the Plains of Blood.

EPILOGUE

Chapter Twenty-two

Vertunda and the good pelots had returned. The city had repented and the words of Vertunda, from the visit in the animal shelter at Farella, had come true. The prophet from Farella had truly come to Rift before the true kingdom began and ended. Yes, the kingdom of Ontelles officially began and ended the moment the people repented. Up till that moment I wasn't a king sitting on a throne and I really wasn't one now. The inhabitants of Rift accepted me as their leader, but a leader sent from God. This expectation that the people had of me was a great and at times a frustrating challenge.

My first act as the prophet-king of Rift was to purify the temple. The walls and floor were scrubbed with sandstones and boiling water. The stone and woodwork was repaired. My second act was to move all the scrolls back to Topaz's study chamber, which became what we termed the Center of Truth. Scribes and secretaries, men from Rift who had been elders, labored day and night in three shifts making copies of all the holy scrolls. Each completed set of copies was then taken to other buildings around the city from where other centers of truth were established. My greater plan was to send copies of the holy scrolls to all the villages in the Lepis and Topan Wildernesses. There was going to be an awakening on Ontelles, and I was preparing and training the workers to accomplish this colossal undertaking. My third and last act was to establish a new priesthood that would lead in worship at the temple and who would also provide as instructors at the centers of truth.

Problems of domestic origin, such as food distribution, maintenance of city buildings and security I placed in the hands of Joba, who reported to me daily on his progress. All seemed to be moving smoothly the rest of that summer, except that I was longing in the evenings and nights for my bride who was still at Farella. I had been too busy to leave and bring her to Rift. I also feared sending someone, thus revealing the location, in case I ever needed to flee there.

It wasn't until an autumn evening when Joba and I decided to take our evening meal with the young elb herders outside the city walls that a plan was set concerning a return to Farella. Joba and I sat around a fire and spoke privately after the herders had gone off to bed or to their turn at watch. The stars sparkled in the clear black velvet sky above.

"What do you know about the stars, Zeb?" asked Joba who always was curious about the heavens.

"We are the fourth planet from our star system's suns in the Tal system. This system is one of innumerable systems that make up the Triad Galaxy," I said smiling.

Joba's eyes grew wide and he looked at me oddly knowing I had never spoken with such knowledge. "All right, explain yourself."

I laughed and slapped him on the back. "I haven't been sleeping much at night lately, so I began walking the streets. One night I saw this old man up on a balcony watching the stars with an eye instrument he had made. I asked if I could use his instrument and he invited me into his house. He said his name was Triad and he was a watcher of the heavens. He had hundreds of charts and maps of the stars. I was amazed at what I saw through his eye instrument and he explained many new things that he had discovered. He said he named our galaxy after himself."

"Tell me what a star system is and what's a galaxy?" begged Joba like a little boy who had just discovered how to talk and wanted to learn more.

"You can ask old Triad, for I'm sending you with him to Farella."

"What?"

"Last night I was at Triad's house and he was saying how he wished he could take his eye instrument up on a high mountain and look at the stars from there. It was then that I decided about Farella. I'm sending you with the old man and his eye instrument to Farella. You can leave him there for the winter, but I want you to return with Desiree and my son, and with whoever else wants to come."

"Good, I'll be glad to get away from this city and get some fresh air with my wife," Joba said with a wide grin. We toasted cups full of cream juice, and I stood and told Joba to be ready in the morning at first light for I was going to tell Triad. Joba said he had much work to do and people to put in command if he was leaving in the morning.

Early the next morning Triad and myself met Joba at the Gate of Virgins as the suns rose and struck the marble walls of the city. I had Triad's eye instrument broken down and tied to my back in a pack, since the crack in the wall was too small to fit a beast through and besides there weren't any beasts at Rift. It took a while shimmying the bundle through the crack but once we made it there was much jubilation.

"By the way Joba, this is Triad," I said realizing I hadn't properly introduced the two. "Also, Triad is Topaz's older brother and I believe that makes him your brother-in-law or some kind of relation."

"Are you serious?" asked Joba. "That is strange that we have never met before, nor has my wife spoken of you."

"Topaz was my brother and so is Topo, unfortunately,

and both would have nothing to do with me. I would be surprised if your wife would even know of me." This was all said in a sad voice.

"Tell me, why weren't you the high priest of Rift if you are older than Topaz?" asked Joba.

"I'm a man of science not of religion. I have nothing to do with the spirit world only the physical realm."

"You will soon learn otherwise, my friend," I gently pointed out. Triad smiled politely but made no comment.

I helped Joba with the heavy pack and wished the two men safety and success. I watched them disappear into the trees as a great sadness filled me. I knew I had to remain at Rift and oversee all my new acts and make sure they were carried out. Had I not abandoned Rift after Joba's and Dee's armies recaptured the city, it possibly wouldn't have fallen to the state of decadence that it did. This was my thought and argument that made me decide to stay and send Joba instead to Farella with Triad. I missed Desiree and my son terribly, yet I reminded myself that they both would be with me soon.

With my sadness temporarily placed aside I turned to squeeze back through the crack in the wall, but instead I was startled by what I saw. For standing at the entrance of Rift was Vertunda. He and the good pelots had vanished from human sight after Topo dropped the Sword of Guile at the temple and ran out of the compound. I had wanted to speak with Vertunda, but this was the first appearance since the day of repentance.

"Greetings and peace be upon you servant of the Holy One," said Vertunda in his soothing and comforting voice.

"I'm glad to see you my friend," I replied in a surprised voice. "What brings you here?"

"I have come to comfort and exhort you. The Holy One is pleased with what you are doing and I'm to tell you that you shall have a long season of peace and rest. The city of

Rift will grow in the direction of right actions and the spread of the holy scrolls has been long awaited. Continue in your labors and I shall return at the end of three winters and will then show you a glimpse of things to come."

"Like what happened to Elan, mentioned in the FARELLA scroll?" I asked excitedly.

"Yes, just like that. Now guard the Sword of Truth and bury the words of the Holy One in your heart. Fear not and always put your eye upon Him." He then vanished from my sight.

I stood there and marveled for a few moments before passing through the Gate of Virgins. On the other side I was struck by a new sensitivity to the beauty of Rift. The golden roofs, the snow white walls, the green meadows dotted with the colorful herds of elbs moving like the gentle lashing of the sea. One of the herders was waving to me with his right arm. I looked and noticed the hand was missing. I squinted my eyes in order to see better and immediately recognized the herder as Peton. He could have become a great hero giving up his hand for the new order but instead he accepted the humble life of a herder of elbs. Maybe there was going to be peace and healing to this old world. I saluted Peton for the hero he truly was and walked over and embraced him as a loving father would his favorite son. I spent the rest of the day helping him in his work as an elb herder. I was a happy man, fulfilled with my life and optimistic about the future. Truly the evil yoke that held my world was now broken. Soon all sons of Ontelles would be able to return to their villages without the fear of death and the scattering of their bodies on the four winds.

THE END

Printed in the United States
141382LV00001B/151/A

9 781591 601586